Lair of the Sentinels

Geoff Palmer

PODSNAP PUBLISHING
WELLINGTON, NEW ZEALAND

Podsnap Publishing Ltd., 17 Moir Street, Mt Victoria,
Wellington 6011, New Zealand.

ISBN: 978-0-473-34890-8

Cover design by David Owen
www.davidowen.co.nz

v12

Prologue

No one spoke. Silence hung over the landscape as they watched Albert's distant figure disappear into the lengthening twilight, an empty petrol can in one hand.

Tim ran a finger over the bonnet of the black Cadillac as a fine grit from the explosion settled on it like a dusting of talcum powder. He glanced at his sister. Coral bit her lip. They both knew that amidst those blasted atoms were the remains of their friends' spaceship.

The Eltherians hadn't moved. Alkemy clung to her brother, her face buried against his chest, crying quietly. Ludokrus stared towards the reserve, his face expressionless.

A tui settled on a power line overhead. The white ruff of feathers round its neck glowed orange in the setting sun. It trilled a string of melodious notes before concluding with a harsh Crrrrhh, a sound like an echo of the explosion. Alkemy looked up at it and bit her lip.

Coral nudged Tim. He followed her gaze in the direction of the farm. The direction Albert was heading. Across the open fields, he caught sight of their uncle's ute heading towards them.

'What are we going to tell the grown-ups?' Coral said.

1

Shatter Day

1 : In Darkness

It was watching him, Tim could sense it. The killer robot. The Emissary. The thing without a face. It stood at the end of his bed, staring down at him through the dozen eyes – large and small – that dotted its pockmarked metal head. It had no mouth, no nose, just grilles where the cheeks should be. Tim could hear air moving through them. Some sort of ventilation, perhaps. It sounded like an old man's rasping breath.

He edged back in his bed, feeling the pillows bunch up behind his shoulders, and kicked down the duvet to free his legs so he could run. But where to? Where could he go?

Suddenly the robot's face began to melt. The grilles merged to form a mouth, a mouth that grinned at him then opened wide. The jaw hinged back revealing row on row of jagged, pointy teeth like those of a shark. Its hands closed around the wooden board at the end of the bed and it launched itself straight at him.

'Whoa!'

Tim jerked awake, unsure if he really had cried out, and lay in darkness as his pounding heart returned to a more normal beat. He switched on the lamp on the bedside table and looked about the room. Dresser, wardrobe, the old kauri desk with his school books scattered over it. Nothing had changed. It couldn't have. The killer robot was gone. Blown up. He knew that. Still, he couldn't help himself. He took out his torch and checked under the bed and inside the wardrobe, just in case.

Sighing, he opened his bedroom door and headed for the kitchen. Starlight streamed through the kitchen windows as he took a glass from the bench, filled it with water and sipped in silence, staring at the stars. The night outside was bright and cloudless. Nothing stirred. He could see the outlines of his uncle's cows huddled near the fence, sleeping. A line from a Christmas carol came to him: *All is calm, all is bright.*

Not even close, he thought.

On the way back to his room he saw a faint glow along the bottom of his sister's door. He paused and tapped and opened it a fraction. Coral was sitting up in bed, her reading lamp on, a book perched on her knees.

'What are you doing up?' she whispered.

'I ... just went to the kitchen. Saw your light.'

Coral nodded and turned a page, barely looking at the text or pictures. Tim recognised the book, *Old Norse Myths and Legends.*

'I had a dream,' he said. 'The killer robot ...'

Coral turned another page. She wasn't really reading. Her eyes were puffy with lack of sleep and her long blonde hair looked like birds had been nesting in it. At length she said, 'It really is gone, isn't it?'

'That's what Albert said.'

'How can he be sure?'

'He analysed the dust. Picked up traces of whatever powered it. Something called a micro-fusion generator. Besides, nothing could have survived that explosion. You saw the crater.'

'So why can't I get that through my thick skull?' She tapped her head. 'Every time I close my eyes, my brain goes into overdrive. The house creaks or a door bangs and it goes, "It's back! It's back!"

'Then I think about how close we were. Five more minutes and we'd have been right there. If we hadn't stopped at Dead Man's Bend, if Albert hadn't run out of petrol, we'd all have been blown to smithereens.' She stared at her brother. 'This is for real, Timmo. Those Sentinels want us dead.'

He went to the window and drew back the curtain. A crescent moon hung in the sky to the east. A thin sliver, like the blade of a sickle. Its cold light glanced off the roof of the caravan parked at the side of the house. Aunt Em had insisted the visitors move it there the night before. Alkemy and Ludokrus readily agreed, even though it had been far enough from the explosion to only suffer a little scorched paint and a dent from a falling branch.

'We should be safe for a while,' he said. 'The Sentinels will think they got us last night.'

'I hope so.' Coral sighed and slumped against her pillows, but her look said she didn't really believe him.

Tim didn't really believe it himself.

2 : Country Air

The sound began as a faint murmur in the distance, growing louder by the second till it hit the house with a full-throated roar that rattled the windows and almost shook the fillings from Tim's teeth. He leapt from his bed, still half-asleep, and raced down the hall towards the kitchen, the roaring keeping pace with him as he ran.

Coral looked up from the breakfast table as he burst in. She was washed and dressed, her hair neatly brushed, her face unconcerned. He suddenly realised it was morning and the house was filled with daylight.

The roaring faded, moving south, and he recognised the *whup-whup-whup* as the sound of a helicopter.

'They must be looking at the crater,' Coral said. 'You know, from that *meteorite* yesterday?'

Her emphasis was slight, but it was a useful reminder for his sleep-fudged brain. Saying the explosion had been caused by a meteorite had been his idea. He even pretended he'd seen a streaking flash in the sky in the seconds before it hit.

'Oh. Right.'

Coral gave him a knowing look. She'd seen the fear in his face. That noise ... Those dreams ... At least she understood.

He returned five minutes later, washed and dressed, and took a seat opposite her at the dining table. Eight places had been laid. Aunt Em and Uncle Frank bustled around at the other end of the kitchen, preparing what looked like an enormous breakfast. Tim realised he was hungry. He'd only pecked at his food the night before, unable to eat properly after all the excitement.

'Well look at this,' Frank said. 'The pair of you, up and dressed at 8:45 on a Saturday morning. A holiday weekend too. I reckon the country air is finally getting to you city-slickers.'

The helicopter finished its business at the crater and returned, the noise of its rotor blades rising to a screaming pitch as it headed north and passed back over the house.

'That must be it,' Coral yelled. 'I mean, IT'S JUST SO PEACEFUL HERE, I'M AMAZED WE DIDN'T SLEEP ALL DAY!'

The *whup-whup-whup* fell away steadily and more normal countryside sounds returned.

'Puss, puss, puss? Come on puss.' Alice's shadow passed the kitchen window. 'Oh, don't be so silly. It's nothing to be frightened of. And it's gone now. Come on. It's all right. You can trust me, Smudge. Smudge? Oh I give up.'

She appeared at the back door carrying a bowl of cat biscuits.

'New diet?' Frank asked.

She ignored him and turned to her sister. 'She still won't come out from under the house. She spent the whole night there after that explosion, and now that thing's gone and frightened her all over again.'

'She'll come out when she's good and ready,' her sister said.

'And hungry,' Frank added. 'Like these two.' He jerked his head at Tim and Coral.

Alice set the cat bowl down suddenly and stared at the dining table with eight places layed around it. Her mouth pursed and she backed away. 'Oh ... I ... um ... ate earlier.'

'Really?' Em said.

'Yes, yes, I'm quite full up.'

Frank inspected the cat bowl and made a face. Em shot him a warning glance.

There were footsteps on the veranda. Alice snatched her car keys from a hook beside the door. 'I think I'll go for a drive instead and get out of your way.'

'Are you sure?'

But she was already gone, heading for the blue Daihatsu parked in the turning circle outside the kitchen window.

'Here comes the rest of the hungry horde,' Frank said, gesturing towards the veranda.

Alkemy led the way, wishing everyone a good morning. She was dressed in jeans and a plain white T-shirt, her wavy hair neatly clipped back, its silvery highlights glinting in the morning sun. She smiled, but it somehow didn't reach her eyes which looked tired and downcast.

Ludokrus followed. He was two years older – Coral's age – a head and shoulders taller. His cargo pants and sweatshirt looked like they'd been slept in, but he moved with an easy grace. Although he never seemed to brush his straight brown hair, it always looked just right, Coral thought.

They were followed by Albert, a tall, lean, middle-aged man with a shock of frizzy grey hair that could do with a trim. His clothes were clean but well-worn, and he had the look of someone whose mind was elsewhere, thinking deep, important thoughts. It was difficult to believe that beneath that haphazard exterior lay a mechanical heart and an electronic brain.

'Sleep OK?' Coral asked as they settled round the table.

Ludokrus blew out his cheeks. His chiselled features looked partially eroded. 'The nighthorse keep me awake.'

'*Mare*,' Alkemy corrected. 'Me also. And Albert work all night,' she added in a lower tone.

'Doing what?'

'He finally have all the part, so he build the Temporal Accumulator.'

'That thing you came here for?' Tim glanced at the microwave. 'Why bother? What good is it now?'

Alkemy shrugged.

Em and Frank began loading up the dining table. Dishes of bacon, scrambled eggs, tomatoes, mushrooms, sausages and hash browns. Pitchers of fresh milk and cream for their cereal. A big yellow slab of butter. Frank manned the toaster, keeping up a steady stream as everyone dug in. Tim licked his lips. His appetite was back with a vengeance, along with everyone else's. Even Albert, who could draw energy from a number of sources – including sunlight – tucked in heartily.

Frank checked his watch, leaned across and turned up the radio in time for the nine o'clock news. It was preceded by a bird call. A tui. Alkemy smiled sadly in recognition.

There was the usual list of troubles from around the country and around the world, and then: 'A family of tourists had a lucky escape late yesterday when a meteorite struck a bush reserve near their camp site. The impact, about forty kilometres south of Haast on the South Island's West Coast, left a ten-metre wide crater. Nearby resident Frank Townsend, whose dairy farm is just a kilometre from the site, spoke to us earlier this morning ...'

Em beamed at her husband. Albert looked up sharply.

'The wife and I were having a cuppa when we heard this terrific bang and the whole place shook,' Frank's voice said. 'We looked out the window and saw this mushroom-shaped cloud rising in the distance. For a moment I thought they'd nuked Rata.'

'Rata?' the interviewer asked.

'Nearest town. Twenty K away.'

Radio Frank went on to describe how some tourists – he didn't say he knew them or that his niece and nephew were with them at the time – had been even closer to the scene.

'The tourists, believed to be Norwegian, were still in shock and weren't available for comment,' the radio concluded.

Frank turned the volume down.

No one spoke.

Coral saw Albert's mouth pursed in anger. Alkemy and Ludokrus had stopped eating.

'When did you do that?' she said to her uncle by way of distraction.

'They called just after six. I was the only one up.' He

turned to Albert. 'I'd have given you a yell, but you said last night you didn't want to be bothered by journalists. I've still got the reporter's number though, if you want to call him back.'

'Thanks, but I don't think I'll bother,' Albert's voice was mild but his features were wooden.

Coral elbowed Tim and whispered, 'What's all that about? What's the big deal?'

'Uncle Frank's just told the whole wide world the Eltherians survived the explosion,' he said grimly. 'Including the Sentinels.'

3 : Out of the Frying Pan

'I'm dying.'

'I wish I only felt that bad.'

'Was it the Snot Champagne? Or the Green Slime cocktails?'

'I think it was your Mucus Beer.'

'You didn't have to drink it all.'

'You didn't have to help me.'

'Still, it was quite a celebration.'

'One of the best. But after fourteen years stuck on this wretched planet we deserved a celebration.'

'Look, another cause for celebration. A message from our masters. Our evacuation craft has been despatched.'

'Our ship! Our good old ship! We're going home at last. I can hardly believe it.'

'There's even a message of congratulations.'

'Yes, yes, very good, but turn it down please. That screen is rather bright.'

'It is turned down. As far as it will go.'

'And turn off that music too.'

'What music?'

'That bee-bop, bee-bop noise. Were we really dancing to that *last night?'*

   'Wait a minute. That's not music ...!'

* * *

Norman Smith rolled over in bed and studied his alarm clock, luxuriating in the thought of the long weekend ahead. Monday was Rata Day, a local holiday to celebrate the founding of the town, so that meant three whole days of idleness. He'd help his mum in the shop of course, but Rata weekend was always quiet as many locals went away. He thought about what else he'd do. Some more on the electronics project he was working on, perhaps a start on next week's homework – he liked to keep ahead – and maybe he could talk his mum into taking the Mini out for a spin. They could visit his friend Tim Townsend at his aunt and uncle's farm out on the coast. It'd be fun to talk over all that happened yesterday and find out how the Eltherians' launch had gone last night.

He reached up and clapped his hands. The radio came on. An electronics project he'd completed the month before. A simple thyristor circuit, but it amused him. Clapping twice turned it off again. It was like having a servant.

He was just in time for the nine o'clock news and listened with half an ear, clapping the radio on and off, on and off. Then he froze mid-clap.

Thirty seconds later he leapt from his bed and raced down the hall. 'Mum! Mum!' He burst through the beaded curtain that separated the house from RAGS, the Rata Area General Store.

Gladys Smith was serving a customer. Daisy Robson owned Feather Willow Lodge, the town's only accommodation. Both women looked round at him and smiled. He was still in his pyjamas.

'Good morning, Norman.'

'Good morning, Mrs Robson.'

'I must say I like your PJs. Rocket ships and moons. Very fashionable.'

'Er ... thanks.' Norman coloured.

As they watched her go, Glad said, 'What's got you so excited?'

'Have you heard the news?'

* * *

The hearty breakfast made a heap of dishes. Alkemy, Tim, Coral and Ludokrus stacked them up as the adults took the coffee pot and retired to the back lawn.

'They have no dishwash?' Ludokrus was incredulous.

'They do,' Coral told him. 'Us.'

He blew out his cheeks and stared at the pile of cutlery, plates, cups, saucers, trays, pots and greasy pans littering the bench.

Tim rolled up his sleeves and started filling the sink. Alkemy picked up a tea towel. She'd hardly said a word since the news broadcast. Coral patted her shoulder. 'It's only a big a deal if the Sentinels listen to Radio New Zealand, you know.'

'But other news will pick up also,' Ludokrus said. 'When we see the helichop before, we laugh because there is no

18

caravan there. No evidence we survive. Now the whole world know the truth.'

'Well it's not Uncle Frank's fault. He doesn't know about you guys.'

'Albert tell him no to journalist last night.'

'For Albert, not for everyone. Anyway, the guy called him. What's he supposed to say? This was always going to cause a stir, Ludokrus. That was a huge explosion. You've seen the crater.'

Ludokrus sighed, picked up a tea towel, then put it down again. 'You have the calculator?' he said to his sister.

'Of course.' She nodded to her pink school backpack slung over one of the chairs. 'Always carry.'

'At least that is not also blowed up.'

He unzipped a side pocket and took out a device that looked like a fancy scientific calculator. It had banks of switches arranged around a central display, each one marked by a symbol that glowed faintly. The switches sat in asterisk-shaped channels, meaning each could be moved in one of eight different directions.

Ludokrus pressed the device against the side of the nearest pot, studied the oval display, and began flicking switches. Then he indicated Tim should hold out one of the greasy pans, pressed a button, and released a small grey-green blob. It dropped from a hatch in the side and plopped into the base of the pan. Within seconds, it began fizzing and bubbling as if the pan was scalding hot.

'Tilt her.'

Tim did so. As the blob moved, the area beneath it shone through, shiny and clean.

'Oh wow! That's neat.'

The blob expanded, an action Tim knew to be the work of the microscopic machines generated by the calculator. They replicated furiously, copying themselves and clearing a path as they went. One quick slosh of the pan and it was spotless.

'That makes it easier. What now?' The fizzing green bubbles reached the rim.

'Pour into next.'

Tim did so and the process continued, except for the residue in the first pan, which continued fizzing, bubbling and expanding. He dipped it in the sink to rinse it. That slowed the process a little, but it continued again as soon as he took the pan out.

'Er ...' he said.

Alkemy looked at the calculator and frowned. 'Where do you tell the nanomachine to get material to make more machine?'

Ludokrus gave her a long-suffering look. 'From the pan of course.'

'... um ...'

She pointed to the display. 'You set it to take the atom from the metal of the surface, yes?'

'A few only. No one will miss.'

'... Hey guys ...'

'Please define "few". And how do they know when they are to stop?"

He looked at her blankly for a moment then muttered, 'Oh.'

With a distinct *bloop*, the bottom fell out of the frying pan Tim was holding. The bulk of the blob landed on the stainless steel bench where it bubbled even more furiously.

Some droplets splashed on to the cream-coloured benchtop where they fizzled out for lack of raw material, but others found the metal parts of the taps, the toaster and the electric jug.

'Oh no!' Tim cried.

The shiny chrome sugar bowl was the first casualty. One thin side vanished, spilling a cascade of sugar across the breakfast bar. Tim grabbed a ladle to stem the flow, but the curved handle had been splashed with a tiny droplet. It seethed greenly for a second, then sagged. He watched in amazement as it bowed, bent, then broke in half.

'Oops,' Ludokrus said.

The whole sink bench was now seething with molecular activity. It looked as if its entire surface was engulfed in a weird green fire as nanomachines consumed the thick metal. Faint pops and crackles sounded as the fizzing mass reached the pots and pans stacked on one side and began dissolving them from below.

'What do we do?' Tim cried.

Ludokrus snatched the calculator back and began furiously flicking switches. Alkemy rushed from the kitchen.

The toaster collapsed in on itself like the shell of a burnt-out building. The electric jug, pulled off-centre by the weight of its plastic handle, tilted sideways and slumped to the benchtop.

'Water!' Coral pointed to the sink where the seething activity around the sides of the basin had stopped at the water line. Tim dipped a hand in and splashed, causing the greenish bubbles to slow markedly. He splashed again, sloshing water round the sink, then grabbed a plastic jug, scooped it full and tipped it over the bench.

The water wiped out most of the activity, washing a grey-green sludge into the sink and revealing deeply scarred metal peppered with small green blotches that flared again as the water drained away. He repeated the process. Again and again. It wasn't a complete cure, but it was slowing them down.

Alkemy returned, dragging the laundry basket. 'Cover, quick!' she said, hurling T-shirts, socks and bed linen on to the bench, piling it as high as possible.

'What ...?' Coral said, but Tim caught on right away.

'Nanomachines get their energy from light. Block it out and they shut down.'

'Right!'

Coral snatched the curtains shut while Tim and Alkemy emptied the laundry basket, covering every available surface and pressing down tightly. The others helped, leaning on it in the semi-darkness, fearful that the damaged bench would collapse beneath them.

A minute later they carefully peeled back the damp laundry. Specks of activity flared here and there but were easily snuffed out. Alkemy gathered up the sodden garments, most now stained grey-green, while Coral opened the curtains to reveal the extent of the damage.

The frying pan was just a handle attached to a ragged circle of wire while the pots stacked on the sink bench leaned like capsized boats, their bottoms and sides partially dissolved. All that remained of the kettle and toaster were odd collections of plastic bits. The sugar bowl had gone completely. The stainless steel benchtop and once-shiny taps were now deeply scored and pitted, as if eaten away by acid.

They stared at the devastation, open-mouthed in shock. 'What the heck do we do now?' Coral muttered.

Tim shook his head as footsteps sounded on the veranda outside. 'Better think quickly. Someone's coming!'

4 : Footprints

Glad stopped her red Mini at Dead Man's Bend, the corner that marked the start of the steep, winding section of road leading down to the coast. At its apex stood Dead Man's Pine, a tree that had been frazzled by a lightning strike years before. Its roots still clung to the side of the cliff, but its blackened top had acted as a signpost; a warning of the stretch of road to come. At least until yesterday, when the rear end of Fitchett's Flyer – driven by Tim Townsend – slammed into it and snapped it off, sending the charred part of the tree plunging down to the rocks far below.

'What have we stopped here for?' Norman said as Glad got out to look.

It seemed incredible. Glad was half-convinced she'd dreamt the whole thing. She went to the fence and leaned on one of the posts, looking out at the view of the rocky coastline and the sparkling blue of the Tasman Sea beyond. The Eltherians had fixed the fence of course, and the damaged bus. Made everything as good as new with those nanomachine things of theirs. But they couldn't do much about the tree.

She looked back at the Mini. They'd fixed that too. And her. She slipped a hand inside her jeans and felt the spot near her hip where the killer robot's bullet had passed straight through. Had she dreamt that too? The pain and shock? There was a faint dimple there now, that was all. After accelerated healing from one of the gel beds in their tiny spaceship, she was as good as new.

'Mum?' Norman got out behind her.

He'd been there as well, but had missed most of the action, buttoned in the pocket of her shirt, his mind still locked in the body of a mouse.

It *must* have been a dream, she thought. It was too incredible.

'Hey look over there. I can see the crater.'

She followed the direction of his outstretched arm. Through the morning haze, she made out a faint indentation in the distance. A bare circle in the bush.

The meteorite.

She hadn't dreamt that.

'It did all happen, didn't it?' she said, partly to herself.

'What? Yesterday?' Norman seemed surprised at the question.

'It's just that everything's been fixed up. Like it never happened.' She rubbed her hip again.

'Almost. But it looks like they missed a bit.'

'What do you mean?'

He pointed to the stump of Dead Man's Pine. A few flakes of green paint were scraped deep into the old tree's bark. It was the same colour as the paint on Fitchett's Flyer.

'So they did.' Glad smiled, relieved. 'C'mon, let's get down there and see what those "tourists" have to say for themselves.'

* * *

'Do something. Quick!' Tim hissed as the approaching footsteps grew louder. He dragged all the mangled pots and pans into the sink and spread a damp tea towel over the damaged bench.

'Why me?' Coral hissed back, but she was already halfway to the door.

In a tone remarkably like her aunt's she said, 'I hope you've not come to disturb my kitchen.'

Frank's voice replied: 'Just come for the Gingernuts, your ladyship.'

'Keep your boots on. I'll get them.'

He leaned against the door jamb while Ludokrus and Alkemy dried already dry plates and did their best to block his view of the sink. Tim scrubbed an imaginary pot. It really was imaginary. It was nothing but a handle.

'I love hard work,' Frank said. 'I could watch it for hours.'

'Don't get comfortable.' Coral thrust the biscuit barrel at him. 'You're upsetting the staff.'

He gave her a mock salute. As he turned to go, tyres sounded on the gravel drive and a red Mini stopped in the turning circle outside the kitchen. A woman in her mid-thirties emerged wearing jeans, T-shirt and a big sloppy bush shirt that she wore like an unbuttoned jacket. A boy Tim's age got out the other side. He had the same unruly mop of gingery hair as his mother.

'Why it's the famous Glad Smith,' Frank said. 'Good morning. What brings our esteemed storekeeper out to these lowly parts?'

'Me? Famous?' Glad said. 'You're the radio star. I've come for your autograph.'

'Well, you're just in time for coffee. If you leave your order with young Coral here, I'm doing signings out the back.'

'Actually, we came to see the crater,' Norman said.

'You mean I'm not the star attraction after all? It really is only fifteen minutes of fame, isn't it?'

Glad saw the faces at the kitchen window. 'I'll join you in a minute, Frank. I'll just say hello to the others.'

'No rush. Stay for lunch if you like.'

'I'd love to, but I could only get Brittany in to mind the shop for a couple of hours.'

Frank headed off, tapping a tune on the lid of the biscuit barrel as Glad climbed the steps of the veranda and poked her head around the kitchen door. 'We heard the radio. Are you all OK?' She looked at the weary faces. 'You scared us half to death. What happened? Did something go wrong with the take-off?'

'We do not get that far,' Alkemy said. 'The killer robot blow up our ship.'

'*What?* But it fell off the cliff at Dead Man's Bend.'

'Must get smash but not destroyed. We think it crawl to ship and self-destruct.'

'Oh god. Does that mean you're stuck here?' Glad stared at Alkemy's pinched face. 'I don't know what to say. But at least you're OK. We should talk later. I better not keep the others waiting.'

'D'you want coffee?' Coral called after her.

'Instant's fine, thanks.'

'Milk, no sugar,' Norman said, taking her place at the door before stepping into the kitchen. 'Holy crap! What happened here?'

'Nanomachine mishap,' Tim said, draining the sink and sloshing away the last of the grey-green residue.

Coral shoved Norman aside and rummaged in the cupboard. 'I need something to boil water in.'

Tim held up a saucepan. Its bottom was sliced off at a forty-five degree angle.

Norman laughed.

'It's not funny you know,' Coral snapped. 'Unless you fancy explaining all this to Aunt Em and Uncle Frank.'

She found an old aluminium pan, filled it with water and set it on the stove.

'Don't stand there gawping,' she told Norman. 'Make yourself useful. Go through to Tim's room and keep an eye on the adults. If any of them makes a move in this direction, report back immediately.'

The Eltherians hunched over the calculator, Ludokrus making adjustments which Alkemy kept correcting. Finally, he gave up, thrust the device at her and stomped out.

'What's the problem?' Tim said.

'We have not enough raw material. All the metal that was dissolve is wash away.'

'So what can we do?'

'Make thin with what we have and hope it will be enough.'

'OK. We should start with the obvious stuff like the sink bench and taps. Then the sugar bowl, toaster and kettle. We can always hide the saucepans till later.'

'Sink and tap, no problem,' she said flipping switches on the calculator, taking a partly melted saucepan, smearing a fresh blob around its bottom edge and setting it on the bench. 'They take the layout from the existing shape and repair.'

The bottom of the pan began to melt, coating the pitted surface of the bench, leaving it shiny and smooth again.

'Shapes of pans are standard also. But the other thing?' She shook her head. 'We have no plans.'

Tim swept up the spilled sugar and found a ragged metal disk buried beneath it. 'Hey, look at this.' He held it up. 'The sugar must've blocked the light and stopped the nanomachines from getting to this bit.'

'Is all we need.' Alkemy took it and pressed it against the calculator. 'Can use for analysis to rebuild her.'

She was right about the kettle and toaster though. Both were now just collections of plastic bits.

Coral came through from the laundry. 'That's the washing on. Now for Glad's coffee.'

Ludokrus returned carrying a cardboard box. He set it on the stove and took out a kettle and a toaster identical to the demolished ones.

'Whoa! Where'd they come from?'

'The caravan. Remember when we first build her? We need many things inside to make her look like she is proper and in use.'

'That's right! You copied Aunt Em's kitchen stuff.' Coral clapped him on the shoulder. 'Good thinking. We'll swap them over and restore your stuff later.'

'Or maybe not,' he said quietly.

'What? Why not?'

'Fix first, news after.'

'News?'

They looked at him curiously as he took the remaining pots and pans from the box, but his grave expression gave nothing away. Still, the mood in the kitchen changed, and they went about the business of comparing and swapping damaged pans in silence. Repairs to the sink bench and taps took longer, but as the minutes ticked past, the missing surfaces reappeared beneath bubbling blobs of foam. Finally, the bubbles died, activity ceased, and Tim wiped away the residue of grey-green dust to reveal shiny unmarked surfaces beneath.

'Well, that only took about twice as long as it should've done,' he said.

No one smiled. All eyes were on Ludokrus as he put away the last of the damaged pans and closed the flaps of the cardboard box. He stood weighing it in his arms.

'So?' Coral prompted. 'What's the news? Why won't you need to restore that stuff.'

'Because we are leaving,' he said.

5 : Bigger Dishes

'If it's not music, what is it?'
  'It sounds like an alarm.'
  'An alarm ...?'

* * *

Alkemy pegged out the last of the laundry as Coral scooped up the empty basket and carried it back inside. The clothesline had a fixed metal pole with a rotating top, and Alkemy, still on the box she'd been standing on to hang the washing out, gave it a push. It turned slowly, squeaking faintly above the whispered argument between Ludokrus and Albert.

'But we are safe here,' Ludokrus hissed as they dismantled the awning.

'We're not safe anywhere, Ludokrus. The fact that the Sentinels sent a killer robot after you all – in public – shows their level of desperation. We're just lucky that this is such a remote spot and no one else saw it.'

'But is gone now, you say yourself.'

'Look at the manner of its "departure". You've seen the crater. There's nothing subtle about that. Do you think for one moment that if the Sentinels had some sort of missile they wouldn't aim it straight at this farm now they know we're still alive?'

Ludokrus said nothing as they folded the heavy canvas and dragged it into the caravan.

'For all we know they may be preparing something as we speak. We can't endanger the people here. They're innocent bystanders. This is nothing to do with them. We *have* to separate ourselves and go back to the reserve.'

'Then what? Sit and wait to die?'

'Not quite,' Albert said, gathering up the support poles.

Alkemy gave the line another push as Glad came around the side of the house to say she had to get back to the shop and that she'd see them later. 'If we are still alive,' Ludokrus muttered.

The Mini departed and Alkemy watched the faint trail of dust as it headed up the road. The brownish plume hung in the still air like the exhaust from a rocket, and she thought again of their lost ship.

She turned at the sound of other voices and was surprised to see Norman Smith still there.

'Your mum has gone,' she said.

'But I'm staying,' Norman grinned. 'The whole weekend. Mr and Mrs Townsend said it's OK. I'm going back with you guys on Tuesday morning on Fitchett's Flyer. How cool is that?'

'Great.' She smiled, but without enthusiasm, thinking of Albert's words and wondering if they'd live to see Tuesday morning.

Albert hitched the caravan to the Cadillac's tow bar and waved them over. 'Can I see you all please, after lunch, once we're unpacked and set up? I have an idea, but it's not something I can develop here, and I'm going to need your help with it.'

'Like a secret plan?' Norman said. Albert nodded. 'Yes!'

The Cadillac departed. Coral, Tim and Norman retired to the back lawn and took over the deck chairs the adults had vacated. Aunt Em brought out a jug of boysenberry cordial and a plate of chocolate biscuits to thank them for their hard work.

'Those pots and pans are spotless. Whatever did you use?'

'Oh, it was just some stuff they had in the caravan,' Coral said.

'I must get the name of it off Albert. It's like having a brand new kitchen.'

Another car sounded in the drive. A door slammed and Alice appeared.

'Have they gone?' she said to Em, staring at the spot where the caravan had been.

'Yes, back to the reserve. Albert insisted. Said he didn't want to be in the way. Silly man.'

Alice looked relieved.

'Do you remember Norman, Glad Smith's son? He's staying the weekend. My sister Alice, down from Greymouth,' Em said to Norman.

'Hi.'

Alice froze. Her eyes widened as they fixed on him.

'Would you mind picking some rhubarb?' Em said. 'I

thought I'd do a rhubarb tart for dessert tonight.'

'No. No, of course not.' Alice dragged her eyes away. 'I'll ... get a basket.'

She scuttled off and Em followed her in.

'What was that about?' Norman said.

Tim shrugged.

'She has a built-in dork detector,' Coral said. 'I guess she spotted one.'

'Ignore her,' Tim said. 'She's weird.'

Norman glared at Coral. 'Yeah, and so is your aunt.'

They settled in the shade of a brightly coloured umbrella, feeling the warmth of the clear blue day around them. Tim and Coral almost drifted off, but Norman was restless. There was a rustling from the undergrowth near the house and a large black and white cat emerged, peering left and right before trotting over to join them. Tim opened one eye and looked down as her tail brushed past his arm. 'Hello scaredy-cat.' He reached out a hand. 'Finally got your courage back?'

Smudge turned and settled on the lawn beneath his seat.

'Wonder what Albert's got in mind,' Norman said.

'Dunno.'

'Tell you what I don't get,' Coral said, opening one eye. 'That explosion only took out their escape pod. They've still got a mothership up there. It must have more than one landing craft, so why not just get it to send another one?'

'*That's* the problem,' Tim said. 'Sending the message. They need a really powerful transmitter to do that.'

'But we build transmitters all the time. *And* we send out space probes. How hard can it be?'

'How far away is their mothership?' Norman asked.

'About seven hours at the speed of light.'

'There's your problem.'

'What do you mean?'

'Light travels about a billion kilometres an hour, so that means their mothership is seven billion kilometres away. You'll need a really big transmitter to send a signal that far. And a really accurate one to pinpoint a spaceship.'

'How big?'

'NASA use the Deep Space Network for their interplanetary craft. They've got stations in America, Australia and Spain. The dish near Canberra's seventy metres across.'

'*Seventy metres?*'

'You could probably get away with something half that size if you aimed it really carefully, with computer controls and everything.'

'Forget computers,' Tim said. 'There's no way they could ever build something that big. The raw materials alone ... And even if they could, someone's bound to notice a thirty-five metre dish, even round here.'

'What about all their advanced technology?' Coral said.

'Apparently they could make one the size of a suitcase – which is what the escape pod used – but it needs all sorts of exotic materials that could take months to refine. Stuff you'd need a chemistry lab to extract, provided you could find the right raw materials in the first place.'

'So they really are stuck.'

'Maybe not,' Norman grinned. 'Remember, Albert said he's got a plan.'

6 : Perfect Spies

The shortcut to the reserve wasn't much of a shortcut. It involved climbing fences, jumping the stream that marked the edge of the Townsend property, then following a winding track through the bush, but it was more interesting than the straight stretch of gravel road that led from the entrance of the farm. Smudge followed them part of the way, trotting along behind like a well-trained dog, and she showed every sign of wanting to continue past the rushing stream if only someone would lift her across.

'Go home, you'll get lost,' Tim said, waving her away.

The track emerged on the seaward side of the reserve behind a low wooden toilet block at the bottom of the circular camping area. The patch of grass in front of it was empty apart for the Eltherians' car and caravan, parked at the opposite end, exactly where they'd been the day before.

At first, nothing looked different. The space where the caravan sat was backed by long grass, bush and tall trees, but looking higher they could see the tops of the trees were scorched and broken. Many were missing branches, as if a barber had shaved the backs of their heads.

They heard Ludokrus's raised voice in the distance. Albert snapped something back. Ludokrus replied. The sounds reached them, but not the words.

'We might be a bit early,' Tim said. 'Let's give them another few minutes and check out the crater.'

They moved on, keeping out of sight.

The damage was more obvious the closer they got to the centre of the explosion. The dense vegetation was scorched and torn. Every tree around the crater's edge had been snapped and flattened. Tim tried to imagine it from the air. It would be like a child's drawing of the sun. An empty circle with lines radiating out from the edge.

The crater itself was ten metres across and three deep, its steeply sloping sides streaked with glassy fragments of rock fused by the tremendous heat of the blast.

'Wow!' Norman muttered.

Tim looked at the wasteland around them. It didn't seem possible that this time yesterday it had been dense bush teeming with bird life. That where he stood now had been the entrance to a glade of waist-high ferns that hid the little Eltherian ship. He and his sister had explored some of the area in the bodies of mice, marvelling at the richness and variety of life in even a tiny patch of ground. Now it was all gone.

'I wonder if Pipi and Paua are OK,' Coral said. She'd been thinking about the mice too.

'They should be,' Tim said. 'Alkemy let them go near the caravan.'

Norman edged into the crater, picking up and studying fragments of fused rock as he made his way towards the epicentre.

'Is it still radioactive?' Coral said loudly.

He squawked and bounded out again to find her doubled-up with laughter. 'I wish I'd got that on my phone,' she said. 'The look on your face!'

* * *

Tempers had cooled by the time they returned to the reserve. One side of the awning had been rolled up to let in light and air, and Albert was busy at a makeshift table. Alkemy and Ludokrus were in the caravan, unpacking and arranging the last of their things.

They spotted the smell as they approached. An odd, dry odour like burnt coffee. It grew stronger, and by the time they reached the caravan it was almost overpowering. Alkemy came down the steps fanning a piece of cardboard.

'What is that pong?' Coral said.

Albert, stooped over the table, lifted a metal rack from a square plastic trough and set it to one side. As he did so, another wave of the burnt coffee smell washed over them and they all screwed up their noses.

'Another reason to move away from the farm,' he said, glancing at Ludokrus.

He took several grey cubes from the rack and inspected them. They looked like dice without numbers on the sides. He nodded in satisfaction. 'Good. Let me neutralise this stuff.'

He poured a bucket of brown liquid into the trough. There was a faint fizzing sound and steam-like tendrils rose above the surface. The burnt coffee smell thinned immediately.

'Go inside. Make yourselves comfortable. We need to talk.'

They squeezed around the caravan's tiny dining table and Albert set three of the grey cubes in front of them. 'Scanner blocks,' he said.

The cubes measured a centimetre on each side. They had rounded corners, a mottled surface, and a texture that resembled compressed sand. Tim picked one up. It was surprisingly heavy and its sides sparkled faintly in the light.

'A quick build from a quick design, but I think they'll do the trick. Before we get on to that though, tell me all you know about the Sentinels.'

Ludokrus crossed his arms. 'Only what you tell us. Almost nothing.'

'Right, well let me correct that.' Albert pulled up a folding chair and settled at the end of the table.

'The Sentinels are agents of the Thanatos. They were sent here to look out for survivors after our ship crashed in your solar system. They're essentially watchers; a first line of defence sent to shield human beings from outside interference. From people like us.

'In appearance, Sentinels are large slug-like beings that live underground, but they have one unique ability; to work their way into the minds of other creatures. Once in, they see what their host sees and hear what it hears. In short, they're perfect spies. And given time, they can even gain limited control of their host.

'Sentinels work in pairs and are creature-exclusive, which is to say they can only monitor and direct one person each. We've identified one of their hosts, Millicent Millais, the principal of Rata Area School, the teacher you call Cakeface. There will almost certainly be another, as yet unidentified.'

'Now, you're aware of the problem we have communicating with our mothership?' They nodded. 'We could spend months obtaining and refining the raw materials we need to build a transmitter. My original plan was to move away and do just that, but now the Sentinels know we're still alive, they'll pursue us. And they'll keep pursuing us until they fulfil their mission. So we don't have the luxury of time any more. We need to move fast and we need to move boldly. We need a transmitter, and it occurs to me that the Sentinels must already have one.'

The idea took them by surprise.

'You mean ... to copy?' Coral said.

'No, I mean to use.'

Ludokrus snorted, 'You think we can go to them and say, "Please may we borrow this?"'

'There will of course be ... contingencies to manage.'

'Contingencies? You mean like the killer robot? How do we *manage* him?'

'Things will become clearer once we've discovered the Sentinels' location.'

Tim gestured at the cubes. 'So where do these come in?'

'The Sentinels monitor their hosts via direct mental links making them almost impossible to detect. But to *control* their hosts they have to send them signals in the form of suggestions and subtle directions. That's what these things pick up.'

'You mean we eavesdrop on them?'

'No, they're not that sophisticated. But what they will

do is pick up those signals, and that will help us pinpoint the location of their transmitter.' He pointed to the rack in the awning. 'I've made a hundred of these things. The wider we spread them and the more signals they intercept, the more precisely we can locate it.'

'Triangulation,' Norman said.

'Exactly.'

'Huh?' Coral said.

Albert pushed scanner blocks into three into different corners of the table. 'Imagine these things detect the same transmission, from this point here.' He tapped his finger on one side. 'Because they're not all at the same distance from my finger, they'll receive that transmission at slightly different times. We know that radio waves travel in a straight line and at a constant speed, so by measuring the angles and distances between the blocks we can pinpoint source of the transmission.'

'OK.'

'The key to this is distribution. We're talking about tiny differences in the time of reception, so the wider they're spread, the better. What I'd like Coral and Tim to do is distribute them around here and around the farm. The rest of us – with Norman's guidance – will do the same around Rata.

'After that, we simply wait for the Sentinels to send instructions to their hosts. The blocks will intercept them, and from that data we can locate their transmitter.'

Norman frowned. 'But what if the Sentinels send Cakeface after us with a gun or something?'

'They can't. It doesn't work that way. If they gave her a direct instruction like that, she'd become aware of them. It would be like having voices in your head. They have to work indirectly, try to make her do what they want without making their presence obvious.'

'How do you mean?'

'Let's say they wanted you to go into the kitchen. They can't say *Go into the kitchen* or you'd become aware of them, so instead they might make you feel thirsty. *Then* you'd go into the kitchen of your own accord to get a drink.'

'Creepy!'

'And that's what the scanner blocks pick up?' Coral said. 'The signals they send to make you feel thirsty?'

Albert nodded

'What about the second host?' Alkemy said. 'You say they work in pair, so there must be one more. But we do not know who.'

'Hopefully, these things will help us pinpoint him or her too.'

'I know already,' Ludokrus said.

'Eh?'

'What?'

'Who?'

They all spoke at once.

'Can only be the Uncle Frank. He who give us away on the radio. Tell the whole world we are OK.'

'If he *was* a Sentinel host,' Albert said evenly, 'there'd be no need to do that since he'd be communicating with them directly. Besides, I checked the farmhouse and all the out-buildings last night. I'm certain that it's no one there.'

'How can you be sure?'

'Once they establish a link, the Sentinel portion inside the host's brain needs regular recharging. They do that by drawing energy from a particular wavelength of light. I've checked the farm thoroughly for coloured light bulbs, stained glass windows and that sort of thing. There's nothing at all that qualifies. It would either have to be a large source in a common area that allows for a slow, steady charge, or a concentrated source in a small space so as to recharge rapidly.'

Ludokrus raised an eyebrow. 'What colour is this light? Pink, maybe?'

'Why yes.'

'A shade like sickly pink?'

'How did you know that?'

'And you will get this charge maybe from a room painted in this colour?'

'As long as the host spends several hours a day in there, yes.'

Ludokrus was silent for a moment. Then he said in a low tone, 'Why do you not tell us this before?' His voice had an edge to it. An ominous quality. Like the ticking of a time-bomb.

'I didn't think it was relevant.'

'You do not think is relevant.' Ludokrus took a breath. 'What colour do you think is the office of the Cakeface, the teacher who lure us into a trap and almost get us killed?'

Albert stared at him.

Ludokrus slammed his fist on the table. 'I tell you what is colour; pink, *sick pink!*'

'You never said—'

'I never say?' Ludokrus leapt to his feet. 'How do I know what is relevant? You want I tell you the colour of her stapler or the type of dress she wear? If we know what we are looking for, we would be on our guard. Instead, you tell us nothing. Leave us to be kidnap. Almost we are killed because you keep us in the dark!'

'I'm sorry.'

'Yeah, sorry. That make it better. I feel so good now. No more nighthorse for sure.' He snorted. 'If you tell us, warn us, maybe we do not even lose our ship. Now you say we are to walk into the base of our enemy. "Please, may we use your radio?" We see already what these Sentinels can do.' He pointed round at the others. '*We* are there, not you. *We* face the killer robot, not you. And when they catch us, kill us, will you say again that you are sorry?'

Albert said nothing.

'You know what is your problem? I think you spend too long to fix our broken ship. I think the space mould get into your brain and make your wiring misfire. A robot will have more sense!'

Ludokrus threw down the scanner block and stormed out of the caravan.

7 : Off Day

'That's ... not ... possible ...'

'What isn't? Show me?'

'The Eltherians. They're still alive.'

'That's not possible.'

'I just said that! And clearly they are. Look. That's what that alarm was trying to tell us.'

'I thought it was music.'

'The Thanatos will make music with our innards if they find out we've failed!'

'But what about our ship? It's coming to take us home. We can't send it back. That'll give the game away.'

'We need another Emissary.'

'There was only one killer robot in the local system, and that blew itself up. The nearest local support post is almost a week away. Besides, our ship is due in sixty hours.'

'Then there's nothing we can do. The Thanatos will find out. We're doomed!'

'Oh no we're not. We still have two-and-a-half days before our ship arrives. That gives us two-and-a-half days to finish the job.'

'But how?'

'Any way we can!'

* * *

'They're gone,' Coral said.

'I hear the car.'

'So it's just you and me.'

'I guess.' Ludokrus didn't turn. He stood at the crater rim, hands deep in his pockets.

'For what it's worth, I thought you were right. If Albert had told us more about what to expect, none of this would have happened.'

Ludokrus said nothing. Coral unzipped a pocket in her backpack and drew out a water bottle, took a swig then offered it to him. Ludokrus wasn't thirsty, but this wasn't about thirst. He took a drink and passed it back.

'Thanks.' He continued staring down at the crater, then sighed. 'I feel bad. Should not say that thing to Albert, but he make me mad sometimes. Always with the logic. Always with the secret'

'You mean about him being as dumb as a robot?'

'Bad thing to say to syntho. They are like real people, only better sometimes. Do not get mad or say dumb thing.'

Coral remembered what he'd told her of the Robot Liberation Movement. A movement not to free mindless machines from the scrapheap, but to liberate synthos from the term "robot" and give them legal rights. Robots did what they were programmed to do, over and over. Synthos thought about things and had minds of their own.

'You're just tired and a bit cranky. We all are. None of us got much sleep last night.'

He sighed.

'Are you going to stand there looking at that hole all day, or are you going to help me with these?' She shook her backpack containing their share of the scanner blocks.

'I help.' He turned to face her. 'But first, there is something I must get.'

She followed him back to the caravan where he opened a drawer beneath the sink and took out a willow-pattern plate. 'I mean to give this back, but last night I forget.'

'Aunt Em's plate,' Coral said. 'The one that got broken.'

The day before, Alice had left a plate of pikelets for them, but when Albert discovered the others were in trouble, he'd accidentally dropped it, shattering it on a stone.

'I fix her with the nanomachine.'

'Good job.' Coral studied it. 'You can't even see the joins.'

'Is fun design, yes? Chinese scene with little peoples. Girl with donkey, men in boat, another fish from bridge.'

'I guess.'

'I make another.' He went to the cupboard beside his fold-out bed and took out a second plate. 'For you.'

'Me? Oh. Thanks.' Coral was puzzled. Why would she want a plate?

He grinned. 'Not quite the same.'

She held them side by side and looked from one to the other. They were identical.

Almost.

'Always I have been good at draw, so change the faces.

See? Albert, Alkemy and me in boat. Tim fish from bridge. The corner of pagoda I make like the fins on the Cadillac. In the clouds, I hide our ship. And you, the main one, I make her best. Leading donkey, looking back.'

Coral looked and saw herself in perfect caricature. The resemblance was uncanny.

'And the donkey!'

'You see that also?'

'Of course.'

The donkey was still a donkey, but somehow, with the addition of a few deft strokes, it had the face of Norman Smith.

'When did you do this?'

'Last night, when I cannot sleep. I think that when we are gone you will have no picture, no photo, only memory. So I make this. Present. So you will remember us.'

'Oh Ludokrus, how could I ever forget you?'

She stared down at her present, not daring to look at him. It was the loveliest thing anyone had ever given her. It made her want to cry.

'We should put out the scanner blocks,' he said at length.

Coral cleared her throat. 'And I'll give this back to Aunt Em.' She hugged the second plate to her chest. 'But I'm keeping this one very safe.'

They headed out, back across the reserve, pausing to place one of the blocks on the roof the communal toilet and another in the fork of a tree. As they started on the track to the farm he said, 'You think these things will work?'

'I hope so. But you missed the next bit. After you stormed out, Norman asked what would happen if this plan didn't work. Albert said you'd have to leave. Go somewhere else for safety's sake. Keep moving until he worked out something else. Maybe even go to Australia and try to hijack one of their satellite dishes.'

Ludokrus swallowed. 'Does he say how long we have?'

'Twenty-four hours. If we've made no progress by this time tomorrow, you're gone.'

Ludokrus bit his lip but said nothing more.

They jumped the stream, climbed the fence, and headed across the fields towards the milking shed. It was unused at this time of day and the perfect spot for another scanner block.

'I guess it doesn't make much difference,' Coral said at length. 'You were supposed to go yesterday, but ... I dunno ... it's fun having you guys around.'

'Is fun to be around,' Ludokrus said quietly.

Several of the grazing cows looked up and watched them cross the field.

'I will come back,' he added. 'Even if we go yesterday, I will come back to see you.'

'Oh god, don't do that.'

'Why not?'

'Because of where you come from. Your home planet's fifty light-years away. You travel at close to light speed, and we both know how that works. If you went home yesterday and came straight back, you'd only be six weeks older, but decades would have passed here on Earth. By the time you got back, Tim and I would be on the pension. Or worse.'

'Albert says he has an idea about this.'

'Yeah, you told us.'

'Now he does more. Says he build new circuit into the

Temporal Accumulator he make last night.'

'What sort of circuit?'

'The accumulator store time to use when we are travelling, yes? He say he work out a way to inject extra when we are moving so that back home the decades do not pass. Weeks only, like you say, so six-week trip will be the same for everyone.'

'But ... that would be like the travellers going backwards in time, and that's impossible.'

'He say no. He show me the math, but I do not understand. Make my brain hurt to even see. He say find a loopyhole in the physic.'

'A loophole? In the physics of Special Relativity?' Coral laughed. 'Did he say he mastered quantum mechanics in his tea break too?'

'Huh?'

'Seriously, Ludokrus. You said yourself he's got a touch of space mould. Do you really think your silly old syntho is smarter than our Einstein, or all of *your* scientists and physicists who made space travel possible?'

They climbed a second fence and Coral slipped around the side of the milking shed to hide another scanner block. Ludokrus watched her, thinking of his argument with Albert. She was right. What could their eccentric syntho possibly come up with that thousands of experts and specialists had overlooked? When Albert said he had an idea, Ludokrus *wanted* to believe him, but that didn't make it true – or even valid.

Coral returned.

Ludokrus sighed. 'I think you are right.'

'I wish I wasn't.' She made a face and looked away as

they headed for the house.

Frank appeared from one of the sheds further up, riding a ride-on mower. He waved and motored on, disappearing around the corner of the house. A few seconds later there was a loud crash and the sound of the mower's engine stopped.

Coral looked at Ludokrus. Ludokrus looked back. Then they both started running towards the house.

8 : A Little Leverage

The Cadillac stopped beside Dead Man's Pine. 'More like Dead Man's Stump,' Tim said as he clambered out and wedged a scanner block in its gnarled bark. 'Should we make a note of where we put these things so we can collect them later?'

'No need,' Albert said. 'They're designed to break down into their constituent atoms after a couple of days.'

'Leave only footprints, eh?' he said, getting back in the car.

'And craters,' Alkemy muttered.

They drove on, gradually descending towards Rata, passing through lush green countryside and rolling hills, pausing regularly so one of them could climb out and place a block.

The town of Rata consisted of a pub, a petrol station, a dozen shops – four of which looked like they'd been closed for a hundred years – and RAM and RAGS, which stood opposite each other on the main road, like guardians at the entrance to the town. Rata Area Merchants stocked farming supplies, tools, hardware and gardening needs, while Rata

Area General Store carried groceries, fruit and vegetables, fresh bread, and doubled as the local post office.

Glad looked up from stacking shelves when the four of them trooped in. 'Don't tell me the Townsends have thrown you out already,' she said to Norman.

He checked the rear aisle. The shop was empty. 'We're on a mission,' he said, then explained what they were up to.

'Sounds like a good plan,' she said. 'There's plenty of places round here to hide your blocks. And you say these Sentinel things live underground?'

Albert nodded.

'Rata's an old mining town. This whole area's littered with abandoned pits. But I hope you're not going with them.'

'Oh? Why not?' he said.

'Three kids wandering about won't draw attention, especially on a holiday weekend. But you're a stranger round here. You'll stick out like a sore thumb.'

'Actually, I was hoping to locate some raw materials.'

'Raw materials?'

'I need to build a receiver to track the signals from the scanner blocks. Norman said you may have some old computer equipment I could use.'

'I've got a shed full. We're the drop-off point for the annual recycling drive. C'mon through, I'll show you.'

* * *

Coral and Ludokrus found Frank scratching his head and studying the clothesline which was now lying in the garden

53

– with the washing still attached. The ride-on mower was jammed up on top of its support post.

'What happened?'

'Some damn fool ran into it,' Frank said. 'Can't have been watching where he was going.'

Coral laughed. 'Which damn fool would that be?'

'Would you believe I swerved to avoid a begonia?'

'I should breathalyse you. What's the penalty for being drunk in charge of a mower?'

'Fourteen years hard marriage, I think.'

'I heard that Frank Townsend.' Em appeared from the other side of the house, garden trowel in hand. 'What have you done now?'

'Ah, hello my sweet. I'm trying out my new invention: the horizontal clothesline.'

'I'll horizontal you! Alice has only just hung that out.'

'Actually, Alkemy and I did that,' Coral said.

'Did you, dear? Well you and Alkemy can have first swing at him.'

'Now now girls, no need to be like that. I just need to get the post out from under the mower.'

'And how do you propose to do that?'

'With the help of this strapping lad here.' He clapped Ludokrus on the shoulder. 'You lift the mower, I'll do the rest.'

Ludokrus frowned. 'Big mower. Look heavy.'

'When I say "lift", I don't mean *lift* lift. Here.' He picked up a length of four-by-two lying in the uncut grass and wedged one end under the side of the mower. Then he took a block of wood and placed it part way along to act as a pivot.

'Press down on this end, and up the mower goes. See? Easy. Now, if you just hold it there ...'

Ludokrus did so, supporting the mower's weight while Frank unbolted the clothesline's rotating top. It came loose, tilted over and fell into the freshly dug garden – along with the remainder of the washing.

'Ah. I should probably have got one of you to hold on to that,' Frank said.

Em glared. 'Yes, you probably should.'

'All right Ludokrus, now for the big lift. As high as you can.'

Ludokrus leaned on the end of the four-by-two and pushed it all the way down. The side of the mower rose smoothly, Frank grabbed the support pole – its base still fixed in a lump of cement – and dragged it to one side.

'There's your problem,' he said to Em. 'Dodgy concreting job.'

'Hmm, I wonder who did that?'

Ludokrus lowered the mower, then raised it again one-handed.

'Easy, eh?' Frank said. 'What was it that Archimedes joker said? "Give me a lever long enough, and a place on which to rest it, and I will move the world."'

'Archimedes?' Coral said. 'I didn't know you'd had a classical education, Uncle Frank.'

'What classical education? Bob Archimedes used to have the farm up the road. He was always saying stuff like that.'

'Did he have any laundry tips?' Em narrowed her eyes. 'Because you're going to need them once you've gathered up that washing.'

'Hadn't I better fix this first? After all, what good's laundry without a place on which to hang it?'

Em said nothing, just stared at him, her hands on her hips.

'No, no. Quite right, my sweet. Laundry first.'

9 : Town and Around

'If higher up is better,' Norman said, weighing a scanner block in his hand, 'then how about RAM's roof?'

'Are they designed to be ...' Tim began as Norman lobbed it, '... thrown?'

They watched it soar through the air then disappear from sight. It landed with a sharp *clack* on the far side of the pitched iron roof and shattered into dozens of pieces, all of which clattered down to the guttering.

'Guess not,' Norman said as the back door of Rata Area Merchants burst open. A wiry figure in a khaki-coloured apron appeared, wielding a broom. He looked up and down the street, snorted, 'Bloody kids,' and went back inside.

'Was that Rambob?' Tim said from the shelter of some bushes. 'I don't think I've actually seen him before.'

'The name is foreign?' Alkemy asked.

Norman pointed to a large cartoon ram painted on the side of the building, its features a caricature of its owner. 'His real name's Bob, but another Bob used to run the garage, so everyone called him Rambob to avoid confusion.'

'Funny to make up such a name.'

'Wait till you meet the guy that runs the Rata Area Tavern. They call him Morrie the Rat,' Norman said, leading them across the road, down a side street and over a patch of waste ground. A few minutes later, they came to a squat concrete structure standing on a low hill.

'The old water tower. Reckon that's high enough?'

A rusty iron ladder ran up one side. It didn't look safe, but Norman scrambled up it without a moment's hesitation. Alkemy put a hand to her mouth. Tim shook his head in admiration. It was like when they were mice. Give quiet, bookish Norman a mission, and he'd throw himself into it with such energy that he hardly gave a thought to his own safety.

'Whoa, it was a bit freaky near the top,' he said, dropping to the ground and shaking out his stiff, rust-coloured fingers. 'Some of those rungs are nearly rotted through. Great view, though.'

For the next hour they zigzagged back and forth across town, slipping scanner blocks onto roofs, tucking them behind signs, or wedging them in tree branches. Everywhere they went they saw evidence of an older and once more prosperous place. Ramshackle buildings with wood bleached almost white. Rusting machinery hidden in weeds. Areas of barren ground, some of it fenced off. Tim knew a little of the town's history. How it had been founded in the gold rush days of the 1860s before moving on to coal. Then that ran out too. Norman added a wealth of detail, pointing out old crushing plants and tailing pits, leading them past abandoned sidings, collapsed buildings and pools of noxious looking waste.

Pioneer Park was a narrow strip of greenery that ran

the length of the town. Two blocks back from the main street, partway up a gentle hill, it ran parallel to the road, continuing on past each intersecting street.

'Used to be the railway line,' Norman said. 'But that got ripped out years ago, so they turned it into a park.'

They stopped at a section containing a play area and stood watching while Alkemy clambered up the climbing frame to place a scanner block on top. She paused, looked about, gave a startled gasp and scrambled down.

'Quick, this way. Someone come.'

'Who? What? Where?'

'Hide. Hurry.'

She steered them to some trees on the northern side where they took cover and watched as a yellow Citroën swung into a car park near the swings.

'The Cakeface car. I see her coming up the hill.'

Millicent Millais, principal of Rata Area School, got out and looked around.

'What's *she* doing here?'

'You think she follow us?'

'What, up the water tower and through the quarry?' Norman said. 'We probably would have noticed.'

'Still, she is a Sentinel host,' Tim said. 'It's a heck of a coincidence.'

They watched as Cakeface walked over to the swings, inspected them and tugged on one of the chains.

'What's she doing?'

'Dunno.' Tim said. Cakeface gave him the creeps. He'd had dealings with her at school and had seen the effects of the Sentinels manipulating her mind and altering her memories, even as she spoke.

'If the Sentinels did send her,' Norman said, 'it's just what we want. The scanner blocks will pick up their directions.'

Cakeface went back to her car, opened the passenger door, and took out a clipboard. She returned to the swings and began examining them closely, checking the wooden seats, peering up to where the chains connected to the crossbar and making notes on the clipboard.

'Ha!' Norman said. 'It's not us at all. She's doing some sort of safety inspection.'

'Why would she do that? It's not her job.'

'I dunno.'

'On a Saturday too. And a holiday weekend. That's the sort of thing the local council should do.'

'Maybe some kid got hurt on the way to school or something and she has to write a report. Who cares? It's just a coincidence. She's not interested in us. She hasn't even looked this way. C'mon, we've still got a ton of blocks left, and now has to be the perfect time to leave a couple up at the school.'

Norman raced off through the undergrowth. Alkemy followed, calling for him to slow down. Tim paused a moment longer, watching Cakeface examining things and writing notes. Something wasn't right. He could feel it in his bones.

* * *

Norman dropped from a tree and landed at their feet. 'That's it, lucky last.' He dusted off his hands. 'Unless you guys have any left?'

Tim shook his head. 'I'm all out.'

Alkemy yawned. 'Me also.'

Norman had taken Albert's request to heart and insisted on spreading the scanner blocks as widely as possible. They'd been all over town, from one end to the other, zigzagging back and forth until their legs ached. Tim was secretly pleased they'd finally run out. If they'd had any more left he reckoned Norman would want to plant them in the next district.

Glad looked up as they trooped into RAGS. 'Mission accomplished?' Norman gave her a thumbs-up. 'Well if you fancy a snack, Albert's out the back cooking burgers. There's plenty to go round. Help yourselves to whatever you like.'

Norman licked his lips and rubbed his hands in anticipation. He was always hungry.

'Albert? Cook?' Alkemy muttered as they went through to the house. 'He does not do this at home.'

They found him in the neatly paved back yard, bent over a barbecue.

'It appears that an internal temperature of seventy-one degrees Celsius maintained for a period of ten seconds yields the best results,' he said, waving a spatula as he turned. 'Oh, it's you lot. All finished?'

He was wearing an apron bearing the legend "World's Greatest Mum".

'What you do?' Alkemy said. 'When we ask, you tell us you do not make the cooking.'

'I don't. Cooking's robot's work. However, Glad had several packets of meat patties nearing their expiry date and she asked if I could determine the optimal timing for

61

heating them.'

Tim smiled. Apparently it depended on how you phrased the question.

'And this?' Alkemy indicated the stack of bread rolls and bowls of sliced tomato, cheese, cucumber, gherkin, beetroot and shredded lettuce.

'Ancillary experiments. It would be a shame to waste the test material.'

'I agree,' Norman said, grabbing a paper plate, a bun and piling food on it.

Tim did likewise. The smell and sound of the sizzling patties made his mouth water. They'd walked a long way this afternoon. Lunch – and breakfast before it – now seemed like ancient history.

'What of the other experiment?' Alkemy said. 'You make a receiver for the scanner blocks?'

'Finished it an hour ago.' Albert gestured at a flat black-glass panel sitting on a chair. It was the size of a serving tray and looked like an oversized tablet computer, complete with shiny chrome edging. 'There have only been two transmissions so far. Both just after two o'clock as I was finishing it off, so not much use to us. But now it's complete, it should start recording useful data.'

'So now we watch and wait?' Norman said with his mouth full.

Albert nodded.

Tim reckoned waiting was a great idea, especially once he'd finished a juicy burger with all the trimmings and found one of the reclining armchairs in the lounge. It had soft deep padding, a rich leathery smell, and seemed to swallow him up. He settled with a sigh and pulled a lever to extend the folding footstool. The night's broken sleep and the long walk around Rata had worn him out, but as he closed his eyes, he thought about Cakeface at the playground, about their morning at the farm, and had a wild, crazy dream in which everything suddenly made sense ...

10 : Right From the Start

Tim opened his eyes and checked his watch. Four-thirty. For a moment, he wasn't sure if it was late afternoon or early morning as the room was in deep shadow. He guessed Glad had seen him dozing and drawn the curtains. He got up and pulled them open in time to see Norman, Alkemy and Albert troop in from the back yard.

Alkemy smiled as he met them in the kitchen. 'Ah, you are awake.'

'Where have you guys been?'

Her smile faded and she slumped at the kitchen table. Norman tossed the receiver down beside her, something in his carelessness giving Tim a clue.

'Not working?'

'It does work. Or rather, did. But it hasn't picked up anything since then.' Norman pointed at two sets of glowing numerals that read 14:07 and 14:22. 'So we went round to Cakeface's place to see if we could get a reaction. She was out in the garden. Alkemy went right up to her and said she was lost and could Cakeface please direct her to RAGS. Albert and I were hiding, watching, just in case. It'd be a perfect chance for the Sentinels to tell Cakeface to grab Alkemy, but she didn't do a thing, just gave her directions and even drew a little map.

'We've triple-checked the receiver and some of the scanner blocks. Everything's working OK, but the Sentinels have stopped transmitting.'

'Actually, I kind of guessed that would happen,' Tim said.

'What do you mean?'

'I have two questions for you,' Tim said to Albert, 'and one for Norman.'

'OK.'

'First, Albert, what would you do if you were the Sentinels and you found out about the scanner blocks?'

Albert crossed his arms. 'I'd stop transmitting.'

He turned to Norman. 'When did we leave that scanner block at the playground?'

Norman glanced at his watch. 'Just after two, I think.'

'So how about this for an idea.' Tim pointed at the receiver. 'At 14:07, the Sentinels send Cakeface out to find us. They've heard, or guessed, that we're in town somewhere, so they send her out, driving around till she spots us at the playground. What does she see? Alkemy climbing a climbing frame while you and I stand watching. Then she climbs back down and we all walk away. Must've looked a bit suspicious, kids in a playground not playing.

'At 14:22, the Sentinels "remind" Cakeface she's supposed to be doing a safety check of the swings and stuff. "And don't forget that climbing frame," they tell her. So after we're gone, she climbs up where Alkemy was, takes a look and sees the scanner block. The Sentinels see it through her eyes, realise what it is, and stop transmitting.'

'Whoa, hold on,' Norman said. 'It's just a grey cube. How would they know what it was?'

'What if they *knew* we had a transmitter problem?'

'How would they know that?'

'I have a nasty feeling we told them ourselves.'

Albert spoke quietly. 'You said you had two questions for me, Tim. What was the second one?'

'I was going to ask what the Sentinels look for in a host? Could they use anyone or anything?'

'Not at all. A host needs a certain level of consciousness and concentration for a start. A sparrow would never do, for example. They're too jumpy and constantly on the move. Plus, they need a good lifespan. It can take months to establish basic mental control, so it would hardly be worth bothering with something that only lived a year or two.'

'What about a cat? They can live for twenty years or more.'

'A cat?'

'I was thinking of Smudge, my aunt and uncle's cat. She was there right from the start, from the very first time I met Alkemy and Ludokrus when they were disguised as mice checking out the microwave. She's there all the time. Never goes on holiday, never leaves the farm. And she hangs around when people are around, yet no one ever really notices her.'

'I certainly didn't,' Albert said thoughtfully. 'Yes, a cat would make an excellent host. What made you think of that?'

'I remembered what Coral, Norman and I were talking about when Smudge finally came out from under the house this morning.'

Norman closed his eyes and slapped a hand against his forehead. 'Oh man!'

Alkemy and Albert looked on, mystified.

'After you guys went back to the reserve, we sat around the back lawn talking about your transmitter problem. Smudge came out and joined us.'

'And I mentioned how Albert had a plan,' Norman groaned.

Tim said, 'After lunch, when we headed to the reserve, Smudge tried to follow us. She only got stopped by the stream.'

'So how did she know we were in town?'

'Maybe she heard the car go or saw Ludokrus and Coral on their own. The Sentinels would wonder where the rest of us were and guess we must've gone into town because the Cadillac never went back past the farm.'

Norman bit his lip. 'It does make sense.'

They turned to Albert who nodded grimly. 'Yes, I'm afraid it does.'

'What now?' Alkemy said.

'I don't know. I really don't. But we should alert the others.'

* * *

The chicken coop had one of the best views on the farm. It sat on a headland and looked out over the sparkling waters of the Tasman Sea. Somewhere to the west, more than two thousand kilometres away, lay Australia.

Coral tucked the last scanner block under a corner of the coop's roof, then she and Ludokrus settled in a patch of sun on the far side, sheltered from the house. It was peaceful with the chickens ranging about. They had free run of the area, but most didn't stray far. Coral watched them for a while then closed her eyes. 'Say the blocks do work, say you find the Sentinels' transmitter and get a signal to your ship. How long then before another escape pod arrives?'

'About one day.'

'So if they don't work, you drive somewhere else tomorrow. And if they do, you go on Monday.' She sniffed. 'Not much difference.'

Ludokrus looked away and said, 'I will come back.'

Coral shook her head. 'You can't. That's crazy.'

'Co-ral!'

The cry came from the house. Long and loud. Frank's voice.

Coral jerked upright and poked her head around the side of the chicken coop. Her uncle was standing on the veranda, his hands cupped around his mouth.

'Co-ral!'

She stood up and stepped into view. '*What?*' she called back.

'*Phone!*'

She started for the house. Ludokrus followed.

'*Who is it?*'

'*Your boyfriend.*'

'Derek?' she muttered to herself. 'But he doesn't even have this number.'

Ludokrus stopped in his tracks.

'*I mean your brother.*'

'*Oh, ha ha!*' she called and hurried in to take the phone. Ludokrus stayed where he was and watched her go.

11 : The Rata Meteorite Mystery

Coral found Smudge lying in a patch of sun in the lounge and stood looking at her, thinking about what Tim had told her on the phone. All along they'd been looking for a human Sentinel host, never considering the possibility that it could be something else. A few days ago she'd even made a list of suspects; her uncle and aunt, Alice, the Robinsons from the farm up the road, Errol Fitchett the school bus driver. And it was the cat all along!

Possibly.

There was no way check now the Sentinels had stopped transmitting.

Or maybe there was, she thought.

'Hello puss.' she knelt and stroked the cat's sun-toasted side. Smudge glanced at her through one half-open eye, closed it again and purred lazily.

'You look comfortable there, but I've got somewhere I think you'll be even more comfortable.' She scooped the cat up in both arms and carried her through to her bedroom. 'How about that?' She set her down on her bed in an equally sunny patch and moved quickly to the door.

Smudge looked around, sniffed the duvet cover, and settled down again.

'That's it,' Coral closed the door on her. 'You stay right there.'

She skipped back to tell Ludokrus what Tim had said and tell him about her idea. He was sitting at the far end of the veranda, swinging his legs and staring out across the fields. She was about to speak when tyres scrunched on the gravel drive and a light green station wagon drew up. A man and a woman sat in front. The back was piled high with black boxes with bright metal frames. For a moment she thought they were members of a band who'd lost their way.

The driver stepped from the car and stretched. He was stocky, with close-cropped hair, jeans, running shoes, T-shirt and a black nylon jacket emblazoned with a 9-News logo. His companion emerged, a striking woman with blonde shoulder-length hair. She was dressed the same – T-shirt, jeans, light nylon jacket – but it all looked much more stylish on her. Designer versions, perhaps. And instead of running shoes she wore a pair of slinky high-heels.

'Oh. My. God!' Coral muttered as Frank emerged from the milking shed and Em and Alice appeared from round the back. 'I don't believe it. It's Crystal Starbrite!'

'Who?'

'The TV reporter. And not just a reporter. She's a real celebrity. She was going out with a guy from *Shortland Street* and their bust-up was on the cover of all the magazines for weeks.'

Ludokrus frowned. 'The news reporter is herself also news?'

'What's she's doing down here?' Coral said, fluffing her

hair and straightening her blouse before stepping off the veranda like a model on a catwalk.

Frank and Em were exchanging greetings.

'Eric Newcombe,' the stocky man said. 'I'm Crystal's OPC.'

'OPC?' Frank said.

'One Person Crew. Crystal reports and presents, I do the rest: video, sound, directing and editing.'

'Emma Townsend,' Em held out her hand.

'And Frank,' Frank said. 'I'm her OPC.'

'Are you the guy from the radio?'

'My fame is spreading.'

'Would you do an interview with us?'

'What, TV?' Frank raised an eyebrow. 'I'll have to talk to my agent.'

'It'll only take a few minutes to set up.'

'Make-up and wardrobe will take a bit longer than that,' Em said, casting a critical eye over her husband. 'You might want to come in for a cup of tea while you wait.'

'Where have you come from?' Frank asked as they ambled towards the house.

'Today? Westport,' Eric said. 'Hell of a drive. You're a long way from anywhere down here.'

'That's just the way we like it. Come on in.'

Crystal Starbrite lingered, looking as though she'd caught a whiff of something unpleasant from the nearby paddock.

'I'm Coral,' Coral said, offering her hand.

The reporter took it limply.

'Oh my god, are they *Italiano's*?' Coral gestured at her shoes. 'That is *such* a fabulous shop!'

'You know it?'

Coral gave a horsey laugh. 'I'd move in there if they'd let me.'

'You're not from round here then?'

'Oh god no! My brother and I are just down for a visit.'

Crystal glanced at Ludokrus lingering on the veranda. 'Oh, so you're an Auckland girl?'

'Born and bred.'

'I grew up in a place like this.' Crystal blew out her cheeks. 'In the middle of nowhere, the back of beyond. A long way from civilisation. I couldn't wait to escape.'

'I know *exactly* what you mean.'

Ludokrus watched them approach, chatting like old friends. Albert had warned them about talking to reporters, so he ducked inside ahead of them and went to the bathroom, waiting with one ear to the door till the others assembled in the lounge. Then he followed Em and Alice as they carried in trays of tea things and slices of cake.

Crystal and Eric had an armchair each. Frank and Em sat on the sofa. Coral sat on the floor near the famous reporter and her adorable shoes, while Alice perched on a padded footstool. Crystal tilted her head and flicked her shoulder-length hair. 'So, we were shooting a package in Westport and ended up ... what? ...' she glanced at Eric, '... two minutes late for check-in ...?'

'More like twenty.'

'... and they went without us! The last flight! Bloody Air New Zealand. We had to stay the night – what a dump! – and the news desk were furious. Then, *poof*, up pops this meteor thing and all of a sudden it's, "Oh Crystal, please get us some aerial shots."'

'So that was you in the helicopter this morning,' Frank said.

'Me,' Eric said.

'*I* don't do mornings.' Crystal gave her hair another flick. 'Anyway, we got their shots and were all set for the 10:40 flight when the news desk phones again. Radio NZ have been talking about a near miss for some tourists. Why don't we zip down and do a story ...'

'And here you are!' Coral beamed.

'... and *then* they phone again when we're halfway here. "There might be more to this than meets the eye. Take a couple of days and do an in-depth. We'll make it a Monday special, call it The Rata Meteorite Mystery." Great, but it's *my* bloody weekend!'

'The Rata Meteorite Mystery?' Frank said. 'I didn't know there was one.'

'Something our archives people came up with,' Eric said. 'Apparently you've had a couple of these things before. They reckon the chance of two coming down in the same area – even years apart – is millions to one.'

Alice set her cup down with a clack. The noise made them all look round.

'Sorry,' she muttered, her pale face paler than usual.

'Hardly a mystery,' Frank said. 'More like a coincidence.'

'Doesn't have the same ring though, does it: "The Rata Meteorite Coincidence"?'

'So you'll be staying in town,' Em said.

Crystal fluttered a hand. 'The office booked it.'

'A place called Feather Willow Lodge,' Eric said.

'Oh, nice. Daisy Robson's place. You'll be very

comfortable there. The rooms are lovely.'

'Is it far?'

'Another twenty K,' Frank said. 'Over the hill.'

'Is that the turn-off just before the campground I saw from the chopper this morning?'

'That's the one.'

'We'll stop and get some ground-level shots of the crater as we go past. Were there any other witnesses apart from you two?'

Alice took a breath then bit her lip.

'We're not exactly witnesses,' Frank said. 'We just heard the bang. But Coral and her brother actually saw it come down.'

'Would you be prepared to tell us about it on camera?' Crystal asked.

'Oh, sure.' Coral flicked her own hair and tried to remain casual, but she couldn't stop a delighted grin.

Eric said, 'How about we interview the kids at the crater after shooting you on the back lawn, Frank?'

'Funny, I felt like doing that myself this morning,' Em said quietly.

'And what about those tourists you mentioned on the radio? Have they moved on yet? I didn't see any sign of them from the chopper.'

'They're … still about,' Frank glanced at Ludokrus standing in the doorway, 'but they're not keen on reporters.'

'They'll talk to me.' Crystal flicked her hair again. '*Everybody* talks to me.'

'I'll put in a word, if you like,' Coral said.

Ludokrus grunted and walked away.

12 : The Interview Express

Glad handed Norman an overnight bag. 'Some things for your weekend away so you won't have to borrow from Tim.'

'Cool, thanks Mum.'

She kissed the top of his head and waved the Cadillac off.

'You have a nice mum,' Alkemy said.

'Thanks. I think so. What are your parents like?'

Alkemy was silent for a moment. 'Always busy. They have not much time for us.'

'Busy?' Tim said. 'I didn't think Eltherians had to work. Can't you just make whatever you want with nanomachines?'

'Of course. The nanomachine mean people are free to do whatever interest them most.' Alkemy paused. 'But our parent have not so much interest in us any more.'

Tim thought about Albert, their guardian, and wondered how common it was for children to have syntho minders on Eltheria.

'What do they do?' Norman asked.

'Study alien archaeology and ancient civilisation on

other planets.'

'That sounds cool.'

'Yeah, cool,' Alkemy sighed, her gaze fixed out the window.

Tim recalled how she and her brother had set out to visit their parents for the Eltherian equivalent of the school holidays and ended up crashing in Earth's solar system. There hadn't been any search parties, and Albert had been forced to rebuild their ship on his own. It had taken him years while Alkemy and Ludokrus were in suspended animation.

The rest of the trip passed in silence. Albert drove steadily. Alkemy kept her eyes on the passing countryside. Tim sensed a sadness in her. That she was looking at this stretch of road for the last time and trying to hold on to the memory of it. With the scanner block plan a failure they'd have to move on, keep one step ahead of the Sentinels and come up with some other way of communicating with their mothership.

Albert slowed as they neared the reserve, then sped up again, accelerating round the bend in Rata Road and sending a slew of gravel and dust over the turn-off.

'What's up? What was that about?' Tim said.

'There's someone there. A film crew.'

'Really?' All he'd seen was a glimpse of green station wagon.

Albert's eyes narrowed on the road ahead. 'And what's Ludokrus doing out here?'

'Ludokrus?'

Tim squinted, but it was at least another two hundred metres before he caught sight of a faint speck lounging by a stand of cabbage trees near the farm gate. The speck straightened and waved as they drew nearer, resolving itself into a familiar shape. Tim glanced at Albert, guessing he must have some sort of built-in telescopic vision.

'You see the TV peoples?' Ludokrus called. 'They wait for Tim. Want to interview.'

'Me?' Tim said.

'Your uncle and your sister also wait.' He gestured towards the house.

'Well if it's all the same to you, I'll let you off here,' Albert said. 'I think Alkemy, Ludokrus and I will do a little touring. In the opposite direction.'

Ludokrus took their place as Tim and Norman clambered out and headed up the drive.

'Ah, there you are,' Frank said. 'I thought I heard the Caddy.' His hair was slicked back and he was wearing a smart, neatly pressed shirt and tie over the top of his black singlet. It wasn't tucked in and he wore his usual tatty shorts and gumboots.

'My new look,' he said, seeing their surprise. 'What d'you think?' He held up his arms and turned left and right like a model on a catwalk.

'Um ...' was the best Tim could manage.

'Radio, now TV. A star is born. I might have to give up the farm.'

'I take it they only filmed your top half?'

'Yeah, like those newsreaders. You don't think they bother with trousers, do you?' Frank rubbed his chin. 'At least I *hope* they only filmed my top half.'

Coral bustled down the steps. 'Tim! There you are! Hurry up now, Crystal Starbrite's waiting for us at the reserve. Uncle Frank's going to drop us off.'

'Is that why you're all dolled up?'

'I'm not dolled up. I just had a wash and changed my blouse.'

'You've done your hair too. And are you wearing make-up?'

'None of your business. You should do something about your own hair. Ever heard of things called combs?'

Frank whistled to them from the ute. 'All aboard the Interview Express.'

'Can we ride on the back?' Norman said.

'I don't see why not.'

Coral travelled in the cab with Frank while Tim and Norman crouched on the tray, hanging on tightly, the wind in their faces. To Coral's disgust, it made even more of a mess of her brother's hair.

The first part of the interview took place near the intersection of Rata Road, right where they'd been when they saw the explosion. Tim and Coral repeated their walk, describing what they'd seen to Crystal Starbrite, while the cameraman walked backwards, filming them. Then they paused and answered questions.

Coral loved it, chatting easily with the reporter, and Tim was happy enough till the attention turned to him and he was asked to describe the flash he pretended to have seen moments before the nonexistent meteorite hit the ground. It was bad enough lying to his aunt and uncle. Doing so on national television seemed even worse.

'Let me get some shots of you by the crater,' Eric said. 'Fill-in stuff. No sound.'

'Can I be in it?' Norman said.

'I don't see why not.'

'You weren't even there!' Coral hissed.

'I'm here now though.'

Eric took shots from several different angles. The three of them standing on the crater rim looking down. Tim pointing, tracing the path of the imaginary meteorite through the sky. A view from the bottom of the crater looking up. The whole scene from a distance.

'That's great. Thanks everyone.'

Back at the farmhouse, they found the Cadillac in the drive being loaded up with provisions; a tray of eggs, vegetables from the garden, a bag of freshly dug potatoes. Albert closed the rear door, thanked Em and told Alkemy and Ludokrus he'd see them back at the caravan.

'Maybe you will start on dinner,' Alkemy called.

'I'll certainly start on something,' he called back.

'Still nothing on the scanner?' Norman asked Alkemy. She had the scanner in her backpack.

She shook her head.

'It's all our fault,' Tim sighed. 'If only we hadn't talked about your you-know-what problem in front of you-know-who. Where is she, by the way?'

'Have not seen her since we arrive.'

'Smudge!' Coral exclaimed. 'I almost forgot. I locked her in my room just before the TV people arrived. She's been in there for ages.'

'What did you do that for?' Tim said.

Coral smiled wickedly. 'I have a cunning plan ...'

13 : Game On!

'What sor of plan?' Tim asked.

Coral beckoned them to the end of the veranda where they wouldn't be overheard. 'I thought about what you said about Smudge, and it all makes sense. The Sentinels have got Cakeface in town keeping an eye on what happens there, but they'd really want someone out here too. After all, this is where the microwave is – the thing they used to lure the Eltherians here in the first place – and Albert said he's sure the second host isn't one of the adults.'

'Still, we cannot prove,' Alkemy said.

'Ah, but we can. That's where my cunning plan comes in.' She crossed her arms and looked at them smugly.

'So what is it?' Tim said. 'Or are you just going to stand there looking pleased with yourself?'

'What do all Sentinel hosts have to do regularly?' They looked at her blankly. 'Recharge, right? Cakeface has a pink office she spends half her days in. If Smudge is a Sentinel, she must have something similar.'

'But what? And where does she get this?' Ludokrus said. 'Albert say he does not find.'

'Albert was looking for something human-sized. Cats are much smaller. They can go anywhere.'

'How does she make? Cats do not build or paint. Also, big farm. If we are looking for a small place, this could be anywhere.'

'*That's* why I locked her up. I want Smudge to lead us to it. She hasn't had a zap for ages. She was in the lounge all afternoon, and now she's locked in my bedroom. I'm guessing it'll be the first thing she does when I let her out. Like a reflex. Automatic. Something she can't help herself doing. And the Sentinels can't tell her not to, not without sending out a transmission – which we'd pick up on the receiver.'

Ludokrus still looked sceptical, but Tim gave his sister a high-five and Coral took charge of the operation. 'Norman, over there behind the milking shed. Alkemy, up the drive. Tim, round the back. Ludokrus, you go over by the chicken coop. I'll give you all a minute to get in position then go in and let her out. I'll cover the house in case she stays inside. Keep your eyes peeled!'

'Yes sir, ma'am,' Norman gave her a mock salute and they fanned out to their hiding places.

There were faint scratching sounds as Coral headed down the hallway and a pink nose appeared in the gap the moment she opened her bedroom door. Smudge sniffed and pawed at the gap. Coral opened it wider and the cat shot out.

'Game on!' she said to herself, following Smudge as she headed down the hall and out through the kitchen, straight past her food and water dishes.

'Oh yeah!'

Coral jogged behind her, keeping a back a little as Smudge trotted across the veranda and disappeared around the side of the house. She directed Alkemy and Norman to close in with waves of her hands before racing after her.

'In the garden. Over there.' Tim said, coming out of his hiding place by the vegetable patch. 'Under those ferns.'

'Does not come out my side,' Alkemy said, joining them from the opposite direction.

Ludokrus and Norman arrived, and they all kept a careful watch, but the cat didn't re-emerge.

The garden at the back of the house was a wild patch bordered by paving slabs. The outer edge was flowers and low shrubs, with larger plants closer in. They'd been trimmed back where they threatened to block windows, but mostly they'd been left to themselves, meaning the vegetation was dense and tangled.

'Spread out, space yourselves equally and move in towards the house,' Coral said.

'Probably she is just going to the toilet,' Ludokrus said.

'Well be careful where you tread.'

Norman sniggered.

'This is serious!'

They moved slowly, one step at a time, a broad semicircle that narrowed steadily, closing in a huddle near the house.

'Nothing.'

'I see no sign.'

'Does not pass me.'

'But that's impossible. She can't have disappeared. Are you sure she came in here?' Coral said to Tim.

'Positive. Right over there. She dived straight in.'

'And no one saw her come out again?'

They shook their heads.

'That's just not possible—'

'Hold on. Look at this.'

Norman squatted against the house, pointing to the low concrete wall that made up the edge of the foundations. The house was timber, set on concrete piles, and the wall formed their outer boundary. It was half a metre high with rectangular air vents spaced along it at regular intervals.

'Look at what?' Coral said.

He pulled back a wiry shrub and revealed a broken air vent behind it.

The opening was a perfect cat-sized hole, but there was no way they could get through it. Coral sent Tim to fetch a torch, but all that revealed was a patch of dusty ground and the undersides of floorboards.

'Over here,' Norman called.

He beckoned them further up the garden to where a human-sized entry hatch was set in the wall below Tim's bedroom window. It was like a miniature gate, closed with a rusty bolt and hasp. He knelt, wiggled the bolt and drew it back. The hinges creaked as he opened it and cobwebs tore away from the sides.

They huddled round the opening, peering into the void. Grilled air vents, most shaded by shrubs, let in a little light, but it didn't penetrate far. All the torch revealed was concrete foundation blocks in neat parallel lines supporting a crisscross of floor joists.

'What is this place for?' Alkemy asked.

'Access to the plumbing and wiring that runs under the house,' Norman said, 'in case you ever need to get to it. Also, ventilation for the floorboards and foundations. Damp timber rots.'

Most of the space was open and empty. Nothing grew in the dark. There were some lengths of timber and old pipe near the entrance, and in the distance they could see the dark square shape of the base of the lounge fireplace. Closer in, away to one side, was another dark shape.

'What's that?' Coral aimed the torch, but the beam wasn't quite powerful enough. 'That's where the laundry is, isn't it? There shouldn't be anything under there.'

There was a length of timber on the ground in front of it. 'Looks like it's been pushed there,' Tim said.

Coral thrust her torch at Norman. 'Here. Go fetch.'

'What? Why me?'

'Because you're the littlest. There's not much space under there.'

'It's all yucky and cobwebby.'

'You've got a change of clothes, haven't you?'

'What about the cat? She must be round here somewhere. She'll probably claw my eyes out.'

'If she does, you'll be a hero.'

'How d'you figure that?'

'Because to make her attack you the Sentinels will have to send her a signal. And if they do that, they'll light up every scanner block in the district.'

Norman hesitated, but he couldn't fault her logic.

'Look, if you're too scared I'll go ...' Coral reached for the torch. Norman snatched it back and scrambled inside. Coral winked at the others.

He kept low, crawling on his knees and elbows to avoid banging his head on the joists. The others crowded round to watch his progress.

It was awkward in the confined space, but the earth was dry and his eyes quickly grew accustomed to the half-light.

'It's a cardboard box,' he called over his shoulder. 'On its side, facing away with the top flaps open.'

'Bring it here,' Coral said. 'Let's see what's inside.'

He dodged a length of sagging wiring and approached the box from behind, intending to hook it towards himself with his free hand. But it was heavier than he expected.

'There seems to be ... something ... in it ...'

'Possibly the—' Coral began as Smudge let out a yowl and bounded away into the darkness, heading for the broken vent.

'I guess we know where she spent last night now,' Coral said.

'That's better.' Norman caught the carton by its bottom edge and dragged it towards himself.

By the time he got it back to the entrance he was filthy and covered in cobwebs. He crawled out first, groaning and stretching, his hair matted with a mass of silver strands. Coral nudged him aside and reached for the box.

It was made of heavy brown cardboard and had black lettering on the side. She tilted her head and read aloud: 'Fieldstar Microwave Oven.'

'Is that the box the microwave came in?'

'I reckon.' Coral stood it upright and opened the flaps. 'And look at this.'

There was an old woollen blanket in the bottom of the box, matted with cat fur. The whole of the interior – sides, bottom, even the insides of the flaps – had been painted pink. The same sickly shade as Cakeface's office.

'Oh, man!' Tim muttered.

'This is it all right.' She turned to Ludokrus. 'What do you say to that?'

'Something is written.' He pointed to one of the flaps. 'Looks like an address.'

Coral turned the box over and they read the faint script on the yellowing label:

Mrs M Millais
10 Fernhill Road
Rata

'Cakeface! It came from her! That's all the proof we need,' she said, turning to Norman, who was still plucking cobwebs from his hair. 'You can put it back now. Exactly where you found it, mind.'

'What?'

'Get a move on. We haven't got all day.'

14 : The Last Piece

'I don't get it,' Tim said. 'I thought Alice gave them the microwave.'

'She did,' Coral said. 'It was a wedding present.'

'But that label was addressed to Cakeface.'

'Did you notice the edges? They were torn, like someone tried to peel it off. There was a squiggly line through it too.'

'I still don't see—'

'Alice gave it to Uncle Frank and Aunt Em, but she bought it off someone in town. Someone who already had one. They won it in a competition, didn't need a second one, so sold it off.'

'OK, so Cakeface set the whole thing up. But how did the box get under the house?'

'It's only a guess, but you know how cats love cardboard boxes. I reckon when they unpacked it, Smudge dived in and just kept going back. But who wants an old cardboard box sitting round? So they shoved it under the house. Somewhere Smudge could still get at it if she really wanted to. Besides, once the Sentinels established that mind-control thing, they'd make her play merry hell if anyone tried to throw it out.'

Norman reappeared, wiggling his shoulders and making a face.

'What's up with you?'

'I don't know. There were all sorts of creepy crawlies under there.'

'If the Sentinels build the microwave,' Ludokrus said, 'how do they get it to the Cakeface?'

'Maybe they delivered it then tweaked her memory to make her think she'd won it. They would have known she already had one and would probably sell it. Maybe they even gave her that idea too.'

'But how do they know who will buy?'

'They didn't, that's the point, and it didn't matter. Whoever ended up with it would become the target for you guys. Every time they used it, it would send out a time signal. Like a beacon. Like the bait in a trap. All they had to do was take over a nearby mind to keep a watch on it.'

'And they chose Smudge.'

'Maybe cats are easier to take over than people. Maybe they're easier to control too.'

'Wah!' Norman leapt back as a large black spider dropped from his shirt and scuttled away across the grass. 'There. I told you! Did you see that?'

'Yeah, whatever,' Coral said.

'There is one problem though,' Tim said. 'The timing's wrong. The Eltherian ship crashed twenty-five years ago, remember? Smudge isn't that old. And Aunt Em and Uncle Frank haven't been married that long either.'

'Fourteen years,' Coral said thoughtfully, recalling

Frank's comment after he crashed the mower.

'So why set this up so long afterwards?'

Ludokrus said, 'Because they do not know if we survive.'

He explained about the crash, how the ship's chronocells – the special batteries that stored spare time – sent out an emergency signal when they were wrecked. Called a Time Scream, it was a signal of distress to all other Eltherian vessels in the area.

'But there are none. No one come,' Ludokrus said. 'Maybe the Thanatos block it.'

The signal alerted would have the Thanatos to the crash, but it wouldn't have told them what the damage was or whether there were any survivors. So they sent out the Sentinels to keep an eye on things, just in case.

'Crash is bad. There is much damage. Many raw materials are lost. It take much time to find and refine these things, and always – away from ship – Albert must go careful in case he is detect.'

The first priority was to fix the ship's engines because, until they were functioning again, it was reliant on power from dwindling electric batteries and carefully positioned solar panels.

'Once the engine is fix, she must be restart. This always give off a telltale signal. Very small. Almost invisible unless you are looking.'

'Which is exactly what the Sentinels were doing,' Tim said. 'They spotted it, saw it meant someone was still alive out there, and realised that to get home they'd need to top up their chronocells. *That's* when they set up the trap.'

'How long did it take to fix the engines?' Coral asked.

'Albert tell us more than ten years.'

'That's it then: the last piece of the puzzle. There was no point doing anything earlier because you might all be dead.'

They grinned at each other, eyes bright, delighted to have solved the puzzle.

'Should we have put that box back?' Coral asked.

'What do you mean "*we*"?' Norman muttered.

'Maybe we should haul it out and destroy it. Deprive the Sentinels of one of their agents.'

'Better, I think, to leave. We know for sure now, but the Sentinel do not know we know. Maybe we can use.'

'Yeah, you're right. Good idea.'

Norman looked relieved.

'We must tell Albert right away,' Alkemy said, getting to her feet. 'Maybe he will make a new plan so we do not have to go tomorrow.'

Frank's voice sounded from the front of the house, a cupped-hand bellow. 'Paging Coral, Tim and Norman Smith. Dinner will be served in five minutes. Repeat, *five minutes*. This is your one and only call.'

'Oh man, dinner,' Norman said. 'I could eat a horse.'

'You can't go in like that,' Coral told him. 'Look at the state of you. You're filthy. And what's that crawling in your hair?'

'What? Ah! Oh my god!' He started a crazed dance, shaking and smacking himself around the head.

Coral sniggered. 'Even though it doesn't work around here, I really have to start carrying my phone. I'm missing some priceless video moments.'

15 : Distant Thunder

The long summer evening was drawing to a close. After saying goodbye to the others, after dinner and doing the dishes – without the help of nanomachines – Tim and Norman sat on the veranda watching black clouds form in the hills on the southern horizon. There was a flash of lightning. Norman began counting, '... twenty-two ... twenty-three ... twenty-four ...' then they heard the thunder, a distant rumbling roar.

'Eight kilometres away,' he said.

'How do you know that?'

'It's the difference between the speed of sound and the speed of light. Sound's much slower so you count off the seconds then divide by three to get the distance.'

There was another rumble. Louder. Tim shuddered. The sound reminded him of the explosion. He thought of Alkemy and Ludokrus back at the caravan and wondered how they'd react.

'Weird storm though,' Norman added. 'It came in really quickly. The sky over there was clear five minutes ago.'

Coral appeared from the kitchen. 'It's nearly nine

o'clock. You did set the video, didn't you?'

'Yes,' Tim said wearily. It was the third time she'd asked.

Em, Frank and Alice were already in the lounge when they took their places on the sofa. 'Are you sure it's recording?' Coral squinted at the unit below the TV.

'Yes!'

'And it's on the right channel?'

'There's only two choices down here.'

'I don't want to save some cooking show.'

'Nine News at Nine,' a booming voice-over proclaimed as dramatic music swelled and surged. 'All the news you *need* to know.'

A series of images flashed across the screen as the announcer said, 'In the news tonight: Can the Minister of Finance really count? ... Will Bubbles the giraffe finally get a hip replacement? ... And could a tiny South Island town be the staging point for an alien invasion?' A clip showed Coral in close-up saying, 'We wouldn't have had a chance. We'd have been blown to smithereens.' The music swelled again, more graphics tumbled about the screen, and the picture finally settled on the two presenters.

'Oh my god! Was that me?'

'Wow, third item.'

'Have you told your mum and dad this is on?'

'Do I really sound like that?'

Their item started six minutes later, beginning with a view from the air. The camera tracked sedately over farm land and bush until it suddenly came to rest at a sunburst-like scar in the landscape. Torn earth, raw and fresh, streams of debris radiating from its centre. It looked like they'd suddenly entered a war zone.

'The meteor came down in a remote area of native bush about forty kilometres south of Haast,' the newsreader said. 'Our news team has been on the scene since first light this morning.'

The picture switched to a nighttime view of Crystal standing in Rata's main street as the words *Live* and *Exclusive* scrolled along the bottom.

'Hey, there's RAGS!'

'Call your mum. Tell her to go out and wave.'

'Ssshh!'

'... and earlier today I spoke to some of the lucky survivors,' Crystal said as the picture switched to the interview with Tim and Coral.

'What about me?' Frank said. 'I put on tie and everything.'

'Ssshh!'

Tim looked uncomfortable describing the streaking light he'd seen in the sky in the seconds before impact, but Coral had no such qualms. She cut him off before he could even finish.

'We were coming down this road here,' she said, pointing, 'and suddenly there was this flash of light. Then about a second later: *boom*. Man, I thought the world had ended.'

'Were you frightened?'

'Not really. Just stunned.'

'What happened then?'

'This sort of mushroom cloud rose up. Like a mini atom bomb or something. Then it started snowing dust and stuff. From the explosion, I guess. It was pretty weird.'

'What if you'd been a bit closer?'

'We wouldn't have had a chance. We'd have been blown to smithereens. I mean, look at the crater and all the trees around it.'

The picture changed to a shot of the three of them looking down into the crater.

The boys laughed and nudged each other. Coral squealed and buried her face in a cushion, half-afraid to look and half-afraid not to.

'A family of tourists also had a near miss. Earlier this afternoon I tried to speak with them,' Crystal's voice-over continued, 'but they were still shaken by their ordeal.' The screen showed pictures of the closed-up caravan and the scorched paint along the back.

Back in the studio, the newsreader said, 'I understand this isn't the first time this area's been, shall we say, *targeted*, Crystal.'

'Quite right, John. This is only the latest in a series of mysterious happenings in an area that some people are already calling Latitude 51 ...'

'What people?' Frank said.

'... a clear reference to the mysterious Area 51 in the US where alien spaceships are supposed to have been captured and alien autopsies performed.'

Alice put a hand to her mouth.

'And just three nights ago, a shooting star startled locals as it skimmed the tree tops before coming to rest in remote bush somewhere to the northwest ...' she gestured.

'That's south,' Frank said.

Norman gave Tim a quizzical look.

'The killer robot's ship,' Tim whispered in his ear.

'… the very *same* area where, twenty-five years ago, yet *another* meteorite came down. Late this afternoon, I spoke to someone who was there.'

The picture changed to a wiry, middle-aged man in a khaki apron with a caption that said Robert "Rambob" Blessed.

'*He's* not wearing a tie.'

'Ssshh!'

'Yes, I remember it well,' Rambob said. 'It came down near an old mining area called Gizzard Gully. We had to go in there about a week afterwards because there were a couple of trampers missing in the bush nearby. I was part of the search party. We actually saw where it came down.'

'Can you describe it?'

'Just a long burnt streak in the ground. Must've come in at a shallow angle because it went on for quite a way.'

'No crater then?'

He shook his head.

'Any sign of what caused it?'

'Whatever it was, it must've buried itself pretty deep.'

'And the trampers?'

'We found them a few hours later. They were out of food and a bit confused. Had some wild stories about lights in the sky and strange noises at night, but they were fine.'

Back *Live* and *Exclusive* on Main Street, Crystal stared intently at the camera. 'So there you have it. *Three* mysterious impacts in the space of just twenty-five years. The experts tell us that the chances of that happening in the same area are more than a billion-to-one. So what is it about this remote town that's drawing the attention of visitors from outer space? Is it, as some claim, pure coincidence? Or is there something darker and more mysterious going on here?'

Alice stared wide-eyed at the screen and made a faint whimpering sound.

'I'll have more tomorrow, and an exclusive Nine News in-depth report on Monday.'

The image cut back to the studio. 'That was Crystal Starbrite, live, from Southland.'

Frank snorted. 'We're West Coast, you chump!'

* * *

Norman unfurled his sleeping bag and climbed into bed. 'So that first, one, the one that Rambob and the search party saw, the one that dug itself in, that must've been the Sentinels themselves, right?'

'Yeah,' Tim said, turning out the light. It had been a long day.

'Fancy Rambob coming across that. Who'd've guessed?'

'Mmm.'

'Oh, there's something I want to check.' Norman's torch snapped on and he leaned across the camp stretcher to examine the bookshelf. He pulled out an atlas and thumbed through it till he found a map of New Zealand. 'Hah! Thought so.'

'Thought what?' Tim muttered, barely able to keep his eyes open.

'That reporter kept talking about Latitude 51, but that's way down south by Campbell Island. We're about latitude forty-four. She's only about six hundred kilometres out!'

Tim grunted.

'If news people can't get their facts right, you don't know what to believe.' Norman put the book back and switched off his torch. 'I wonder what Albert said about Smudge. It's a real breakthrough, eh? Maybe he's come up with another way to get a message to their mothership. How many escape pods does it have, d'you know? Maybe they could send for a couple and we could go with them and have a look at it. Imagine that, a real live interstellar spaceship. How cool would that be?'

A faint sigh was Tim's only reply.

'Tim?'

Norman flashed his torch around and saw his friend was sound asleep.

16 : Absent Friends

Tim woke with a start, his heart pounding. The thump of it seemed to fill the silent room around him.

A flicker of moonlight hung around the edges of the curtains. Drizzly rain sounded on the iron roof. But that hadn't woken him. Norman gave a half-snore and turned over in the camp stretcher on the other side of the room. It wasn't that either.

His racing heart began to slow and he was half-convinced it had been a dream when it came again.

Tap. Pause. *Tap-tap-tap*.

He sat up in bed.

'Norman,' he whispered, 'did you hear that?'

Norman didn't stir.

'Norman!' he whispered as loud as he dared, but Norman's breathing carried on, slow and steady.

The sound had come from somewhere outside. Tim thought of the hatch beneath the house, right below his bedroom window and the vision of a Sentinel-controlled killer robot bursting through the floorboards filled his mind for a moment.

Then it came again.

Tap. Pause. *Tap-tap-tap*.

No, it wasn't the floor. It was coming from the window. And he recognised the pattern. What Ludokrus jokingly called his secret knock. The one he'd used to open the escape pod when he showed it to them.

Tim sprang out of bed, hurried across and snatched the curtains aside to reveal two pinched faces staring back at him through the rain-streaked glass.

* * *

The tea candles were Coral's idea. She said the room light might draw the attention of someone using the bathroom, so she sneaked them in from the kitchen and arranged them in a circle on the floor. Tim wedged his pillows against the bottom of the door in case even that flickering light was visible from the hallway, then the conference began.

'Start from the beginning,' Coral said. 'Right after you guys left us before dinner.'

Alkemy combed her damp hair back with her fingers. 'When we return to the caravan, Albert study a map book, one of the whole area he borrow from Glad. He read it like he is scanning to memorise. We tell him what we learn of Smudge and he is much pleased. Says that maybe we can use this information, but for now he must make more of the scanner block.

'He work for maybe two hour. Much intense. When he is finish he say he go for walk. Need to stretch. Will place more of the scanner block because there are not so many near the reserve.

'But we left heaps around there,' Coral said. 'And why bother anyway? They're useless.'

Alkemy shrugged. 'He go, and we do not see him since.'

The rain outside intensified, surging against the roof with a sound like a breaking wave. Alkemy and Ludokrus stared at the candles. The others exchanged worried glances.

'You went back to the reserve about six o'clock,' Tim said. 'How soon did he go out before that storm hit? Do you think he might have got caught in it?'

'It does not reach us, but we hear the thunder. Much loud. He go maybe one hour before it break.'

'Well that storm started just before the nine o'clock news, which means he left about eight.' Tim checked his watch. 'He's been gone for four-and-a-half hours.'

'He say he will be only one,' Alkemy said.

'Which direction was he heading?'

'Toward the resource pit.'

'What's past there?' Coral said to Tim. 'Just bush, isn't it?'

He nodded.

'Maybe he's lost. It does happen, you know.'

'Maybe. But I do not think. He have very good direction. Remember, he is part machine.'

'Could he have had an accident? Be lying injured somewhere?'

'Maybe he got struck by lightning,' Norman said.

They all stared at him.

'It does happen you know. Dozens of people get hit by lightning every year.'

'Not if the storm was eight K away like you reckoned,' Tim said. 'He was on foot, remember? He can't have gone that far. And it would have been getting dark.'

'You will be surprised,' Ludokrus said. 'Syntho may cover much ground quick. Machine part does not tire. Go maybe thirty kilometre in this time.'

'Even in dense bush?'

'In bush, maybe half of that.'

Norman reached for Tim's calculator. 'So fifteen K ... pi times radius squared ... That makes a search area of about seven hundred square kilometres. Halve that because we're on the coast – he's not likely to be at sea – but it's still a big area.'

'What if he's not lost or injured?' Coral said, choosing her words carefully. No one wanted to say it, but they had to consider the possibility. 'What if the Sentinels got him? Or a killer robot?'

Ludokrus shook his head. 'The robot blow himself up with our ship. They have no other.'

'Are you sure?'

'If they do, it would come for us also.'

'So your no-robot theory is based on the fact that you're not dead yet?'

Ludokrus made a face. 'Albert say they have only one.'

'And Albert was always straight with you guys, right?'

He pursed his lips and looked away.

'What about the Sentinels themselves?' Tim said. 'Could they have caught him?'

Ludokrus shook his head. 'They live underground. Avoid the sun.'

'The sun's not up now,' Coral said.

'It was still light when he leave.'

'They might have set a trap.'

'How can you make a trap if you cannot go outside?'

'How do you deliver a microwave if you can't go outside? They must have machines and stuff to do things for them.'

'How do they know where he is? Where he go?'

Coral shook her head and they lapsed into silence.

'He must be lost,' Tim said, though he wasn't totally convinced. 'Look, we're all pretty tired, and we can't mount a search in the dark, so the best thing to do is get some sleep and start first thing in the morning. He'll probably be back by then anyway.'

'You are right. We can do nothing now.'

Alkemy and Ludokrus got to their feet and retrieved their raincoats.

'Maybe he return while we are gone,' Alkemy said, forcing a smile, 'and now he worry that *we* are lost.'

'Yeah, maybe.' Ludokrus patted her shoulder and adjusted her hood, but when he looked back at the others his expression was grim.

2

Sunday

17 : Only Two

Alkemy woke several times in the night thinking she sensed Albert returning, but it was either the wind in the trees, the intermittent rain or shifting patterns of light and dark as heavy clouds scudded past the moon. Between each hopeful start she somehow drifted off again, sleeping in spite of her worry and disappointment. Now, studying the empty awning in the light of dawn, those snatched moments of rest felt like a betrayal.

The rain had ceased, but the sky was as grim as her mood. She retraced the steps she'd seen Albert take the night before; walked past the Cadillac and headed up the grassy knoll on the reserve's south-eastern boundary. At the top, she paused to look around. Here, after a short flat stretch, the ground dropped away into a shallow valley that formed the resource pit. Humans called it a rubbish dump because they hadn't yet mastered the technology to allow them to reuse discarded things.

She surveyed the piles of junk, half-expecting to find Albert studying some piece of primitive technology, careless of the time and bemused by her concern, but all she found were gulls fighting over scraps.

To the left was the gravel track that led back to Rata Road. To the right, a long stretch of gorse that eventually gave way to rocky coastline. In between, just beyond the dump itself, lay a succession of bush-clad hills, misty and still in the morning drizzle.

She thought of his last words – 'Won't be long, Alkemy' – words she'd barely paid attention to. Now he was out there somewhere, lost or injured or ...

'Hey! Hey!'

For a moment, her heart skipped a beat. For a moment, she thought ...

She turned to find Ludokrus running up the slope behind her.

'What you think you do?' He shook her shoulder, still breathless, still in his pyjamas. 'I wake and you are gone also.' He stood there gasping, staring at her angrily.

'I just come to look.'

'No. No, you do not. You do not go alone. We are only two now. Understand? Must always wait for other. Must make plan first, go careful. Not alone. Never!'

Tears started. She looked away. Ludokrus put his arms around her.

* * *

Frank was hosing down after the morning's milking when he spied Em leaning on the rail that ran around the holding yard. 'Gidday stranger. Been there long?'

'Long enough to see you missed a bit by the milking

parlour.'

'And there I was, thinking you were here for the pleasure of watching a craftsman at work.'

'Tricky is it,' she said, 'aiming that hose?'

'Wouldn't want it to run away with me.' He gave it a flick in her direction. 'These high-pressure things can easily slip out of your hand.'

Em narrowed her eyes. 'So can carving knives.'

He grinned and shut off the valve. 'Did I just see the kids heading off to the reserve?'

'They're getting an early start. Meeting the others at the caravan then doing a walk to Fantail Falls.'

He checked the sky. 'Good day for it. It'll be spectacular after that rain last night. The country air really is getting to them.' He looked at his wife. 'But something tells me that's not what brought you out here. What's on your mind, my sweet?'

'Alice,' Em said with a sigh. 'She'd like a word, she says. With both of us.'

'This isn't about the other night is it? When she came back babbling about spaceships in the reserve and alien mice being held prisoner?'

'I hope not. But she's got a bee in her bonnet about something.'

'Remind me again of the difference between having bees in your bonnet and bats in your belfry?' Frank said as they walked back to the house.

Alice was at the china cabinet in the far corner of the kitchen when they entered. The glass door was open and she was checking and replacing the willow-pattern dinner plates one by one. When she was done, she closed the door and turned to face them, frowning.

'Tea?' Em said.

'What? Oh, no. No, thank you.'

'What's on your mind, Alice?' Frank said.

Alice took a moment to compose herself then settled at the dining table, gesturing they should do likewise. 'I know you think I imagined what happened the day before last. I know you think I fell and banged my head or something. I started to think I must have imagined it too. Like an unusually vivid dream. But then other strange things started happening.

'First there was that explosion, or meteorite, or whatever you want to call it. What a coincidence! Hours after I tell you I saw a spaceship at the reserve – *poof* – it's gone. Almost as if someone was trying to cover something up. You heard what they said on the news last night. The experts reckon the chance of three meteors landing the same area in a short space of time is a billion-to-one.'

The kettle boiled and clicked off. Em made no move towards it.

'The second odd thing happened yesterday morning. I come down to visit you two at least once a year, but I hardly ever go in to Rata. I haven't been there for years. And I haven't seen Norman Smith since he was running around in jodhpurs. And yet when I saw him yesterday, sitting out there on the back lawn, I recognised him at once. Do you know why? Because he was there too. Standing by the spaceship with the others. In my "dream". All grown up. Exactly as he is now. That same unruly hair, the same T-shirt, everything.'

'So ... what are you telling us all this for?' Em said.

'Because I'm going to speak to that reporter. I thought about it all last night. I thought about what she said about the meteorite mystery and that Latitude 51 business, and I think it's important that people speak up and tell what they know.'

'Well don't involve us,' Em said.

'But you *are* involved, Em! You were the people I first told about the spaceship. Before it got blown up. Before there was any talk about meteorites or mysteries. I want you to back me up; about what I saw and when I saw it. Remember how I told you about it? I was standing right over there.'

'You told us a lot of things, Alice. You were in a frightful state when you got back here. And no wonder. You must have got lost in the bush and somehow found your way out again. To be honest, the way you were talking, we thought you were a bit hysterical.'

'I suppose you think I'm being hysterical now.'

'Not at all.'

'So does that mean you'll back me up?'

'No, because it really doesn't prove anything. What about the other things you said?'

'What other things?'

'I noticed you were checking the willow-pattern plates when we came in. Those heirloom ones of Mum's. You said one of them got broken at the reserve. That that was one of the reasons you ran off into the bush.'

Alice said nothing.

'Did you count them?'

'Yes.'

'How many are there?'

'Eight.'

'Just like always. And do you know how I know? Because Coral returned it yesterday, with thanks from Albert and the children. It got overlooked in the subsequent excitement. I rinsed it and put it away myself. There wasn't a mark on it.'

'I ... I can't explain that, but I did tell you about the ship, didn't I?'

'You did, yes, but it was one story amongst several. You must see how this plate business makes it look. We just don't want to get involved.'

'How would it involve you?'

'I've seen the sorts of books you read, and I know the sort of people that follow those ... ideas. They'd be pestering us for ever and a day. We don't want that. We just want to carry on with our quiet lives here.'

Alice pursed her lips. 'I won't be put off, Em. I'm going to talk to that reporter anyway.'

'You've always did have a stubborn streak, but you're a free agent. You can do as you like. Just don't involve us. Or the children.'

'But they *are* involved. They were there, standing round the spaceship.'

'They're still children. And not our children. Or yours. I don't want them caught up in this. Is that clear?'

'But—'

'No buts. You do whatever you see fit. But you do it on your own.'

18 : Leaping Frog

Tim saw Alkemy's pinched face at the caravan window as they crossed the circle of grass. She was brushing her hair and fastening it back with hair clips. She glanced up, saw them, and came out to greet them.

'Still no sign?'

She shook her head.

He eased off his backpack and set it down. 'Well we've got all day to help look for him. We told Aunt Em we're going on a tramp to Fantail Falls.'

'She's given us enough food for a month!' Coral groaned, dropping her own pack.

'Well, maybe a week,' Norman said. He was carrying a shoulder bag as he didn't have a backpack. 'We could use some of it for an after-breakfast snack.'

'We've just eaten!'

'It'll lighten the load.'

Ludokrus came from the awning. Coral greeted him warmly but he looked distracted and gestured to the trestle table in the corner where the calculator was completing a collection of ropes, torches, compasses, first aid supplies, energy biscuits, whistles and waterproof markers.

'Hey, nice work.'

'Should divide between. Share the load.' He began separating the things into four piles.

Tim picked up the receiver. 'What happened to this? Someone leave it out in the sun?'

What had once been a flat black rectangle was now dish-shaped. It looked like a fancy rectangular fruit bowl.

'Albert remake her yesterday,' Alkemy said, 'when he make more scanner block.'

Tim touched the power switch. The screen lit up. The same display as before, except the lines of the spreadsheet now bowed with the bowl shape. 'It's no improvement. It's actually harder to read now. And still nothing since 14:22 yesterday.' He turned it off again and put it aside.

Norman was watching Ludokrus separate the search supplies. 'You're only making four piles There's five of us.'

'Only four must go.'

'What? Why?'

'Because we must work in pair, like the soldier. Two pair of peoples, two group. Go two-by-two. First group move ahead while the second watch from behind. Then stop and swap. Like leaping frog, yes?'

'So ... who gets to stay behind?'

'Behind person is important also. In case Albert come back. Or we do not.'

'Couldn't we just leave a note?'

'Also to watch receiver in case the Sentinel again begin the broadcast.'

'We could take it with us.'

'Should not put all the egg in one basket.'

'So who ...?' Norman's repeated, his voice trailing off.

Ludokrus continued sorting the supplies. Coral fiddled with the straps on her backpack. Alkemy picked up the calculator, tucked it inside her pink school backpack and put that inside her larger backpack. Tim looked away across the reserve.

'What are you telling me here?' Norman said.

'You've only got a shoulder bag,' Coral said. 'And you do know how to work that receiver thing.'

'Yeah, like an on-off switch is really complicated. You could always make another backpack, you know. With the nanomachines.'

'Still, someone must stay. Like command post, yes?'

'No,' Norman said, 'I want to help too.'

No one spoke.

'It's not fair.' He snatched up the receiver and stomped off into the caravan.

'This is also help,' Ludokrus called after him.

There was no reply.

'OK.' He turned to the others. 'We make two team. Brother, sister. Yes?'

'Better to mix and match,' Coral said. 'The Sentinels are after you guys. If you travel together, you make a single target. Besides, you should go with someone who walks about the same speed you do, so it should be Tim and Alkemy, and me and you.'

Ludokrus shrugged.

Coral looked puzzled. 'Don't you want to walk with me?'

'Do we need that?' Tim pointed to Glad's map book lying on one side of the table.

'Too heavy. Take only essentials.'

Tim called goodbye to Norman as he and Alkemy followed the others, but Norman didn't answer.

* * *

The day was clear and fine. The night's rain was now a misty memory on the northern horizon and they could already feel the heat building as they climbed the grassy knoll and skirted the perimeter of the rubbish tip. They proceeded as planned; one party leapfrogging the other with what Tim at first, thought was unnecessary caution. But even here, out in the open, it had its advantages. Four pairs of eyes – two looking ahead, two scanning from behind – meant that the intervening territory was thoroughly surveyed. If it hadn't been for that, he might have missed the first clue.

The boundary of the rubbish tip was marked by a pyramid of appliances piled haphazardly on top of each other. Old stoves, fridges, freezers. Discarded whiteware that was rapidly becoming rustware. Pausing to beckon the others, Tim adjusted the straps on his backpack, glancing up as he did so. Something caught his eye in a V-shaped hollow near the top and he immediately took off his pack and began to climb.

'Hey, this is no time for—' Coral said as she and Ludokrus brought up the rear, but she stopped mid-sentence when he dropped to the ground and held out a scanner block.

'Ah ...'

'We do not place this,' Ludokrus said.

116

'Nor did we,' Tim said, 'so it looks like we're heading in the right direction.'

He slipped it in his pocket and they moved on.

Beyond the resource pit, things got more difficult. There was no boundary fence, but past the appliance pyramid the ground became rougher and the weeds thicker till they finally gave way to a stand of kanuka at the base of a steep hill. Tim sighted back along the way they'd come. It seemed logical to continue up the hill, but there was no clear path. If Albert had left any tracks, the overnight rain would have washed them away.

They moved into the forest. The bright day disappeared beneath the dense canopy overhead, and five metres in the distant sound of the sea vanished, muffled by thick bush. They found themselves in a dense, green, twilight world.

Travelling in a straight line became impossible. They had to skirt, climb over or clamber under obstructing branches, and fight their way through tangles of supplejack and kiekie. There were fallen trees, rotted and damp, and broad ponga fronds that brushed past their faces like gigantic fans. It was like negotiating a complicated three-dimensional maze. Only the rising angle of the ground told them they were moving in the right direction.

Fifteen minutes later, they struggled to a small clearing at the top where a gap in the trees showed an endless progression of similar hills ahead, all as densely wooded as the one they were standing on.

'This is hopeless!' Coral dropped her pack to the ground and slumped down on it.

'I have no idea would be so thick,' Ludokrus said. 'Good job we have the compass.'

'You're not seriously thinking of carrying on, are you? Look at this place! He could have angled off in any direction. He could be lying unconscious a couple of metres away and we'd walk right past him. What did Norman reckon? Three hundred square kilometres? Of this? We've travelled about three hundred metres. We'll end up getting lost ourselves. In fact, I'm not sure we aren't already.'

Tim and Alkemy came up behind them and took off their packs, staring glumly at the view. No one spoke as they pulled out their water bottles. Tim handed round some snack bars. At length, Alkemy said, 'He say he will not be long.'

'How long, not long?' Ludokrus said gently. 'Ten minute? Half one hour?'

'One hour. He say one hour only.'

'He can go fast. You know this. Even in this he maybe cover five, ten kilometre. But which way? We do not know. Maybe we already pass. As Coral say, bush so thick we would not see.'

'We could spend all day just searching this hillside,' Tim said.

Alkemy lowered her head. A tear ran down her cheek. 'We cannot give up.'

But what else can we do? Tim thought. Search parties – proper ones – involved dozens of people, sometimes hundreds. And even specialists like Search and Rescue – highly organised and properly equipped – might spend days or weeks and still turn up nothing. What could four kids hope to achieve in terrain like this?

'What was that?' Coral cocked her head. 'I heard something. Listen.'

They listened, straining their ears. There was nothing but a distant bird call. The dense bush seemed to swallow sound. Then they heard a snap and crack and rustle of undergrowth somewhere on the hill below them.

'Someone's coming,' Tim said.

'Or some *thing*.'

Alkemy got to her feet. 'Maybe is Albert.'

Tim put a hand on her arm. 'And maybe it isn't. We should be careful.'

'Whatever it is, it's coming this way,' Coral said.

They stared at the wall of undergrowth around them. The sound was getting louder, which meant that whatever was making it was getting closer. Fast.

'What shall we do?'

'Split up. Hide,' Tim hissed. 'Now!'

19 : Stalker

Em called to Alice saying that Frank had made coffee and that they were having it on the back lawn.

'I'll join you in a moment,' Alice said, reaching for the phone book and watching her sister go. She found the number she wanted and dialled.

'Feather Willow Lodge. Daisy Robson speaking.'

'Oh hello. Could I speak to Ms Starbrite please?'

'Who's calling please?'

'My name's Alice.'

'Alice ...?'

'Just Alice.' Daisy Robson always was a nosy old biddy, Alice thought.

'One moment, please.'

It was a long moment. It went on and on. Alice strained on the end of the phone cord, keeping an eye on the veranda in case Em or Frank came back in. Eventually, another voice came on the line, but it wasn't Crystal Starbrite's.

'Eric Newcombe speaking.'

'Oh ... I wanted to speak to Ms Starbrite.'

'She's not up yet, I'm afraid. Can I help?'

'My name's Alice Jones. We met yesterday at—'

'The Townsend farm, of course. Sorry, I should have recognised your voice. How are you, Alice?'

'I'm well, thank you. Look ... I ... have some information. About what you came here for.'

'Let me grab a pen and paper.'

'It's ... rather more than that. It's things I've seen. Personally.'

There was a pause. 'You didn't say anything yesterday.'

'No ... well ...I couldn't really. Not then.' She took another look at the veranda. 'Not with my sister and brother-in-law around. They ... wouldn't approve.'

'You mean they're hiding something?'

'In a way, I suppose. But that's not what I want to tell you.'

'What *do* you want to tell us?'

'Everything that's happened. All I know.'

'You mean an interview?'

'That's really why I called.'

'And on a scale of one to ten, how big would you say this is?'

'Oh, nine-and-a-half at least.'

'Really? OK. Look, Crystal's not up yet. She rarely surfaces before ten, but for "nine-and-a-half at least" I'll put a stick of dynamite under her. Can we meet you somewhere? Not at the farm, obviously. How about the reserve? I want to try and catch those tourists too. We could meet you there at, say, ten-thirty. How would that work?'

Alice checked her watch. 'Perfect. I'll see you then.'

* * *

Tim, Coral, Alkemy and Ludokrus snatched up their packs and scattered to opposite corners of the clearing, diving into the dense bush. Whatever was pursuing them suddenly changed direction and headed Tim's way.

Or did it?

He paused, wondering if it was an acoustic trick caused by the undergrowth. Perhaps the others were experiencing the same sensation; that whichever way they turned, the stalker seemed to follow them.

The crack of small branches and rustle of dry leaves sounded like it was directly behind him. He darted left around a clump of kanuka. The sound moved too. It was still directly behind him. And getting closer.

He worked deeper into the bush, moving as quickly and as quietly as he could, cursing the awkward pack and wishing he'd left it at the clearing. It wasn't fair, he thought. He had to move carefully, but his invisible pursuer was doing the opposite. Charging through the undergrowth, heading straight towards him whichever way he turned, as if it could see him through the foliage. What's more, it seemed to be taking at least two steps for every one of his.

He spun round looking for something to defend himself with, a weapon of some sort – a stick, a lump of wood, anything to fend it off – but as he did so his backpack snagged in a tangle of supplejack and wouldn't pull free. He tore at the buckles and loosened the straps as the crashing pursuit reached a crescendo behind him, and he'd just slipped one shoulder free when a hand shot out from the undergrowth and seized his arm.

'Gotcha!'

'Whoa!' He almost jumped out of his skin before he

recognised the voice. 'Norman! Jeez! What the hell ...?'

Norman laughed, delighted with his prank.

'Where ...? What ...? How did you ...?'

Norman held up the receiver cradled in his left arm. He'd obviously been studying it, oblivious to his surroundings. His face and arms were scratched, there were twigs and leaf litter in his hair, and he was panting with the effort, but he didn't seem bothered by any it. He looked around and said, 'Where are the others?'

Tim explained as they worked their way back to the clearing.

'You know you were heading in a circular direction?' Norman said.

'How would you know?'

'People do that when they don't have clear visual references, like when they're lost in fog or dense bush. It's because most of us have one leg slightly shorter than the other. In your case, it must be your right leg because you were going clockwise.'

'What?'

The others responded to their calls and returned to the clearing. Coral glared at the new arrival. 'What are you doing here? You were supposed to stay in the caravan.'

'I thought you could use some help.'

'Listen, any time we want—'

'I think you should listen,' Tim said. 'He did just track us down, in this,' he gestured at the dense bush.

'Track *you* down, you mean. What was it? Did you leave him a paper trail or something?'

'Nope,' Norman beamed. 'I used this.' He held out the receiver. 'I figured out why Albert changed the design. I thought you might be interested.'

'It doesn't even work!'

'Ah, but it does. Sit down and I'll show you.'

They arranged their packs in a semicircle. Norman sat cross-legged on the ground in front of them, the receiver perched on his knees. He tapped the on-off switch and the column of figures appeared. The last entry still read 14:22.

'This is the original display. It lists messages received from the scanner blocks and – hopefully – the timing of the signals. With some fancy calculations and a bit of triangulation, we'd be able to work out a map reference. But we'd need a separate map, right? Which is why Albert borrowed Mum's map book. He rebuilt the receiver to incorporate the map.'

Norman dipped a finger into the shallow basin formed by the sides of the device and made a circular gesture. The figures vanished, replaced by a glowing display of whorls and lines that filled the interior space and seemed to rise above the dished surface.

'Remember you said you thought the figures were actually harder to read in this version?' he said to Tim. 'You're right. They are. And that got me wondering why he went to the trouble of making something inferior. The rest was just a matter of experimenting.'

He made a flattening gesture with his hands and the image zoomed out to reveal what at first, looked like a weather map made up of a series of concentric circles, but when he tilted the device and showed it from the side, they could see it was a profile of the terrain.

'Oh wow!'

'It's a kind of holographic 3D effect,' Norman said.

Tim stared at the image, moving his head from side to side. It looked like a finely detailed wire-frame model sitting in the bowl of the receiver. He could make out the shape of the hillside they were on. A pair of targeting arrows pointed to a glowing dot.

'Is that us?' he asked.

'You, actually. Did you have a scanner block left over?'

'No, but I picked one up at the dump.' He took it out of his pocket.

'Good job you did because that's how I tracked you. I saw it moving.'

Norman plucked it from Tim's hand and studied it, then threw it over his shoulder into the bush behind him. 'Whoops, lost it.'

He got to his feet, turned round and, guided by the receiver, retrieved it again. 'But not for long.'

'OK, very clever. But what use is that?' Coral said.

Alkemy hunched forward and peered at the screen. 'You can see where is Albert from the block he carry?'

'Not quite, but look at this.'

He put the receiver down where they could all see it and zoomed the image out until the jagged edge of coastline became visible. There were three bright clusters of dots within it.

'This thing picks up all the scanner blocks we've put out. You can see the clusters. There's the ones around the farm. Those one's there are round the caravan. And over there are the ones around Rata.'

'Got it!' Tim said, his excitement rising. He could see where this was leading.

Norman put thumb and forefinger around the second

cluster and expanded them. The receiver zoomed in until each individual dot was visible.

'The caravan's about there, see?' He pointed to a neat cluster centred on the reserve then moved the image down to one dot on its own. 'That's us. Or rather, Tim.' He dragged the image down further. 'So what are those?'

A trail of dots led away to the southeast.

The others looked at each other in puzzlement.

'It's Albert!' Tim exclaimed. 'He went out last night placing more scanner blocks, remember? He's left us a trail!'

20 : Bonus

'Earth Eater is almost through. Look, camera nine.'

'Lights. More lights! Is that ..?'

'Yes! We got it! We got the synthetic! I told you they'd do anything to get our transmitter.'

'Is it dead?'

'Wait, let me send a probe in ...Yes, quite dead.'

'You know, if we retrieved its memory unit, we could see what the monkey people were really up to.'

'Excellent idea, and it will only take a minute ...'

'What's the problem? Why has the probe stopped?'

'That's odd. The synthetic appears to be booby-trapped.'

'Booby-trapped?'

'Look at those readouts. Sensors indicate the memory unit is inaccessible to anyone but an Eltherian. If there isn't one present the thing will self-destruct.'

'Are they normally wired like that?'

'Not at all. The fact that this one is suggests it's valuable and important.'

'Something our masters would like to see?'

'Definitely.'

'But we can't extract it without an Eltherian present.'

'No. Still, if it's that valuable and important, perhaps the Eltherians would like to retrieve it too.'

'You mean, use the synthetic as bait?'

'That's exactly what I mean.'

* * *

They plunged back into the undergrowth following Norman who, unburdened, set a cracking pace. He forged ahead, following a straight line towards the next scanner block, careless of the terrain. Several times they came across rocky patches which he'd had simply scrambled down or jumped – not so easy carrying a heavy pack – and they were forced to skirt around them and work their way back. They'd find him, leaning against a ponga or waiting for them in clearings, grinning. He'd barely give them time to regroup and catch their breaths before saying, 'All set? This way,' and go crashing on ahead.

Tim suspected he was having a little revenge for being left behind, but without him, without the receiver, they were lost. It was obvious from the terrain that they'd gone down one hill and partly up another, but he had no idea which way they were heading or how to get back to the reserve. He thought of Albert the previous evening, going through here on his own. Yes, he was part machine and probably had in-built satellite navigation and night-vision eyes, but with the sun going down this place would have been pretty creepy.

Where was he heading anyway? This wasn't going-out-for-a-stroll terrain. He must have had some aim in mind.

Tim thought of the map book back at the caravan and wondered.

He heard a shout somewhere to his right, muffled by the bush. 'This way!' He changed direction, pushed past long ribbons of supplejack and shouldered his way through a stand of horopito to find himself climbing a short steep bank that opened on a narrow grassy clearing. He staggered to a halt, dropped his pack and sat on it, gasping for breath. The others emerged behind him and did the same.

'Good place for morning tea,' Norman said, looking around.

He was right. The clearing was narrow and flat and curved around the side of the hill they were on. One side was in shade, the other in dappled sunlight – a welcome sight after the gloom of the bush, even if it meant shielding your eyes while they adapted to the glare.

'Bit early for morning tea.' Tim checked his watch. 'We've only been going half an hour.'

'You're kidding!' Coral groaned. 'It feels like we've been going half the day. How far is the next block?'

Norman checked the receiver and pointed up the hill. 'In a straight line, it's about two hundred metres that way. Over that ridge then down the other side.'

Coral looked up at the densely bush-clad slope above the narrow clearing and blew out her cheeks.

'Although …' He swivelled left and right and looked around. To the right, the clearing ended in a jumble of rocks. A recent landslide by the look of it. Norman walked over and began climbing the reddish coloured jumble. Tim followed.

'Although what?'

'I was wondering if this might be some sort of track. Look.' He held out the receiver and traced the line of dots stretching ahead of them. 'This wire-frame model makes it look like the scanner blocks follow a contour line along the hills, but maybe not.'

They got to the top of the slip and looked ahead. He was right. There was a track, overgrown but still distinct, winding away into the hills.

'Which means the next block should be over there.'

They made their way down and, fifty metres on, found it wedged in the fork of a tree.

'That was easy,' Tim said, looking back the way they'd come. 'Instead of going up and over the hill in a straight line, we've come around it.'

'I reckon this is an old miners' track.'

'Meaning it leads to an old mine?'

'That would explain why we can't see a collection of scanner blocks at the end of the trail. We should if Albert had any left.'

'You mean he's gone underground? Maybe looking for the Sentinels' transmitter?'

'There's only one way to find out.'

They hurried back and told the others.

'If the rest of the track is like this, it'll be easy going from now on,' Norman said.

'How far?'

He checked the screen, measuring off the distance with his thumb and forefinger. 'About eight kilometres.'

'Eight kilometres?' Coral said. 'There's no way we can walk that.'

'It's not that far,' Tim said. 'Two, maybe two-an-a-half

hours?'

'*And* back? Possibly with an injured man? Then back down through the bush to the caravan?'

She was right. It would be a sixteen kilometre round trip just to get back here. They were already exhausted.

'From what you said about Albert, that would have taken him about half an hour,' Norman said. 'Which ties in with what he told Alkemy.'

'Except he didn't come back,' Tim said.

Ludokrus studied the receiver, tracking back and forth along the line of dots. 'I can see where this track lead. But where does she begin?'

Norman peered over his shoulder and scrolled the display, tracing back with his finger. 'It must branch off Rata Road about three K from the reserve. But there aren't any side roads there. Not even walking tracks.'

'Old path, so maybe the entrance is overgrown,' Ludokrus said thoughtfully, handing the receiver back. 'How far to go back along this track?'

'Hard to say,' Norman said. 'Maybe four or five kilometres.'

'Plus three more to the reserve. Quicker, I think, to go home in the straight line.'

'Home? You mean you're giving up?'

'No, but I have idea. Less work. But first we need resource so must go back.' He opened the top of Alkemy's backpack and took out her pink school pack. 'Need only the calculator.'

'What about the other gear?'

'Leave. Collect later.'

'We're going down *and* coming back again?' Coral

131

groaned.

'Yeah, but travel back in style. You wait.' He looked around for Norman. 'Lead, please. Quickest path.'

21 : Wired for Sound

It was easier going without the packs, especially the downhill sections, but they were all relieved to finally emerge in the open ground behind the rubbish dump. Ludokrus directed them to the pyramid of appliances and dragged an ancient washing machine from the stack.

'Need more like this. Four at least. Bring here and make five separate pile.' He marked out an area on the grass with the toe of his shoe. 'Tim and Norman can do this, please?' They set to work. 'Then help Coral and me to collect more resource from the tip. Need old tyre, plastic, metal, fabric and electronic.'

'And me?' Alkemy said.

'You also, but first we need the green bag from the awning. Inside is leftover from the build of the Temporal Accumulator. Very useful. You will fetch, please?'

She headed off as the others began ranging far and wide over the tip, which lay in a shallow depression. There was lots of smelly stuff, mostly in plastic bags so it was easily avoided, but they had to be careful where they stepped because the surface was unstable. Most of the things they were after were easily recovered, although at times it took two of them to drag them free.

The five mounds grew quickly. Ludokrus paused now and then to run the calculator over them and call out requirements to the others. Then Alkemy came bounding back, breathless but empty-handed.

'Could not get,' she said. 'The TV peoples are there. And the Aunt Alice. Looks like they are making video.'

Coral set down a box of glass jars she was carrying 'What, of Alice?' The others stopped and joined them. 'What's she doing with Crystal Starbrite?'

'Alice has been acting a bit weird lately,' Tim said. 'We should check it out.'

They moved to the top of the slope that ran down to the reserve and took cover in some low scrub. They could see Eric setting up a tripod and camera down below, opposite the caravan. In front of him, Alice and Crystal faced each other across one of the reserve's wooden picnic tables.

'It looks like they're setting up for an interview. I wonder what that's about. Pity we can't get any closer.'

'Maybe we can.'

Ludokrus darted back and grabbed the remains of an old cassette recorder from one of the junk piles. He punched some keys on the calculator and tapped a blob of nanomachines on to its exposed circuit board. A few seconds later, its built-in microphone came free and fell into his hand.

'Need something to put her in. Small, light, easy to throw.'

'Got it!' Norman raced back to the resource pit and returned carrying an old tennis ball with a split along one side.

'Perfect.'

A second blob was at work on the cassette recorder's speaker, adding an aerial and some circuitry to its base. The microphone now incorporated a power source and sported a metre-long strand of aerial wire hanging from one side. Ludokrus stuffed it into the tennis ball, trailed the wire out behind it, then edged towards the brow of the hill overlooking the caravan and picnic table. He took careful aim and let fly.

The ball dropped sharply, landing in some scrub to the right of the picnic table. They saw Crystal look up at the faint rustle of undergrowth. Then Alice said something and she turned back.

'Close enough, I think.'

Ludokrus picked up the modified speaker and turned it on. There was a crackling hiss as he tuned it in, then they heard Crystal saying, 'Sound check. Testing, two, three, four.'

'All good.' Eric's voice. 'We're rolling.'

'Yes!' Coral hissed and went to give Ludokrus a high-five. He didn't respond. He was focused on the tiny speaker.

'Interview with Alice Jones. Time: the crack of dawn. Date: Sunday, the blah-blah of whatever. Location: the back of beyond.' Crystal sounded bored and weary. Then she drew a long breath and said in her professional voice, 'So, Ms Jones, you have some information for us about The Rata Meteorite Mystery. Why don't you tell us all about it?'

Alice fiddled with her necklace. 'I suppose it really began with the pikelets.'

'Pikelets?'

'Yes. I left a batch out for the tourists – that's Albert and his niece and nephew. We were quite friendly, you see. My sister's niece and nephew are going to the same school as his children and—'

'What were you saying about pikelets?'

'I left a plate of them over there on the step outside the caravan. A little treat for them. But when I came back later in the day, the plate was broken and the pikelets were all scattered and pecked by birds. It looked like Albert had just thrown them away.

'I was upset, of course. They were home-made wholemeal pikelets. And the plate was one of my sister's favourites. I didn't want to go straight back to the farm, so I went for a walk and got a little lost in the bush. Where that crater is now. That's when I saw the spaceship.'

'Spaceship?' Crystal perked up. 'You saw a spaceship?'

'Yes.'

'Can you describe it?'

'It was like a flying saucer, really. Just like you see in the movies. Three or four metres across and about one-and-a-half metres high.'

'That doesn't sound very big.'

'That depends on the size of the inhabitants, doesn't it?'

'Inhabitants? You saw them too?'

'Yes.'

There was a long pause. Eventually Crystal said, 'What were they like?'

'I don't know for sure. I'm guessing they took on a special shape to explore the planet so they wouldn't arouse suspicion if they were seen.'

'What shape was that?'

'Well they looked mice.'

'*Mice?*'

'Yes.'

'I see.' There was a long silence. 'Any particular sort of mice? House mice, field mice, harvest mice ...?'

'I ... I don't know. Just ordinary looking mice. One fawn, one grey.'

'They weren't wearing little clothes, were they?'

'What?'

'Did they communicate with you?'

'They couldn't. They weren't in a position to.'

'Oh, why was that?'

'Because Albert had them in a cage.'

'A cage?'

'Like a birdcage.'

'Why did he—?'

'I don't know. I couldn't ask. I just came across them by chance. He didn't see me and I was shocked. I didn't know what was going on.'

'But you've seen him since?'

'Yes.'

'And you haven't asked him?'

'No. Not after what happened.'

Crystal gave her a curious look.

'The explosion. Or whatever you want to call it. You've seen the crater. That was where the ship was!'

'You said "explosion". We have a witness who saw a meteorite come down.'

'Yes ... well ... I really can't comment on that.'

'But you don't believe it was a meteorite?'

Alice pursed her lips and shook her head.

'What do you think really happened? Speculate.'

'I think ... I think the spaceship was a reconnaissance craft, sent here to check us out. See what human beings are really like. You know, before establishing proper contact. Learn our language, observe our customs, see how we behave. But something went wrong. Albert – whoever he really is – got wind of them and caught them. Took them prisoner.'

'What on earth for?'

'I don't know, but they must have all sorts of advanced technology. That spaceship for a start. I think that's why they blew it up.'

'Wait a minute, you're saying they blew up their own ship. Why would they do that?'

'That's what I couldn't work out, until I thought about it. Imagine you land on a primitive planet in a fancy ship. You want to go out exploring, but you don't want to leave your ship in case something happens to you. If you're caught or killed, the ship's still there for the local inhabitants to find. So you add a remote control or a timer or something. Perhaps you have to call in every hour and say you're all right. If you don't, or if you trigger the remote, the ship self-destructs.'

'And you believe that's what happened?'

'Yes.'

'Isn't it more likely to have been a meteorite?'

'You said yourself it's a billion-to-one to get three of them coming down in the same area.'

Crystal said nothing to that.

'You don't have to believe me, but I know what I saw.'

Crystal cleared her throat. 'Have you ever had any other

alien encounters, Ms Jones?'

'What do you mean?'

'Seen UFOs? Been kidnapped by them, perhaps?'

'Of course not.'

'They don't communicate with you in your sleep? Tell you to do things for them?'

'No!' Alice bristled. 'I know what you're implying. I just ... Other people know about this too, you know. You should talk to them.'

'What other people?'

Alice bit her lip. 'I've said enough. I can't say any more. I don't think this was a such a good idea after all.' She got to her feet. 'I've changed my mind. Can you please not use this?'

'You called us, Ms Jones. You were the one with the story, remember?'

'I've changed my mind. There isn't one.'

Alice pulled off her microphone and stomped away. Crystal sighed and turned towards the camera. 'I guess that's a cut.'

* * *

'Oh man,' Coral clamped a hand to her mouth. 'That is so funny! She's got it all backwards. She thinks the mice are the aliens.'

'She got a lot of it right though,' Tim said, looking concerned.

'Yeah, but she can't prove any of it. The spaceship's gone. The broken plate's fixed and back in the kitchen cupboard. It's just her word against ours.'

'She said other people know about it.'

'Us, presumably. And Glad was there too, remember?'

'So why didn't she say so?'

'Hey, I don't know. I'm not—'

A ringing sound came from the speaker and Coral sat up with a start. 'Is that ...'

She peered over the brow of the hill and saw Eric packing up. The ringing continued, getting louder as Crystal took something from one of the bags. It stopped when she put it to her ear.

'... a cellphone?'

The others looked down too as Crystal took the call.

'It can't be. They don't work here. I thought this whole area was in a black spot.'

'It is,' Norman said. 'But that's not a cellphone. See the chunky aerial? It's a satphone.'

'A what?'

'Cellphones need cellphone towers. There aren't any round here. Satphones use satellites. They work anywhere on the planet. That's how they did that live broadcast from Rata last night. Via a satellite link.'

Ludokrus, who'd been heading back to the resource pit, stopped and turned. 'What you say?'

'You mean about satellites and satphones?'

'This is what they have?' He hurried back and peered down the hill.

'Yeah. See?'

'Oh man, we are so dumb! We do not think. Should not avoid this journalist at all.'

'What? You don't mean you want to talk to her now?'

Coral said.

'Not me. You. You are friend. Go. Make delay. Hurry. Give me two minute.' He snatched up the calculator and began furiously punching buttons.

'What are you—?'

'Quick please. And borrow phone. You must get hold of phone!'

22 : Girl Talk

Ludokrus worked frantically, setting switches and studying the calculator's tiny screen.

'I'm guessing you'll need raw materials.' Tim said.

'No, nothing thank you. Code only. Please, I must concentrate.'

Tim left him to it, went back to the brow of the hill and looked down to see his sister greeting Crystal and Eric.

'When I am done, you will deliver?' Ludokrus called.

'Yeah, sure.'

'Almost there ... OK. Quick.'

Ludokrus held the calculator out, Tim cupped his hand beneath the little trap door and a blob plopped into his palm.

'Access port will be in the base. Sit phone on the blob. It will do the rest.'

He raced off, not fully understanding what was going on, but fired with the urgency of the task.

Ludokrus blew out his cheeks and watched him go.

Alkemy said, 'Explain please. What do you do?'

'We need to send a signal to our ship, yes? We thought

we need very powerful transmitter, also much precise. Normally, we would need the big dish. And computer. And machine to make steer. But think; there are satellites all around this planet for these phone. Already they link together, so we can use. Make one big planet-sized transmitter. Send our signal to all corner of the solar system at the one time.'

'But they point down here. They send signals down to Earth,' Norman said.

'We need to change. My program do this. Tell them all to turn from Earth, send our signal, then turn back. Take ten, maybe fifteen seconds at the most.'

'And then our ship will come?'

He nodded and Alkemy's face lit up. 'Then we must work hard to find Albert. He will be pleased with us.' She nudged Norman and the pair of them raced back to the resource pit.

* * *

Tim heard Coral and Crystal's voices as he approached the caravan. He kept it between them so he wouldn't be seen, his left hand cupped tightly round the blob.

'Any idea what time they'll be back?' Crystal said.

'Won't be till late this evening. I didn't fancy such a long walk. That's why I came back early.'

'I don't blame you. That outdoors stuff is wildly overrated. Give me a shopping mall any day.'

'Me too!'

'Tell me, do you know much about the tourists? That

Albert character, for example? What's he like?'

'Just ... ordinary. Middle-aged. A bit eccentric. Nothing special.'

'D'you know what he does for a job.'

'Um ... architect, I think.'

'He's not a government agent or something?'

'What, Albert?' Coral laughed. 'No, why do you ask?'

'Oh, no reason. Small town gossip.'

Tim edged around the side of the caravan and caught his sister's eye. When Crystal turned to talk to Eric, Coral sidled over and he handed her the blob. 'Set the base of the phone in it. Stay on the line for at least a minute. It'll do the rest.'

Coral nodded. Tim ducked away and headed back to the reserve.

'Do you mind if I ask you something personal?' Coral said when Crystal turned back. 'Only, there's no one cool round here I can talk to.'

'Sure, doll.'

'I've got this ... friend back home. But I've been stuck down here for weeks now and ... well, you know what guys are like. There's no computer at the farm so I can't email him, and the only phone's right in the middle of the kitchen – where my aunt and uncle practically live. Plus, the whole area's a black spot for mobiles. I was wondering if I should write to him.'

'Write? You mean a letter? My god, how positively Victorian. Do men still read?'

'Pretty sad, eh? But what else can I do?'

'Take it from me doll, you can't beat the direct approach. Here.' There was a rustling sound. 'Use this.'

'But cellphones don't—'

'It's a satellite phone. You can use it anywhere. Just don't be too long. The calls cost a fortune.'

'Gosh. Thanks. You don't mind?'

'Go for it. Who am I to stand in the way of young love?'

Coral checked the bottom of the phone. There was a socket for a power lead and wide connector slot. She pressed the nanomachine blob against it and, like a tiny creature seeking shelter from the light, it slurped inside and vanished.

She studied the handset. Nothing happened. Then it gave a faint beep and the screen lit up. She guessed that meant it was ready.

Derek's number was about the only one she knew by heart. When they first started going out, she hadn't worked out how to use speed-dialling on her new phone so she'd carefully memorised it. The thought made her cringe now. How could she have been so soppy?

She dialled.

The ideal situation would be for him not to answer. She could just leave a voice message. Something cool and enigmatic. But when a giggly female voice said, 'Hello,' all she could manage was, 'Derek?'

The giggly voice assured her it wasn't Derek.

Tim said to stay online for at least a minute.

She checked her watch but suddenly couldn't think of anything to say.

'Who's this?' the voice enquired.

'Is that you, Mel?' she managed at last. 'What are you doing on Derek's phone? ... Who's asking? It's Coral ... Coral ... *Coral Townsend* ... Ha ha ha. Yeah. Hi ... So where's ...? Gone for a swim? ... Oh, you're at Piha? Nice. What, with the whole gang? ... Oh, just you and Derek? ... No, no, of course I don't mind. Not if he asked you ...'

She snatched the phone from her ear.

Melanie bloody Johnson! How dare she?

'What? Yeah, yeah, I'm still here ... Oh, probably till the end of term now ... Actually, it's quite cool ... No, really ... Oh, this and that. Hey, you didn't see the news last night, did you? Nine News at Nine?'

The phone was getting warm. She checked her watch and changed hands.

'Sorry, you went where last night?'

Come on time, hurry up!

'And they let you in? ... No way! ... Really? ... Just you and Derek ...?'

The phone gave a low beep and particles of dust drifted from the connection socket.

Finally!

'Sorry Mel, Crystal's calling. I've got to dash. She wants her satellite phone back. I just borrowed it to say hi ... Yeah, satellite phone ... Crystal Starbrite ... Well of course *the* Crystal Starbrite. How many do you think there are? ... No, really. You should watch the news some time ... Oh, we were just having a girlie chat, but I can't stop now, we've got another interview to shoot. Tell Derek I said hi. Bye!'

She stabbed the disconnect button and added, 'Cow!'

23 : Nanomachines at Work

Ludokrus shouldn't have been listening. He didn't mean to. He forgot the speaker was still on. In fact, he only heard the first part of the conversation and really only registered two words of it: 'Hello, Derek?'

Then he realised his mistake and stomped on the speaker, hard, smashing it with his heel and grinding it into tiny pieces before kicking the remains into one of the recycling piles. Alkemy was right. They should focus on what they were doing. Albert was depending on them.

Coral returned to the resource pit as the green station wagon nosed out of the reserve and headed back up Rata Road. The others gathered round her as soon as she appeared, eager to hear how it went. 'Good. No problems.' She told them about the beep and the dust being expelled. 'Was that right?'

Ludokrus nodded.

Alkemy clapped her hands in delight and gave her a hug. 'Thank you! Thank you!'

'Why? What was that all about?'

Coral's spirits sank as Alkemy explained, right when

147

she thought they couldn't get any lower. She'd just helped summon a ship that would carry away the only other guy she'd ever cared about!

She drew a breath and made the best of it; forced a smile and pretended to be pleased.

'Oh, here, I brought you this.' She handed Ludokrus the green canvas bag he'd sent Alkemy to collect.

'Thanks.' He took it with barely a glance.

'Well, back to work, I guess.'

'Yeah, we need to work.'

She hurried off to the tip face and got busy sorting rubbish. A little later Tim asked, 'Are you OK?'

'Yeah, I've just got something in my eye. Dust, I think.'

Ludokrus called a halt after twenty minutes. They'd accumulated enough raw materials and the construction phase was now well underway.

'So what is it you build?' Alkemy asked.

'Can you guess?'

She moved around the five piles, restless, keen to get going, but also smiling. Their signal had gone! Right now, right at this moment, it was racing through space at three hundred thousand kilometres a second. In seven hours it would reach their mothership. Their mothership would respond and send another escape pod. It wouldn't travel as fast as the signal. It would go more slowly, being careful to avoid detection by Earthlings or Sentinels or the Thanatos, but in little more than a day they'd be on their way home.

Norman knelt, studying the nanomachines closely. He couldn't see much as things were happening on a subatomic level, but it was still fascinating to watch the streams of raw materials moving about, being channelled and shaped by instructions from the calculator.

'Don't get too close,' Tim warned. 'They'll have your nose off.'

Norman lurched back. Tim grinned, looking to his sister for some follow-up remark, but Coral was distracted, staring into the distance.

'Do not believe,' Alkemy told Norman. 'Nanomachine will not hurt the biologic.'

The five blob-like clusters began taking on definite shapes.

'Wheels and handlebars,' Norman said. 'You're building motorbikes!'

'Not "motor", "electric". But you are right.'

'Like the bike you came to school on?'

Tim recalled how Alkemy and Ludokrus first arrived at school riding a motor scooter. A farm-bike version of that would be fun – and a lot quicker than walking or fighting their way through the bush.

A sixth pile began forming as the bikes were finished off; a collection of what looked like spare parts.

The bikes were identical apart from coloured flashes on their sides. Each one was a cross between a scooter, a farm-bike and a low-rider. They had small front wheels angled a metre ahead of their curving handlebars, and a larger, fatter rear wheel. In between was a u-shaped frame that supported a wide comfortable seat, foot pegs and an aerodynamic faring. They had carriers on the rear – presumably for when they collected their packs – and looked sleek and sturdy, but there was something missing.

'Where's the engine?' Tim said.

Ludokrus took one of the bikes off its side-stand and

wheeled it closer. 'Here.' He pointed to the thick hub in the centre of the rear wheel. 'Built-in.'

He turned the handlebars and pointed out the thumb-switches beside each grip. 'Only two main control. Accelerate on right, brake on left. Easy, yes? On-off switch is here.' He pressed a button in the middle of the handlebars and they heard a faint hum.

'Hard to tell if she go or not,' he said, turning it on and off a couple of times. 'Here is way.' He let go the handlebars and the bike stayed upright. 'When she is on, she is auto-stabilise.' He gave it a push. The bike rocked sideways then righted itself. He shoved it harder. A handlebar scraped the ground before it bounced upright again.

'Does it do that while you're on it?' Norman said.

'Of course. The ride is very easy.'

'How fast can they go?' Tim asked.

'Up sixty kilometre per hour. But not so fast on this ground.'

'And for Albert?' Alkemy asked.

'If can ride, he take one for himself and you and I will share. If cannot,' he gestured at the collection of spare parts, 'we make him trailer from these.' He singled a bike out for himself. 'Will make a tow bar for this one in case we need.'

One by one they took a bike and made a slow circuit of the resource pit. It felt odd to be held upright when stationary or nearly stopped. To begin with, Tim kept his legs stretched out on either side, but each time he changed position the bike gently compensated and he soon got used to the idea of it staying upright on its own.

The bikes were light, easy to manoeuvre and their near-silence made them feel like push bikes – at least until you opened the accelerator – but there was something solid about them too. The seats automatically adapted themselves to the shape of the rider, and the suspension was astonishingly smooth. At one point Tim found himself heading for a nasty pothole and braced for the jolt, but the bike flowed in and out of it so smoothly he couldn't have been more comfortable if he'd been riding a feather bed. After that, he began aiming for the bumps.

They moved out on to Rata Road with growing confidence and picked up speed. The loose gravel surface posed no problems, but they kept alert for other traffic in case their unusual transport drew attention.

Norman led the way. Ludokrus had made a special support for the receiver and fixed it between his handlebars. He studied the track on the screen, trying to find the point where it once must have intersected with the road.

They crossed a bridge and followed a gentle incline as it led up into the foothills where the road began to twist and turn. Norman slowed, pausing now and then to check out possible spots.

'It must be round here somewhere. On the right.'

It was easily missed. An overgrown V angled between two steep hills on the outside of a sweeping curve. At some point there'd been a signpost – a rotting stump masked by weeds was all that remained – and the start of the track was obscured by a mound of road workings and a tangle of blackberry. But fifty metres in, the trail became clear, dropping into a valley of amber grasses then climbing up into the bush and disappearing into the hills beyond.

'This is it!' Norman gunned his bike.

'Hold on Albert,' Alkemy muttered. 'We are coming.'

24 : Over the Edge

'What's the matter?'

'I've been thinking. If we do recover the synthetic's memory unit using one of the Eltherians, we won't be able to take it with us anyway because our ship doesn't have room for passengers. Life-support systems for monkey people take up too much space.'

'Who said anything about life-support?'

'But the module will self-destruct without the presence of an Eltherian.'

'It doesn't have to be a whole Eltherian you know ...'

* * *

In some places the track was wide enough to ride two abreast but they stuck to single-file, still getting used to the unusual machines. Norman steadily increased the pace. The ride was so smooth that it hardly felt like they were connected to the ground at all, more like floating a few centimetres above it.

'They should call these things glide bikes,' Tim said.

Then they came to a halt. The track stopped at the edge of a massive slip. An overhang of rock had collapsed, tearing away the cliff face and taking twenty metres of track with it. The dull brown smear of rubble stretched all the way to a stream bed far below. The way ahead was suddenly steep and treacherous. Difficult enough on foot. Certainly no place for the bikes.

'What now?'

'No problem, just go slow to start.'

Ludokrus stood up on the foot pegs, leaned back, and guided his bike over the edge of the cliff, keeping it angled and parallel to the face. The wheels slid a little then gripped, pushing aside loose gravel, and he eased his way down to a relatively level area three metres below. He puttered across then accelerated hard, racing back up the other side, bouncing over boulders and fish-tailing up a gravel slide till he reached the continuation of the track on the other side.

'Who's next?' he called.

Norman didn't need any encouragement. He headed down, across and up, following Ludokrus's trail, but doing it in half the time. Tim and the others followed at a more steady pace, but it was amazingly easy with the bike's auto-stabilisers.

'Are these tyres made of glue or something?' Norman asked.

'Good guess. Original design say must go places where there is no road, so wheels adjust for each terrain. Automatically change pressure, traction and surface stick to suit.'

'I've *got* to get me one of these!' Norman said to Tim as they continued on, following the track as it wound deeper into the hills.

They paused for a drink and a quick snack when they reached their backpacks, then strapped them on to the carriers and carried on, checking off each scanner block as they went.

'That's number fourteen.' Norman pointed out one propped on a ledge part way up a cliff. 'One to go.'

The last kilometre involved a steady climb up a rock-strewn track that wound between two barren cliffs. It zigzagged left and right, into shadow so deep that the air around them felt like winter, then out again into sun-blinding corners that made them blink and squint. The gradient eased as they reached the top, and they found themselves on a barren plateau that ended at two ancient, weather-beaten signs before dropping down into a narrow gorge beyond. One sign said:

TRESPASSERS WILL BE SHOT
AND PROSECUTED.

The other, even older judging from its flaking paint, read:

GIZZARD GULLY
ABANDON HOPE ALL YE WHO ENTER!

25 : Second Sign

Norman checked the scanner block wedged between two warped boards of the *No Trespassing* sign. 'That's it. That's the last one.'

'But no Albert.' Alkemy said.

He zoomed out the receiver to include the valley below. 'He would have gone on, which means he must have gone down there.'

A broken fence, now little more than a tangle of rotten posts and rusted wire, lay beyond the signs, and past that the track narrowed and dropped, following a series of curves down to the gully floor. The gully ran due south, a rocky V-shaped gash in the rolling hills, its sides steeply angled and dotted with diggings, its floor littered with bits of abandoned machinery. Tim counted a dozen mineshafts on the eastern face alone, but apart from a dry creek bed and a handful of exhausted weeds clinging to shady crevices, the place was lifeless and deserted.

'There's some sort of hut down there.' Norman pointed to a broad flat area directly below, now partly in shadow. 'We should check it out.'

Tim hesitated, looking at the second sign. The name seemed familiar, but he couldn't remember where he'd heard it before.

'Should go careful,' Ludokrus said. 'Two-by-two again.'

'Yeah, whatever,' Norman said, accelerating away down the hill on his own. He was still annoyed at being left behind earlier, but riding alone, fast, without having to wait for the others was some compensation.

The electrobikes were fun on the flat, perfect for uphill work and great for rough terrain, but downhill they were astounding. Corners that looked too sharp, that would have had the back wheel skidding on a regular bike, that common sense said would end in a nasty crash, simply required a little extra lean and a firmer grip on the handlebars. The automatic stabilisers and feather-bed suspension made it ridiculously easy. And exciting.

He brought the bike to a skidding halt at the bottom, raising a great cloud of dust. He imagined riding to school on one. What would the other kids think about his skill and prowess? Norman Smith, who didn't even ride a push bike?

'Oh yeah! Gotta get me one of these,' he said, patting his trusty steed.

Up above, Ludokrus and Coral were just starting out. A minute later, Tim and Alkemy followed. Going carefully, two-by-two. Slowly. He sighed, dismounted and checked out the hut.

It was ancient, the size of a garden shed with a not-so-ancient roof. Sheets of corrugated iron had been nailed over sagging timbers and there was a stout modern padlock on the door. Round the side he found two steel drums – one of diesel, one of petrol – both partly full judging by their weight. Both were stencilled with the name Occidental Mining Corporation.

The others finally arrived and switched off their bikes.

'Wonder how they got these here,' Tim said, slapping a hand on one of the drums.

'Helicopter, probably,' Norman said.

Round the front, Ludokrus was examining the padlock. 'Nanomachine will open.' He reached for Alkemy's backpack.

'There is an easier way.' Norman gave the door a nudge with his shoulder. The hasp creaked and wisps of wood dust drifted from the screw holes. Another firm shove and the hasp, complete with padlock, broke free and was left dangling from the jamb. He pushed the door open and they peered inside.

A clipboard and a pair of dusty overalls hung from a nail on the opposite wall. There was a calendar by the door, the paper yellowed, but they could make out the logo – OMC, same as on the drums – and a date: 1991. Apart from that, the hut was empty.

'He can't have come in here,' Tim said. 'Not with the door locked from the outside.'

Alkemy stared up the gully. The sides looked steeper from ground level. One half was in shadow, the other in daylight. The walls were barren and lifeless. 'So where does he go?' she asked.

26 : Hope and Sanity

'Is everything ready? The lights, recording system, the access passage?'

'Yes, yes, all set. I've even charged up Storm Bringer.'

'Excellent! Then I think it's time for a little incentive ...'

* * *

Norman insisted they break for lunch and consider the situation. The others swore they weren't hungry, but once he began unpacking the food Aunt Em had prepared for them – ham sandwiches in soft home-made bread, rolls stuffed with lettuce, tomato and cheese, pottles of coleslaw, fresh fruit, bags of nuts, raisins, chippies and tubs of yoghurt – they managed to work up an appetite. Still, they ate mechanically and mostly in silence.

Tim felt uneasy, unsure why the Gizzard Gully sign bothered him, trying to force the memory of where he'd heard of it before, but failing. Alkemy was impatient to get moving. She surveyed the valley ahead, studied every rock and fissure, feeling in her bones that Albert was somewhere nearby. Ludokrus paced about as he ate, restless, unhappy and impatient now for their ship to arrive, while Coral stared into the middle distance, still numb, still assimilating what had happened back at the reserve. With a single phone call she'd lost her best friend *and* her boyfriend *and* helped the only other guy she'd ever cared about leave the planet.

Norman wasn't worried about anything. He belched and helped himself to another sandwich as Tim knelt beside him and studied the receiver. It showed a 3D model of the way ahead. Grids of lines indicated the contours of the valley walls. They curved left, the gradient increasing a little before ending abruptly at a cliff face.

Tim looked from the virtual landscape to the real one. At the cliffs and the dark mouths of the mineshafts. 'How do we know he didn't just run out of blocks at the top of the gully and turn round?'

'Because we'd have met him on the track. No point going on if he didn't have any more blocks. And if he did go on placing them, we'd see them on the receiver.'

'OK, so the logical explanation is he came down here. But then where did he go? There's at least a dozen mines up there,' Tim pointed to the sunlit side of the valley. 'And if he went down a mineshaft, wouldn't he leave one outside?'

'Why even go down one in the first place?' Coral said. 'He knows the Sentinels live underground.'

'He should have been all right. It was still daylight when he got here.'

'Only just. It would have been fading fast. And speaking of fading daylight.' Coral pointed to the sky further up the gully where the light had taken on a coppery colour. At first it looked like a reflection from the rocky walls, then Tim saw dense banks of bruised clouds rolling up towards the face of the sun, like smoke from a forest fire.

'Whoa! Where's that coming from?'

'It's another of those sudden storms,' Norman said. 'Like that one last night.'

'Except we're right underneath it this time.'

'Should've brought some wet-weather gear.'

Alkemy leapt to her feet, pointing into the valley. 'There! Look! You see?'

They looked, but all they could see were ominous cloud shadows rolling over the sunlit face of the cliffs.

'What? Where?'

'A flash of light. Come from mine.'

'Which one?'

'Number seven. On left. Up high. Past the big rock slide. You see?'

It came again.

'Is it some sort of reflection?'

'No, is regular. Like a signal. Watch.'

And again.

'Is him!' She got to her feet. 'Is Albert!'

'Wait.' Ludokrus put a hand out to restrain her. 'Remember the rule: must go careful. Two-by-two.'

Alkemy looked to Tim.

'Coming.' He got to his feet.

'We go like before,' Ludokrus said. 'Separate. OK?'

'I guess that doesn't include me.' Norman gulped down the last of his sandwich, reached for his bike and raced off into the gully.

Norman stopped beneath the mineshaft, circled the

valley floor a couple of times, then raced back.

'All clear. No booby-traps. Nothing happened.'

'That was stupid and dangerous,' Coral said. 'Besides, they're not after you.'

'Well why don't *I* go up there and check it out?'

'He is ours,' Alkemy said. 'We are responsible.'

'She is right,' Ludokrus said. 'We move from the farm so we do not put our friends in danger. Besides, he hardly know you.' He turned to the others. 'We go. Leaping frog.'

'So how come it's OK for Tim and Coral?'

'He know them, and this is how we start. Danger shared. We look out for each other. Four pair of eyes.'

'That's just dumb!'

'Are you going to stand around arguing, or can we get on with it? There's an injured man up there,' Coral said.

Norman snorted and shook his head while the others moved up the gully in stages. He followed them, keeping back this time, letting them play their silly game.

The ground was gravelled with loose scoria that crunched beneath their wheels. Like riding over old bones, Tim thought as they paused to let Coral and Ludokrus catch up then move on ahead.

The flashes from the mine came at regular intervals and he counted the time between each pulse. Twenty seconds, give or take. A call for attention? Or the beacon of a lighthouse warning ships away?

The silence and the shadows deepened as they moved between the high rock walls. They passed a weather-beaten sign leaning at a drunken angle. One finger pointed up the gully and bore the peeling legend "Hope". The other pointed back the way they'd come. It was labelled "Sanity".

Coral and Ludokrus stopped at the base of an incline of tailings that led up to the mine. Tim and Alkemy drew up beside them. Faint remnants of a switchback track ran up to the entrance, worn into the cliff face by weary miners and their mules.

'Now us,' Alkemy said. She took out her pink backpack and handed it to Ludokrus.

'You may need the calculator to help fix if Albert is injured.'

'Then we will come back for it. Must check first it is safe.'

He nodded, and without another word she gunned her bike and headed up the switchback trail. Tim followed.

The track was narrow, steep, and patches of it were missing completely, wiped away by small rock slides, but the bikes made steady work of the gradient and it was only mildly alarming when he glanced down and saw how high they'd climbed.

At the top, the track opened on to a semicircular ledge that had been scraped out around the entrance to the mine. They parked their bikes and got off.

'Thirty-two ... thirty-three ... thirty-four ...' Tim continued, counting out loud now. 'The flashes have stopped.'

'Is him. He see us come.'

The others watched anxiously from the valley below. Tim waved. 'Nothing yet. We'll take a look inside,' he called down.

'Five minute only,' Ludokrus called back, tapping his watch.

'OK.' Tim checked his own and said to Alkemy,

'Anything we need from the packs?'

'Have torch and spare battery. Maybe also jacket. May be cool, I think.'

Tim pulled on a light nylon jacket and joined her.

Moving cautiously, they approached the mineshaft and peered into the inky blackness. All they could make out was the start of a narrow-gauge track that looked like a miniature railway leading into the mine that was used for hauling out debris. It was very old and very rusted. Two lines of crumbling ochre etched into the grey rock floor.

'Hello?' Tim called quietly.

There was no response.

He tried again.

Nothing.

'*Hello!*' he yelled, making Alkemy jump.

'O ... O ... o ... o ... o ...' The sound echoed into silence.

'Maybe he is hurt and cannot speak.' A strand of her hair had come loose. She brushed it back.

A second later a light flickered in the distance. A faint glimmer that moved from side to side like a signal. Then it dimmed and faded away like the echo.

'Albert!' Alkemy yelled and raced towards it.

* * *

'*Only two? How disappointing.*'

'*It's enough, but let's give the others a little encouragement to join them.*'

27 : Drowned Rats

The air grew colder and the light – filtered by the racing clouds – shimmered and shifted. It was like being underwater. Coral looked from the mineshaft to the steep cliffs above it and picked out spiralling dust devils being whipped up by the wind.

'Three minute.' Ludokrus was studying his watch.

'I think we might need to find some shelter,' she began, but her words were drowned by a crash of thunder like the boom of heavy guns.

A searing flash of lightning danced along the cliff top to their right, almost as if it had been aimed directly at them. Norman didn't even have time to start counting. A second gun-like roar hit them, making the earth tremble and bringing with it waves of stinging rain.

'Back to hut!' Ludokrus shouted.

'The mineshaft's closer.'

'No, two-by-two, remember? Not all at together.' He turned his bike and raced off at full speed. The others followed.

Coral cried out as the first fat drops struck her back,

but no one could hear her above the angry downpour that engulfed them. They hunkered down over their handlebars, focused on the hut that seemed to grow more distant in the dimming light.

The dusty track was suddenly slick. Puddles appeared out of nowhere, and the dry creek bed that ran along one side boiled into life. Ludokrus, leading, brought his bike to a skidding halt at the back of the hut and leapt off to help the others. Coral simply abandoned hers, stepping off it before it had completely stopped, using its momentum to propel her into the shelter. Ludokrus caught it and switched it off.

They left the bikes beside the fuel drums where the overhanging roof gave them some protection. Round the front, they huddled in the doorway, staring out like three drowned rats, barely able to think above the pounding on the iron roof.

* * *

Tim adjusted the slider on the barrel of his torch, narrowing the angle of its beam until it became a spotlight stabbing into the inky blackness ahead.

'Off one moment please,' Alkemy said.

He clicked the switch and they stood in darkness, peering ahead. Waiting. One full minute this time. But there were no more flashes. Not so much as the flicker of a glowworm.

A roar behind them made them start. A deep bass rumble followed immediately by pounding rain. They edged deeper into the mineshaft and Tim turned his torch back on, widening the beam to illuminate rough-hewn walls and sturdy pit props while Alkemy kept hers on narrow beam and directed it ahead.

They moved in silence, shapes and shadows dancing in the torchlight. The sound of the pounding rain faded to a murmur.

'Albert?' Alkemy called.

A muffled echo was the only reply.

There were no footprints on the rock floor. It was hard and smooth, marked by parallel streaks of rust from the long-vanished tracks. Trickles of water caught them up, overspilling the furrows and racing ahead into the eerie gloom.

'Some storm,' Tim said, thinking of the others.

They moved slowly and carefully, examining the pit props on each section of the ancient mine before continuing. Everything seemed stable and solid. It was odd to think it must have been this way for a hundred years or more.

Alkemy stopped, steadying her beam. Tim narrowed his own. Five metres ahead, the shaft ended in a broad T-shape where the miners had hacked about, searching for the dying remnants of the gold seam before finally giving up.

They glanced at each other in the pale backwash of light. That was it. Nothing else. A few scattered rocks, but no sign of Albert.

* * *

They ran away, the cowards!'

'Never mind, they'll be back. Especially if we give them a little incentive. Switch on the recording equipment.'

'Recording now ...'

* * *

'What was that?' Tim heard a faint whisper of sound. He turned and played his torch beam over the walls of the dead-end.

'Like something move,' Alkemy said, doing the same. 'There! What is that? I do not see before.'

Her torch lit up the left branch of the T, playing over a dent in the wall partly masked by a rocky outcrop. Behind it was a circular shadow, dark and silent. They approached and saw what looked like a small side passage angling up and away from the main shaft.

'Albert?' Alkemy called again, louder this time, her words flattened by the dead-end.

'Looks like some sort of ventilation shaft,' Tim said.

It began partway up the wall, a hole a metre in diameter. Perfectly circular, its sides glassy smooth. 'Looks like has been melted.' Alkemy touched the surface and pointed to the puddle of congealed rock they were standing on. 'Is still warm. Feel.'

'Melted? How?'

She shrugged and peered in.

He played his torch around the smooth walls. The light reflected back and forth a thousand times, playing off the glassy sides.

'Looks fresh all right. Could Albert have done this?'

'I do not know.'

She called again.

No reply.

'Only one way to find where it goes.' She eased herself inside.

Tim followed, clambering in after her, his rubber-soled shoes squeaking on the surface of the melted rock. It was like climbing up inside a water slide.

After a long straight section the passage curved right, growing steeper, then angled sharply left. Alkemy's voice came back to him. 'Can see the end. Looks like it come out in another mine.'

There was a faint scuffling sound as she exited, a moment of silence, then a cry. 'Oh … oh … *Oh no!*'

28 : West Coast Sunshine

Alice parked her blue Daihatsu in front of a fading picture of a ram and tried to remember the last time she'd visited her old home town. Years, she thought, and in all that time nothing had changed. That was the trouble with Rata. It wasn't a dynamic, happening place like Greymouth.

She'd driven aimlessly, not wanting to go back to the farm. Not wanting to go anywhere. The interview with Crystal Starbrite played on her mind and she shuddered at the idea of it being broadcast. Em had been right. She shouldn't have done it. At least not, without proper preparation.

Of *course* they'd want evidence. Of *course* they'd want other witnesses. Why hadn't she thought of that before? But there was one way she might redeem herself.

She took a deep breath, got out the car and marched across the road to RAGS.

She stood at the open door a moment. Glad was serving a customer. Alice entered, took a Sunday paper from the rack and stood in line at the counter.

One other thing hadn't changed, she thought; Gladys

Smith. She was still slim, athletic-looking, and still had that unruly mop of gingery-coloured hair. It was as wild as it had been in their school days.

'Good heavens, Alice Jones!' Glad exclaimed when she looked up. 'I don't think I've seen you since Bob and Muriel's wedding. It is still Jones, is it?'

That was uncalled for, Alice thought, suddenly conscious of her left hand around the newspaper.

'I've never bothered with those old patriarchal customs,' she said grandly, dropping the paper on the counter. 'I suppose that's one thing we have in common.'

Glad smiled, either missing or ignoring the veiled reference to her own single-parenthood.

'Have you just arrived? I never saw you at Frank and Em's.'

'I was out for a drive.'

'Sorry I missed you.'

'Actually, I caught sight of you the other day,' Alice said. 'Just in passing.'

'The other day?'

'Mmm. Friday afternoon. Out near Em and Frank's place. How's your leg, by the way?'

'My leg?'

'Yes. You were walking with a stick.'

For an instant, a disconcerted flicker passed across Glad's face.

Gotcha! Alice thought.

'Only, I was going to suggest Arnica gel,' she said aloud. 'It's wonderful for aches and pains, you know.'

'I ... think you must've mistaken me for someone else.'

'No, it was definitely you. And your boy Norman. Gosh,

hasn't he grown! Last time I saw him he was barely walking.'

Glad stared at Alice. Alice glanced over her shoulder to see if they were alone, then smiled. 'I know all about it Glad. The mice, the spaceship. Everything.'

'I ... don't know ... what you're ...'

'Oh yes you do. You were there. I saw you. Hobbling about with a gammy leg. With your son. And Albert. And the children.'

* * *

'Isn't this what you call West Coast sunshine?' Coral yelled above the thunderous drumming on the tin roof.

'Not like this,' Norman shouted back. 'I've never seen rain like this.'

They stared towards the doorway of the hut where the rain was falling with such force that when a flash of lightning froze the scene outside, the droplets looked like long steel bolts suspended in mid-air. They braced themselves and held their breaths as another bone-juddering boom echoed round the gully.

Ludokrus upended his backpack on the floor and began sorting through the collection of parts he'd brought with him.

'Lost something?' Coral had to shout above the din.

'Need to cover the bike.'

'Don't tell me they shrink if they get wet.'

'No, but rain is not good for the electric.'

'You mean they're not waterproof?'

'Not this-proof.' He jerked a thumb at the drumming

171

on the roof.

Finding nothing suitable, he gave up and went to the door.

'See anything?' Coral joined him, but they could barely see two metres.

There was another flash of lightning and another clap of thunder. Coral shivered and stood in silence, dripping and cold, staring at the rain.

* * *

Alkemy's cries grew stronger as Tim forced his way up the last few metres of the smooth-walled passage. 'What is it? What's happened? Alkemy, what's wrong?'

She was on her knees when he emerged. At first, he couldn't see what the matter was. The circular passage ended in a closed chamber, a small rock room like the dead-end tunnel they'd just left. At least it was on three sides. But where Alkemy crouched was a jumble of boulders that looked like the result of a cave-in.

He moved to one side, broadening his torch beam so it flooded the chamber, and found her kneeling, helpless, hands outstretched, crying quietly before a fallen figure.

Albert's head, part of one shoulder and an outstretched arm were all that were visible beneath the fallen rock. He lay face down, head to one side, and might have been resting if it hadn't been for the collapsed roof burying the rest of his body and the puddle of machine fluids in which he lay. From his position, Tim guessed he'd been running from the cave-in. He'd almost made it.

'Albert, Albert, Albert,' Alkemy wept, reaching out to touch his head with trembling fingers.

Tim felt a lump in his throat and looked away. Then Alkemy gave a startled cry as Albert's hand twitched and his eyelids flickered open.

29 : Evidence

Glad stared at Alice then came to a decision. 'So, you know all about it. So what?'

Alice blinked. She hadn't expected that. Not at this stage. Not so easily. She gripped the newspaper she was holding. 'Then you don't deny there's something going on?'

Glad smiled. 'There's always *something* going on *somewhere*, Alice.'

'I mean in that clearing in the bush.'

'There's no bush now. Or clearing.'

'Yes, well, we both know about *that*, don't we?'

'Do we?'

How much does Alice really know? Glad wondered. OK, she saw us in the clearing. But she couldn't possibly know about the killer robot. Or the way it chased us. Or me getting shot. Could she ...?

Emboldened by Glad's reaction, Alice leaned forward confidentially and added, 'It's all right, you know. We're on the same side. Albert's told me everything.'

'Oh, has he?'

'Of course. We're ... well ... we're good friends, if you

know what I mean.'

'I see.' Glad nodded. She knew exactly what she meant. 'In that case ...' she leaned in herself. Alice leaned closer in expectation, '... since you and Albert are such close friends ...'

'Yes?'

'... you must know everything already, so there's nothing I can add.'

Alice straightened and pursed her lips.

Glad smiled and raised an eyebrow.

The entrance buzzer buzzed and the TV cameraman strode in.

'You again?' Glad grinned at him.

'Yeah, I know. It's a filthy habit.'

'Another pack of ten?'

'Please.'

'Twenty-packs are more economical.'

'I'm trying to cut down, but I reckon I picked the wrong weekend for that,' Eric said.

Glad turned to the cabinet where the cigarettes were stored. Alice focused on her newspaper, pretending to read it.

Eric nudged her.

She ignored him.

He nudged her again.

She looked up, frowning, making out she was surprised to see him.

He held a finger to his lips, jerked his head towards the door and waggled one eyebrow.

Was he being silly? Making fun of her? Alice scowled.

Glad turned back with his cigarettes, and he snapped

his attention back to her, holding out a twenty dollar note. As she was making change, he glanced at Alice again and jerked his head towards the door.

'Thanks. See you,' he said to Glad, took his change and left.

Alice gave Glad a haughty look, paid for her paper and followed him out.

She found him standing by the closed-up tearooms up the road. He held up the cigarette packet. 'I really am trying to give these things up, you know. I almost didn't buy them. I stopped by the door wondering if I should. I'm glad I did now because I caught the tail end of that conversation you were having.'

'You did?'

'And before I say anything else, I have to say I think Crystal was a bit hard on you earlier.'

Alice shrugged as if she didn't care, but her face glowed with embarrassment.

'I spend a lot of time looking at people, you know. Through the lens. Often in close-up. I can usually tell when someone's making stuff up. But I didn't get that feeling about you.'

'You didn't?'

'No. And from what I heard back there, it seems the RAGS lady knows more than she's letting on.'

'Yes, she does,' Alice said.

'Was she one of those *other people* you mentioned?'

Alice hesitated. 'She won't admit it.'

'Maybe Crystal can persuade her.'

'Do you think she can?'

'Worth a try.'

'Well, thank you for believing me anyway,' Alice said.

'Not so hard when you have evidence.'

'Evidence?'

'I saw something back at the reserve when we were packing up.'

'What?'

'Crystal saw it too – or rather, them. She's as blind as a bat without her glasses, but they were so close even she could see them.'

'What?' Alice said again.

'A couple of mice under some bushes near the caravan. Looked pretty tame. One fawn, one grey. Just like the ones you described.'

* * *

Norman paced up and down studying the receiver. The thunder and lightning had subsided. All that remained was the lashing rain.

'Is that thing showing anything?' Coral asked.

'I expect they're waiting it out.'

The scanner block Tim was carrying had faded as soon as they entered the mine, but Norman would spot them the moment they re-emerged.

Coral turned to Ludokrus. He was busy assembling the spare parts from his backpack. They snapped and screwed together, making a rickshaw-like stretcher on wheels.

'You think they've found Albert then?'

'Hope so,' he said.

* * *

The voice wasn't Albert's. It had an odd robotic tone and came from his partly open, barely moving lips. As if, since being crushed, he'd learned ventriloquism. 'Perimeter defences activated. Please identify yourselves,' it said.

Alkemy stared, speechless with horror.

'Please move beyond a three metre perimeter or provide valid identification. Failure to do so will result in unit termination. You have ten seconds. Commencing countdown.'

Tim stared too. The shock of finding Albert's crushed remains was bad enough. But finding someone – some *thing* – still active inside him made it even worse.

'Seven seconds till unit termination. Please vacate the area or provide valid identification.'

'How do we do that?' Tim said. 'What do we do?'

'Invalid voice pattern. Five seconds till unit termination. Warning: blast radius three metres.'

He looked helplessly at Alkemy, who sat stunned, her face a mix of grief, shock and horror. 'Say something!' he yelled.

'Commencing termination sequence,' the voice said.

A series of low tones started, increasing in pitch and frequency.

Bip ... bip ... bip ... bee-bip ... bee-bip ... bee-bip ...

'Alkemy!'

'A ... Albert?' she croaked through her tears. 'What happen?'

The tones stopped. Tim closed his eyes and held his breath.

'Voice pattern matched. Perimeter defence deactivated,' the voice said.

Albert's head stirred and he sighed, though how that was possible with a body buried under tons of rock Tim didn't know. 'Alkemy?' he said in his normal voice. 'You and your brother are unharmed?'

'Y ... yes.'

'Caution, sensors indicate the presence of a second life form,' the other voice said. 'Possible coercion.'

'Who is with you?'

'It's me, Tim,' Tim said, moving closer.

'And are you both acting of your own accord?'

'Yes,' they replied, exchanging puzzled looks.

'Voice stress analysis indicates truthful responses. Threat assessment: low.'

Albert cleared his throat. 'Sorry about that. Come, sit where I can see you both and tell me your current status.'

They moved to the side he was facing and sat on the cold rock floor. Tim dimmed his torch and turned it away so it was possible to imagine Albert was simply lying in bed beneath a pile of blankets.

'We ... we are OK.' Alkemy wiped her eyes, but her voice was still shaky. 'Everyone is fine.'

'We got a signal to your ship,' Tim said. 'It turned out that reporter had a satellite phone, so we borrowed it and Ludokrus made a thing and ...'

'Ah,' Albert sighed and closed his eyes. 'Something else I didn't think of.'

They thought they'd lost him for a moment, then his eyes opened again and he added, 'But that is excellent news. Well done!' He smiled which, considering his predicament, seemed bizarre. 'What time was that?'

'About eleven o'clock this morning.'

'Then if all goes well the new escape pod should be here about seven tomorrow evening. It'll still be daylight, so be prepared. The ship is programmed to avoid potential witnesses. You may need transport to get to it.'

'L ... Ludokrus make electrobike,' Alkemy said. 'Is how we come here.'

'Very resourceful. I see you really don't need me any more. That's a great comfort.'

'But you—'

'Keep in mind the escape pod will only wait a short time before returning to the ship. If you miss it, you'll have to summon another. We can't leave advanced spacecraft lying around, can we?'

'But ... you will be coming with us. We can dig you out.'

'No, I'm afraid you can't. The damage is too severe. My situation is terminal. However, I am equipped with a special storage and recording module. It's new technology and highly secret, which is what all that validation and voice analysis was about. We don't want it falling into the wrong hands.'

'I do not understand.'

'I can't explain now, only that you must retrieve it and take it back with you. It's very important that you do. It is, however, in a rather awkward spot.' As he was speaking, his free arm began twitching but not fully engaging, like a machine with a broken gear. He rolled his eyes towards Tim and said, 'Would you mind pressing down on my shoulder?'

Tim got to his feet and, directed by Albert, cupped his hands over the shoulder and gave it a downward shove.

'Harder, please. Use all you weight.'

Tim did so, and something graunched into place. The

sound made him wince, but Albert thanked him, flexed his fingers and reached up to the back of his head where he began tearing out lumps of hair.

'Aaarrgghh! What do you do?' Alkemy cried.

'Just ... trying ... to get at ... ah!' There was a tearing *slurp* and he withdrew a thick wad of hair matted at the roots with blood and tissue.

Tim groaned and looked away.

'I'm sorry. It might be less disturbing if you turn your lights down.'

It was hard to say if it was better or worse. The enclosed space seemed to amplify the smallest sounds; gooey, squelchy noises followed by tearing, like a knife slicing through taut fabric. Then there was a click and Albert muttered, 'There, that's it.'

'Can we turn up the light, now?'

'I wouldn't advise it. But if you'll oblige me Alkemy, give me your hand.'

She felt for his fingers in the semi-darkness. They were moist and sticky.

'My cranial chamber is designed to be accessed from the top,' he explained, 'but we don't have the proper tools. You should however be able to reach up along my spinal duct and get at it from there now that I've cleared the way.'

'No!' Alkemy tried to withdraw her hand, but Albert held it firmly.

'It must be you. It needs to be an Eltherian. More of those defence systems, I'm afraid. But you will need to roll up your sleeve.'

Alkemy did so.

'Extraction of the memory core must be done in one

181

swift movement. The instant it's removed, defensive enzymes will activate and try to destroy it *and* whatever has removed it. If your hand gets stuck for even half a second, you might lose your arm – or worse.'

Alkemy whimpered.

'Don't worry, we'll rehearse the movement first.'

He guided her to a position behind his neck, then lowered her hand on to what felt like the lip of a fleshy crater. She gasped and tried to draw away again, but he gently steered her back.

'Can … you feel that?' she asked.

'Faintly, yes. But it won't be for long.'

He guided her fingers into the crater and up a narrow channel to what felt like a small tunnel. The edges were smooth and rounded, like highly polished metal, but she had to squeeze the sides of her hand together to get it in. On the other side, she pushed through a thin membrane and into what felt like a chamber filled with warm, lumpy custard.

'Move your fingers up and to the right until you encounter something the shape and size of a miniature light bulb,' Albert said.

Alkemy did so, her eyes screwed tight in concentration. Her forearm was almost at full stretch now, but she focused on the sensations from her fingertips and the finely detailed landscape they were exploring.

The inner surface was concave and crowded with components. She could make out shapes. A latticework of triangular bumps, a rough patch of wiry bristles, a smooth expanse pitted with random indentations. And then she found it, quite distinct, an elongated globe the thickness of a whiteboard marker sitting proud of the surface on a finely ribbed mound that felt both fleshy and metallic.

'That's it,' Albert said quietly.

'What do I do now?' she asked, the pounding of her heart almost drowning out his reply.

'Do nothing. Just feel its shape with your fingers, pretend you're holding it, and withdraw your hand as rapidly as possible. *Now!*'

Alkemy snatched her arm out, her fingers round an imaginary bulb.

'Perfect,' Albert said. 'Do exactly that. Do you want more practice?'

She shook her head then, realising it was dark, said, 'No.'

'Very well.' He guided her hand back again. 'Exactly the same procedure as before, except this time grab and pull the bulb.'

'What will happen then?'

'I believe I said my situation was terminal,' he said. 'Pull the bulb and out go the lights.'

'How can you make jokes at a time like this?'

'Because I am content. Knowing that you and your brother will escape this planet is all I could wish for.'

Alkemy stopped. 'No, I cannot do. I cannot kill you.'

'I'm already finished, Alkemy. If you leave me, I'll just die more slowly. Besides, you won't really be killing me. On the contrary, you'll be preserving my essence and everything I've learned. You will be doing me – and, more importantly, Eltheria – an incalculable service. That's another reason I'm content: I have completed my mission to the best of my abilities.'

'You mission?'

'One more thing. Keep the memory bulb with you at all times. It's set to detect the presence of you or your brother. If anything happens to you, or if you drop it or move more than a metre away from it, it will self-destruct. It's only small, but most of its mass will be converted into energy. I estimate a blast radius of at least a metre.'

Alkemy said nothing. Hot tears ran down her cheeks.

'Do you understand?'

'Yes.' She closed her eyes, swallowed hard, then said with quiet concentration, 'Thank you for all you do for us, Albert. I will miss you.'

'I'll miss you too, Alkemy.'

She leaned forward and kissed the side of his head. Then she took a long slow breath and reached for the narrow opening.

'All set?' he said. 'You'll need a tight grip. Don't worry, it's quite robust. One sharp tug and pull your hand straight out. OK?'

'OK.' Her voice wavered.

'Away you go ...'

Alkemy closed her eyes and tugged. Hard. There was a muffled snap and the custardy substance around her hand began to boil, even as she was withdrawing her arm. She snatched it free as a rush of hot, acrid-smelling liquid surged from the cranial opening, overflowing the spinal channel and bubbling up over Albert's neck and exposed shoulder. He arched slightly, gave a tiny grunt, and seemed to sink into the ground.

30 : The Stuff of Nightmares

Tim turned up his torch when he heard the grunt and saw a seething, bubbling, greenish stew around where Albert lay. Alkemy, in a state of shock, stepped back, trembling as choking fumes rose round her. He seized her by the shoulders and steered her towards the side passage where a waft of fresh air from the other mineshaft helped revive her.

'We should go. Quick,' he said as more fumes billowed towards them.

She nodded, dived into the passage and disappeared. Tim glanced back. The noxious fog parted for an instant and he glimpsed metal stripped bare and a bubbling eye socket. He shuddered and dived after her.

The side passage curved down, its glazed surface like the polished metal of a playground slide. An exhilarating ride in darkness, but one that ended at a cold stone floor. Tim picked himself up and found Alkemy wiping her bare arm with a handkerchief.

'Are you OK? That stuff didn't get you?'

She shook her head then opened her hand to show what she'd recovered. Tim aimed his torch at it and saw a miniature version of an old fashioned light bulb, still draped with tendrils of tissue. The base was an ornate circle of metal and the bulb swirled with mottled grey clouds that seemed to absorb the light and act as a kind of camouflage, making its edges difficult to see. At times it almost looked as if there wasn't anything there at all.

She wiped it carefully with her handkerchief then tucked it in the button-down pocket of her blouse. The one over her heart.

Tim touched her shoulder. She looked at him, her mouth puckered, then she burst into tears. He put his arms around her and patted her back till the sobs subsided.

'Looks like it's still raining,' he said at length.

'Yeah.' She wiped her eyes with the back of her hand and they stared at the rocky floor where a film of water cascaded from the entrance, pooling in a corner by the dead-end before draining away through some unseen fissure.

There was movement behind them, a sliding sound, followed by a soft click. Tim turned, but there was nothing to see.

Nothing at all.

'Where did that side passage go?'

He played his torch over the wall. The entrance had vanished. A faint circular outline was all that remained, as if it had been closed off by a shutter. He ran his hand over the surface and could make out the iris-like segments that sealed it off.

'You think maybe the fume trigger something?' Alkemy said.

'No, something isn't right. When we first saw that

passage I assumed Albert had cut it. But he couldn't have. He was coming the other way. Running *away* from that cave-in.'

'I do not understand.'

'Remember that rock slide outside, the one just before this mineshaft? That must have been the one Albert went down. The mineshaft next door.'

'But if he does not cut this hole—' Alkemy began.

'Gizzard Gully!' Tim said. 'The name on the signpost. I *knew* I'd heard it before.'

'You know this place?'

'There was a story on the TV news last night. About the first meteorite to hit this area twenty-five years ago. They interviewed Rambob. He was part of a search party looking for some missing men. He said they found them near Gizzard Gully. *Near where the meteorite came down.*'

'And this meteorite ...?'

'I think it was the Sentinels' ship.'

Alkemy put a hand to her mouth.

'We've got to get out of here.'

He grabbed her hand and was about to add that they should run for it when a section of the wall opposite slid back. A rock shutter, perfectly disguised, rose smoothly and silently, flooding the bottom of the mineshaft with a dazzling pink light. A light broken only by the shapes of two large silhouettes advancing towards them.

Tim recognised them in an instant. They were the stuff of nightmares.

* * *

Rata Area Merchants was like the town itself, Alice thought as Rambob climbed a ladder to a high shelf. It needed a good shake up and a few modern ideas.

'How about this one?' he said, coming back down and holding out a metal contraption the size of a shoe box.

'I want a *humane* one,' Alice said.

'The WhipItOff 2000's pretty humane. Look at that little guillotine. They won't feel a thing.'

'But I don't want to behead them. I want to keep them. Alive.'

He gave her an odd look. 'What on earth for?'

'I ... well ... I don't believe in killing things.'

'So what do you propose to do with them?'

'I want to ... relocate them.'

'Vermin are vermin in my book,' Rambob said, rubbing his chin. 'But if you want to relocate them, try a cat.'

'A cat?'

'One whiff of a cat and mice will run a mile if they know what's good for them.'

'Well, thank you anyway,' Alice said. 'I'll just take the birdcage. And some of those muesli bars over there. And a handful of straw, if I may. How much is that?'

She carried her purchases to her car, thinking about what Eric had said. The mice had shown themselves! They'd escaped from Albert, but they'd lost their ship and were now trapped, friendless, on an alien planet with no way home.

'Not quite friendless,' Alice muttered as she drove quickly out of Rata.

* * *

Shock and fear anchored Tim to the spot. He felt like a possum caught in the headlights of a fast-approaching car. Alkemy yanked his hand, tugged him sideways and dragged him back against the wall where the side passage had been. It hardly provided any cover, but there was nowhere else to go in the flood of pink light.

Pressed flat against the wall, willing themselves to sink into it, they felt the cold dampness of the rock seep into their bones. The swaying shadows loomed larger, accompanied by a throaty chittering – like the sound of birds being strangled – and slowly, as if in a dream, Tim's mind began to clear.

Days before, the Sentinels had tried to coerce him and his sister into becoming their agents; wearing them down with sleeplessness; pursuing them through nightmares every time they closed their eyes. He recognised them at once, even in outline. Creatures that resembled gigantic slugs. They moved with a rippling and frilling of their slimy undersides and could reverse direction in an instant by simply slurping their insides about so they faced the other way. Now they were approaching in the oozing flesh, moving to block off their only escape route.

The chittering grew louder, the shadows loomed larger, and a musty stench rolled over them. A mix of rotting compost, rubbish tips and stagnant ponds. Tim held his breath. The smell grew more intense.

Pressed there, not daring to breathe, he became aware of the tiniest sensations. Moisture seeping into the fabric of his clothes. A faint squelching audible between the rasping chitters. The scurrying of a weta as it sought refuge from the glare. And the looming shadows that blotted out the light before suddenly receding again.

He risked a peek. They were moving away. The silhouettes were heading up the mineshaft. Blocking the exit, certainly, but at least they were moving away.

They hadn't been seen.

He nudged Alkemy. She stared at him and he read the words in her frightened expression: 'What now?'

He felt about the closed-off side passage, seeking some switch or lever that would open it again. If they could just get back down there. Hide. Take cover. To hell with the fumes. It was their only hope.

He found nothing.

The Sentinels reached the entrance, stopping under the curtain of water running down from the cliff above. The sky outside was black with thunderclouds, but he could see it spattering off their outlines. They were revelling in it, slurping from side to side like a couple of fat disco dancers. Their rasping chitters dropped an octave and the sound that came back down the shaft was slower and more sensual.

He shielded his eyes, looking about helplessly, blinking at the blinding light. Recollections of the nightmare pursuits were still fresh in his mind. He knew how the Sentinels worked. They were relentless. Tireless. In his dreams, they wore him down until he knew he'd eventually have to submit.

He looked around desperately, but they had no choice. The moment the Sentinels turned back they'd be spotted. There was nowhere else to go.

He seized Alkemy's hand and dragged her towards the source of the pink light. Back towards the passage they'd emerged from. Right into the Sentinel's lair.

31 : Signs of Life

Tim and Alkemy kept low, shielding their eyes. The light from the passage was so intense it was like a physical presence. Tim felt it as he moved. Like battling a strong wind. Then it dimmed and the pressure eased and they found themselves in a circular tunnel similar to the one that had led to Albert's final resting place. It was darker here and cool. Looking back, he realised they'd pushed through some sort of force field.

This passage was twice the diameter of the other shaft – they could easily stand upright – but it was damp. Two centimetres of water lay in its base. It also had its own internal illumination. The glassy walls gave off a faint pinkish glow, filling it with a soft, uniform light that made their torches unnecessary.

They edged forward, sloshing through the water.

After a short straight stretch, they came to an intersection where the tunnel split into four separate passages, two curving away to the right, two curving to the left.

'Which way?' Tim said.

'Here,' Alkemy said.

Immediately to their right was a gap in the tunnel wall, a broken section where the curving passage had clipped the corner of a natural fissure in the rock. The opening was small and dark. Tim moved towards it without hesitation.

Easing through the irregular opening, they found themselves in a deep chamber plastered in soft green fungus. Stalactites of it hung from the ceiling, stalagmites of it rose from the ground. At first, Tim thought they were rock formations covered in the stuff, but when he brushed against one it yielded, soft and springy, swaying back and forth in the humid air.

'At least is warm in here,' Alkemy whispered.

Tim realised how cold he was. The mineshaft had been cool. Their clothes were damp from where they'd pressed against the wall, and now their feet were soaked too.

They crawled in – there wasn't room to stand upright – then sat and waited. A minute passed. Two. Three. Then shadows flickered in the outer passage. Tim pressed a finger to his lips and they edged further back into the chamber. They saw a rippling pressure wave pass the entrance. Faint chittering sounds grew steadily. The Sentinels were returning.

They took cover behind a mound of fungus as a slimy, elongated shape slid past the opening in the wall.

Tim was surprised at how big they were. It hadn't registered in his dreams or even in silhouette. Height and width were arbitrary measurements for such amorphous creatures, but in terms of bulk, they must have been the size of small cars. The one passing filled the passage completely, moving with surprising speed.

They waited.

The second one began gliding past. Then it paused. Something happened to the side pressed against the opening of the fungus chamber, and Tim realised it was oozing itself into their space. He touched Alkemy's arm. She'd seen it too and they inched back further, keeping low as a bulbous head extruded through the creature's side, swelling up before them in monstrous outline.

* * *

Glad looked up as the door buzzer sounded and Crystal Starbrite stepped into the shop. She was dressed in jeans, a 9-News T-shirt, a pair of expensive looking shoes, and carried a brown leather bag over one shoulder.

'Hi. I'm Crystal Starbrite.' She held out a limp hand.

Glad wasn't sure whether she was expected to shake it or kiss it. She opted for a shake.

'Glad Smith,' Glad said, for once not adding her usual follow-on, 'and I'm glad to meet you.'

Crystal looked about the shop, her eyes lingering briefly on her own picture on the cover of a weekly magazine. 'Nice place.'

'Thanks.'

'Quiet little town, isn't it?'

'I like it.'

'I don't expect much happens round here that you don't know about.'

'Oh, I wouldn't say that.'

'Really?'

'If you're looking for town gossip, you've come to the wrong place.'

'I was wondering what you thought about that meteor impact the other day?'

'Why would you be interested in my opinion?'

'I'm canvassing townsfolk, building up background.'

'Looking for a story, you mean?'

'If there is one.'

They locked eyes for a moment and Glad had a sudden intuition about the leather bag. It didn't fit with the expensive shoes and the designer jeans. It was plain. No fancy label. Nothing exclusive about it. Hardly the sort of thing a celebrity like Crystal Starbrite would carry. And there was something about the way she held it too. Something in the way she kept it level when she moved.

Glad thought about Alice and the cameraman. She'd seen the look that passed between them. Had seen them huddled in a doorway up the road.

'So, you were telling me about the meteorite.'

'Actually I wasn't.' Glad resisted the temptation to straighten her hair or duck out the back and put on a bit of make-up.

'You don't think it's curious that this place seems to be a magnet for that sort of thing? I mean, two in the space of a week ...?'

Glad shrugged. 'Coincidence.'

'What about the spaceship?'

'What?'

'The spaceship, Ms Smith. You know all about that. You were there.'

'I don't know what you're talking about.'

'Come, come, we have witnesses.'

'Witnesses? Plural? You don't need me then.'

Crystal said nothing. She looked about the shop then leaned in confidentially. 'Look, this could be big. How much do you make from a place like this? Open all hours, seven days a week? I bet it's a lot less than what my network would pay for an exclusive story.'

Glad studied her briefly, then reached over to the rack at the end of the counter and picked up a copy of the magazine with Crystal on the cover. 'I just realised. That's you, isn't it?' She held it up in clear view of the leather bag. 'Is that an old photo or have they done something to it? They've made you look ten years younger.'

* * *

'Mine's dead too,' Coral said, trying the starter.

Ludokrus sighed and looked up the gully.

'So much for fancy high-tech bikes,' she said to Norman. 'Looks like we'll be walking home.'

'Is not the bike's fault, is mine,' Ludokrus said. 'Quick build. Need to make fast. I leave off some parts.'

'Like waterproofing.'

'Only some. Should be rainproof. I do not expect the flood.' He gestured at the brightening sky. 'Will come dry if we leave up the seat.'

'How long will that take?'

'One hour, maybe.'

'What are we supposed to do in the meantime?'

'Walk. Like you say.'

Rain had done little to improve the appearance of the gully. Before it had looked dry, desolate and foreboding. Now it looked damp, desolate and foreboding. Most of the downpour had vanished so completely that Coral found herself wondering if she'd imagined it. The foaming drainage ditch still contained a handful of puddles. There were a few more on the track itself and evidence of another slip further up the valley. But apart from clamminess in the shaded sections and a faint steaming from the rocks on the sunlit side, the place had hardly changed.

Timeless, she thought as they started up the track to the mineshaft. If they returned in a hundred years, or even a thousand, it wouldn't look much different.

Norman kept one eye on the receiver as they headed for the mineshaft. 'Nothing yet, but they may be just inside the entrance.'

'Why wait there?' Ludokrus said.

'Water-logged bikes, perhaps?' Coral muttered.

They passed the Hope and Sanity signpost and stopped at the bottom of the switchback track.

'I'll go this time,' Norman said.

'No, we should go two—'

'Two of you are already missing, remember?' Norman headed off without waiting for an answer.

He climbed. Coral and Ludokrus followed his progress, watching every step. They saw him reach the plateau at the entrance to the mine, then heard his voice echo up and down the shaft. He came back to the edge and called down, 'Still no reading on the receiver. I'll go in further.' He pulled a torch from his back pocket. 'Give me a minute.'

Ludokrus kept an eye on his watch. Norman

reappeared, shaking his head. 'Nothing. No sign of them.'

'What? That's not possible.'

'Come up and see for yourselves.'

'But we saw them go in there,' Coral said as they reached the plateau.

'I went right to the end.' Norman said. 'It's a single shaft about sixty metres long. Ends in a sort of T. No side tunnels, no signs of a cave-in. Just a dead-end.'

'Footprint?' Ludokrus said.

'Rock floor.'

'Is this even the right mine?' Coral said.

Norman gave her a pitying look. She was standing right beside the parked bikes.

'Yeah, well, those things don't work in the wet, do they? Maybe they went down on foot.'

'And left their packs behind?'

The packs were still strapped to the back of the bikes.

'Even if they do, where can they go?' Ludokrus looked up at the slope above them. 'Hard to climb, and why would they? Nothing is up there. So must go down. Then is only left or right. One way go back to hut, the other is dead-end.'

They stood in silence, searching the barren gully below for signs of life, but finding nothing.

32 : Whispering Ghosts

Tim and Alkemy ducked below an outcrop of fungus as the Sentinel forced its head through the opening in front of them and expanded like a balloon. At first, it was a grey patchwork of slimy cells, then features appeared, slurping into place. Black nodules the size of tennis balls that might have been eyes popped into position, first one, then the other. Two antenna stalks pushed out from the jelly-like head and began feeling around. Their ends moulded themselves into hand-like shapes, patting and squeezing the hanging blobs of fungus before snapping one off and drawing it to its mouth. It snapped off a second one, pressing this to the top of its head where what must have been a second set of mouthparts ground and chewed in unison with the first. It paused, slurped from a mossy puddle with a sound exactly like someone sipping hot tea, then continued grazing.

Tim and Alkemy watched, alarmed but relieved. They thought the Sentinel had sensed their presence and was pursuing them, but it had really just stopped for a snack. There was nothing to do but lie still, keep quiet and wait for it to finish.

The room was warm, the fungus soft and spongy, and up close it gave off a pleasant, herbal smell. The sound of chewing grew monotonous, almost comforting. Like one of Uncle Frank's cows, Tim thought, closing his eyes for a second.

He opened them again with a start. Something had disturbed him. Like a half-remembered dream. It felt like a wet slap from one of the Sentinel's antenna stalks, but it couldn't have been. The fungus chamber was empty.

Alkemy sat up. 'What? What happen?'

'Nothing.'

'Why you shake me?'

'I didn't.'

'Someone did.' She looked around.

'You must have dreamt it.'

She brushed back her hair then drew her hand away. 'Ugh!' It was damp. Slimy. 'Something drip on me. Look, you too.' She wiped her hand on the fungus and nodded at his shoulder.

Tim looked at a gooey patch on his jacket. 'Oh yuck, what's that?' He wiped it off then checked his watch. Half an hour had passed since they'd entered the mineshaft. They must have fallen asleep while the Sentinel grazed. The Sentinel was gone, but ripples in the water in the passage outside suggested it hadn't been gone long.

It's like it woke us up before it went, he thought. But why would it do that?

Alkemy stretched and yawned, brushing at the fungus. While they'd been dozing, long tendrils of the stuff had reached out and attached itself to their clothes. Hundreds of elastic, web-like filaments that intertwined and formed a dense mat. The threads peeled away easily enough, releasing a faintly soothing odour. Alkemy closed her eyes again and breathed deeply. 'Make me feel sleepy,' she said, flopping back on to the soft mound.

Tim yawned. 'Me too. But we've got to get out of here. Come on.'

They made their way out, moving slowly, listening for sounds of movement and studying the surface of the water. All was still and silent.

Back in the circular tunnel, they returned the way they'd come, sloshing through the water as they went, but the door they'd entered by was closed. The tunnel simply ended at a rock wall.

Tim ran his torch over it. 'There must be a switch or release lever or something.'

He searched but found nothing.

'Maybe further back.'

They checked as far back at the intersection. Still nothing.

He returned and tapped the door with the butt of his torch. It sounded like solid rock. If they hadn't just passed through it, he wouldn't have believed it was anything but a dead-end.

The ground suddenly shuddered. Alkemy grabbed his arm. For ten long seconds, the earth trembled ominously.

'What is that?'

'Felt like an earthquake, or maybe it was a landslide after all that rain.'

Alkemy said nothing. They were both thinking of the mineshaft next door to theirs. The one Albert had gone down. The one that was now closed off by a smear of debris on the hillside.

* * *

'It doesn't make sense.' Norman said. 'Why would they abandon the bikes? Even if they didn't work, they could still coast down the hill on them.'

Ludokrus moved to the mouth of the mineshaft and held up a hand. 'Listen. You hear?'

Norman and Coral joined him, cupping their ears.

There were murmurs in the darkness, like the whispering of ghosts. It sounded like speech, but the words were indistinct and they couldn't make them out.

'I thought you checked in there?' Coral said to Norman.

'I did! That didn't happen when I was—'

'*Ssshh!*' Ludokrus snapped.

More whispers, like quiet conversation, then a sudden cry, loud and clear: 'Oh ... oh ... *Oh no ...!*' followed by Tim's voice: 'What is it? What's happened? Alkemy, what's wrong?'

'Is them.' Ludokrus said. 'In trouble. Quick!' He raced into the mineshaft with Coral at his heels.

'Wait!' Norman yelled. 'Stop!' But his voice was lost in a jumble of echoes. He ran after them. 'No, no! Come back!'

It was only a small explosion. Barely enough to dislodge a few tons of rock above the entrance to the mine, but once released, it set off a chain reaction. Ancient pit props, bearing the weight of a hundred years, sighed and collapsed at the unexpected strain, each one setting off the next. Falling boulders overspilled the narrow ledge, pulverizing the bikes parked there, before sweeping on to the valley floor. When the dust settled and silence returned to the gully, there was no sign there had ever been a mineshaft there at all.

33 : Cages and Bars

Alice turned off the engine near the gate and let her blue Daihatsu coast quietly into the reserve. The tyres made a faint scrunching sound on the gravel as the car rolled to a stop. There was no one else about.

The caravan's windows were closed, the awning zipped up tight. The children weren't back from their walk yet. Good. But they might return at any time. Fantail Falls was several hours south, and they'd left early. The walk ran along a coastal track that started just beyond the crater. The bare, blasted ground would make it easy to see them returning. She kept one eye out as she moved across the campground to the patch of bush where Eric said he'd seen the mice.

'Hello ...?' She cleared her throat and addressed the trees and ferns. 'Hello visitors. My name is Alice. Welcome to Earth!'

A faint breeze stirred the undergrowth.

'Look, we don't have much time. The others could be back at any moment. I know what they tried to do to you and what happened to your ship, and I know what this looks like,' she held up the birdcage she was carrying, 'but you have to trust me. I'm a friend and I really want to help.'

She set the cage behind some ferns at the edge of a clearing.

'I don't think the others know you survived the explosion yet, but when they find out, they're going to start searching for you. Thoroughly. They've probably got all sorts of radar and stuff, so we have to get you away from here. Then we can work out what to do next.'

She crumbled half a muesli bar in front of the open cage door, put the rest inside and backed away.

'There's food and water and a place to rest in here. I think you'll find it very comfortable. And safe.'

There was a cardboard box on one side of the cage. She'd lined it with cotton wool and straw.

'There must be all sorts of hazards out there for mice – and that's without Albert and the children.' She glanced back across the waste ground. 'But I expect you'll want to think about it first. Discuss it amongst yourselves. Please do. But please hurry too. I can only give you half an hour. I'll keep watch while you decide. If I see the others coming back, I'll try to delay them.

'When I return, I'll take the cage with me. If you're inside, I'll take you to safety. If you're not, I'll assume that you have other plans. OK?'

There was no reply from the bush, not even a bird call.

'OK,' Alice said to herself and headed off.

* * *

A rush of air, choking dust, and Norman Smith were Coral's

last impressions. For a moment she thought she was dead. She railed against the thought of being buried with *him* sprawled on top of her. What would future archaeologists think? Then he stirred and coughed and rolled aside and Coral struggled to her feet.

Ahead of them, lit by his own torch, Ludokrus was shaking off dust and grit. He looked dazed. 'What happen?'

'I'll tell you what happened,' Norman said angrily. 'You came rushing in here like an idiot, she followed you, then the Sentinels set off a landslide.'

Coral recalled a shove from behind, driving her forward, away from the crashing debris. 'Does that mean ... you just saved my life?'

'Yeah, whatever,' Norman said, striding off into the darkness. 'Not that it'll make much difference now.'

Ludokrus played his torch over the jumble of rocks behind them. The first five metres of the mineshaft was gone.

'What do you mean it won't make much difference?' Coral called.

'Do you see any other way out?' Norman's voice echoed back.

They followed him down the shaft, catching up with him at the far end, adding their torch beams to the light of his.

'See? I told you there was nothing here.'

'But—'

'And don't forget, I still have this.' He held up the receiver. 'If Tim was anywhere nearby it would have picked him up.'

'But we heard—'

'Recordings,' Norman said.

'What?'

'Do you still not get it? The Sentinels played recordings of Alkemy and Tim to lure us in here. Then they set off that landslide.'

'Recordings?' Coral said. 'But that must mean—'

'Yeah, obviously. They've already got the others.'

* * *

A metal grille blocked the end of the passage. Solid steel. Thick vertical bars ten centimetres apart. Too narrow to squeeze through. Like the bars on a prison cell.

'Just like the others,' Tim said, giving it a shake. It didn't budge.

'That make three in a row,' Alkemy said. 'Maybe fourth time is lucky.'

'I hope so.'

They sloshed their way back to the junction then headed off down the rightmost passage, the only one still unexplored.

It began like all the others, curving and snaking, seemingly at random. The tunnels were monotonous and the pinkish half-light made him feel sleepy, but the source of it was interesting. It came from strands behind the glassy surface of the walls. They seemed too random and organic to be light fittings. Tim guessed they were some sort of alien glowworm.

Up ahead, Alkemy paused at the next bend and let out a sigh.

'Don't tell me. Another grille.'

She shook her head and stood staring as he came up behind her.

'Oh wow!'

The tunnel opened out into a cathedral-sized cleft in the rock where jagged sloping walls rose to a point high above them. The filament-worms had colonised the entire space, clustering so densely near the top that it seemed as though it was lit by a ribbon of light. The rough walls shimmered and glowed. Except for a u-shaped channel etched into the floor – a continuation of the passage they were standing in – the formation looked entirely natural.

They stood entranced, staring up at the magical light show.

'Is beautiful,' Alkemy said.

Tim looked about in wonder as they moved slowly through it. 'To think, this is buried under that barren valley. Amazing!'

'The little worm go everywhere except for here.' Alkemy stopped at a seam of whitish-yellow crystals different from the surrounding rocks. The u-shaped channel skirted round it too, doubling back on itself to avoid it, leaving a drab grey island in a wilderness of pink. Tim picked at the outcrop as they passed and broke off a couple of pieces. It was dry and crumbled easily. He wondered what it was.

They followed the channel to the other side of the fissure. There the circular tunnel began again. Five minutes later, they came to a Y-junction. The passage to the left was barred – Tim tested the grille, but it was fixed solid – and they moved on. After another bend, they found an unusually straight section that ended at yet another grille.

Tim stopped and slumped against the curved wall. 'That's it. This really is a dead-end. There's no way out of here.'

'The Sentinel must pass,' Alkemy said.

'Yeah, but they must carry remote controls or something.'

Alkemy pressed on, seeing it through to the bitter end. He watched her test the grille then turn to one side and examine a section of the wall that was lost in shadow. That was unusual. Everywhere else the light was boringly uniform. He roused himself and sloshed after her.

'Must be fresh,' she said, taking out her torch. 'The glow-strands do not grow here yet.'

This section of tunnel had been widened and there was a trough cut in the floor filled with a milky-looking liquid. Tim knelt and touched a finger to the cloudy surface. It had a consistency like custard and gave off a faint vinegary smell. He rubbed a little between his thumb and forefinger. It felt slimy and unpleasant and stuck to his skin, and after a few seconds he felt it burning. The pain grew sharply and he spun round and doused his fingers in the water in the bottom of the tunnel. He ran them back and forth till the stinging subsided, then took out his hand and studied the tips of his fingers. The skin was red and tender.

'Wonder what that is,' he said. 'Like some sort of acid. Maybe we could use it to eat through the bars.'

He looked up to find Alkemy staring past him, her face frozen in shock.

Following the direction of her gaze, he saw a Sentinel watching them, its bulk filling the tunnel they'd just passed through.

'Where the hell did that come from?' he said, then remembered the Y-junction further back.

A movement to his right caught his attention. He turned to find a second Sentinel pressed against the grille at the end of the straight section of tunnel. As he watched, it pressed harder. The metal bars made indentations in its slimy surface. Then all at once it oozed around and through them, reforming on the other side before slithering straight towards them.

34 : Camouflage

Coral slumped against the side of the mineshaft. The rock was cold and hard. 'That's it then. They've got us all. Game over.'

'You should not come in here,' Ludokrus said.

'I was following you! If you hadn't gone charging off like that—'

'I tell you to go careful from the start. But you, you do not listen.'

'Yeah, *go careful*. Pity you didn't take your own advice.'

'I hear my sister is in trouble. What you think I do?'

'Well I heard my brother—'

'He does not cry out like she. Not upset cry.'

'No? So where is he then? I can't seem to see him at the moment.'

'Jeez, you two,' Norman said. 'Give it up! We've only got about twenty-four hours worth of oxygen in here.'

They fell silent.

'Is that all?' Coral whispered. 'Really?'

'Nah. A space this big will have enough breathable oxygen for weeks. We'll die of thirst first. Or starve.'

'Oh, you're a bag of laughs.'

'I try,' Norman said.

Coral turned to Ludokrus and added in a lower tone. 'Anyway, if I had stayed outside, that landslide would have hit me.'

He looked up. He hadn't thought of that.

A long moment passed as they stood staring at each other. Then Coral said, 'Oh Ludokrus!' Ludokrus said, 'Oh Coral!' And they fell into each other's arms.

'Oh jeez,' Norman groaned, 'if you're going to get all soppy, go up the other end, please. I'm trying to work here.'

'Work?'

'Yeah.'

'At what?'

'Trying to find a way out.'

'We know the way out. It's kind of blocked right now.'

'I mean the other way out.'

'What?'

'Well there must be one. Where have the Sentinels taken Tim and Alkemy? We saw them come in here, but we haven't seen them leave.'

'Oh, I never thought ...'

'What a surprise,' Norman muttered.

'So what exactly are you looking for?'

'I dunno.' He studied the wall with his torch. 'But I'll know it when I see it.'

'Care to give us a clue?'

'Some sort of door or hatch would be my guess. It must be camouflaged because it's not obvious, but there'll be a seam or a gap around the edge where it slots against the real wall.'

The others joined him in his search. Ludokrus started at the dead-end. Coral took the opposite wall. Five minutes later, Ludokrus called out, 'You mean like this?'

He held his torch flat against the side, swivelling it left and right. The beam picked out ridges in the roughly mined surface, highlighting a small flat rectangular patch high up in the middle of the wall.

'Yeah, that's the sort of thing ...'

The smooth patch was mottled with shades of brown and grey so it looked like the rest of the rock wall. It was easy to see how it would escape a cursory glance.

Norman reached up with the butt of his torch and tapped it. 'It's metal. Listen.' He tapped the rock beside it for comparison.

'It's a bit small,' Coral said. 'They couldn't get through there.'

'It's not exactly what we're looking for,' Norman said, 'but it's a start. Remember the flashing light that brought Tim and Alkemy here in the first place? That had to come from somewhere. It must have been pointing directly out the shaft, which would make this an ideal spot for it.'

'OK, but how do we check? That cover sounds pretty solid.'

'I know,' Ludokrus said, reaching for the calculator. 'Remember my dishwash formula?'

* * *

Tim watched with a mixture of horror and fascination as the Sentinel slurped through the bars in front of him, oozing and reforming on the other side. He took a step back and collided with Alkemy, who was edging away from the Sentinel coming from the other direction.

'Go away!' he yelled.

Two gelatinous antennas snaked out, hovering near his face, gliding to and fro, seeming to examine him, their ends forming suction cup-like pads that pulsed greasily. After a brief exchange of chittering, the Sentinel thrust its antennas at Tim's chest, their ends spreading, pushing him back against the wall of the passage. At the same moment, the other Sentinel thrust its antennas at Alkemy, pushing her back towards the trough. She stumbled and threw out a hand, trying to find something to hold on to, and ended up grabbing the Sentinels antenna, but the glutinous substance simply oozed through her fingers and left her clawing empty air.

She tumbled backwards.

Tim cried out and struggled harder, but the antennas pushed him away, sliding him along the smooth-walled passage to where the second Sentinel took over his ejection. He tried fighting back, punching and kicking, but the few jabs that connected ended in dull splats. It was like trying to punch a gigantic jelly.

His last view of Alkemy was of her dancing on the surface of the trough. Something about the liquid resisted sudden impact and she kept switching from foot to foot, taking steps forward and back, then from side to side, but the Sentinel's bulk blocked her from exiting. It thrust an antenna at her, making her stumble. Immediately one foot sank into the murk. She tried to pull it free, but it locked against the movement. Her other foot went under, and all was lost. She sank slowly, crying out, clawing for the side, but each time the Sentinel pushed her back.

Tim fought harder, punching, kicking and tearing at lumps of the gelatinous goo, and it seemed for a moment he was having some effect. Then the Sentinel drew back, reshaped its antennas into a pair of needle-sharp points and stabbed them at him half a dozen times in quick succession. One struck his forehead, one his cheek, one his neck. It was like being machine-gunned with pins and he was forced to back away.

Sensing its advantage, the Sentinel advanced, stabbing again and again with the pointed antennas, forcing him further and further back as Alkemy's anxious cries turned to screams. He remembered the burning sensation on his fingers. Her whole body was sinking in that stuff.

'Stop it! Stop it! Leave her alone!' he yelled, tears of desperation running down his cheeks. But the pointed antennas kept stabbing at him and the Sentinel kept advancing, forcing him away.

35 : Batter Up!

Rivulets of nanomachines ran down the little hatch door, eating deeper and deeper into the metal surface, leaving a fine dust that drifted to the floor. Once they'd eaten away enough to leave a lip, the dust began piling up along the lower edge, so Ludokrus took a piece of paper from his pocket, folded it in a V, then carefully brushed the powder into it.

'What are you doing?' Coral said.

'Saving the raw material. Maybe we can use.'

'Raw material?' She laughed. 'We're in a mine. We're surrounded by raw materials.'

'Yeah, but much rock must be refine to get at them. And to refine, the nanomachine will need the light. Our battery will not last so long.' He stooped, made a neat pile of what he'd collected, and went back to gather more.

'Almost there.'

He picked a large chunk of loosened metal free to reveal a square cut-out set into the wall.

'Hah!' Norman said. 'Look, there's the flashing light. The speaker too.'

'Also microphone and camera.'

'Camera?' Coral said. 'D'you mean they've been watching us?'

'Not likely, the hatch was closed.'

'Well make sure they don't.'

'Easy.' Ludokrus grabbed the camera and wrenched on it. Something snapped and it came free. He did the same with the other items, adding them to the recycling pile.

'Right.' Norman dusted off his hands. 'That hatch is the sort of thing we're looking for, just on a larger scale. Big enough for Tim and Alkemy to get through.'

* * *

Tim continued to retreat, the Sentinel continued to advance, stabbing its pointed antennas like a pair of spears and chittering a series of menacing screeches. He tried to force his way past, moving one way then darting back the other, but the Sentinel was too quick and stuck him in the side several times. Pin pricks, certainly, but still painful. Even if he could avoid the stabbing points, he'd still have to get past the creature's bulk. It could easily squash and suffocate him against the tunnel wall.

Alkemy's screams faded – that was one small mercy – but his feelings of helplessness and rage continued. He was furious at himself for not recognising the name of the gully, for not insisting on more caution, for not making some sort of weapon. But most of all he was furious at what these monsters were doing to his friend.

He stumbled backwards and found himself in the

broad, cathedral-like fissure with its ribbon of light high above. Here he *could* get past the Sentinel, he thought. If it kept following him, he could simply step out of the u-shaped channel and run past it. But the Sentinel spotted that weakness and stopped, blocking the mouth of the tunnel and expanding to fill it completely, like an enormous slimy plug.

Tim tried jeers and feints, tried running towards it then backing away, but apart from steadily tracking his movements with its pointed antennas, the Sentinel showed no reaction.

He was desperate now. The memory of Alkemy's screams burned into his brain. He considered a reckless, suicidal charge. But that would be useless. He'd be stabbed a hundred times even before he reached the Sentinel itself.

He turned in fury to the fissure, seeking something, anything, to throw, and spotted the crumbly crystals by the kink in the channel. Seizing one of the larger lumps, he rushed back and hurled it at the Sentinel.

It didn't bounce or shatter, but struck the creature's upper edge, passing into the gelatinous membrane and causing the tissue to pucker on its passage through. The frequency of the menacing chitters went up a notch and he realised he'd hurt it. He rushed back and gathered more.

'Come on! Come on, what are you going to do about it?' he yelled, holding up another piece of rock.

The Sentinel suddenly seemed wary. It flattened the pointed tip of one antenna, transforming it into a paddle that it used to deflect the second rock.

Tim threw two more in quick succession. The first was knocked aside, but the second struck the paddle squarely and shattered. Fragments of the backscatter pierced the Sentinel and caused tiny puckers in its flesh.

'Ha! Don't like that, eh?' Tim called. 'Ready for another? Come on. Batter up!'

This time, he hurled it deliberately high. The Sentinel tracked it for a second, saw it would miss then dropped its paddle, expecting a second, lower one. None came. The rock shattered on the wall above the passage, releasing a rain of small fragments. The Sentinel gave an alarmed chirrup and backed away.

Tim paused. The reaction seemed out of all proportion. The rock hadn't hit it directly, yet small fragments seemed to do more damage than a large rock. Most curious of all was the way the Sentinel's frilly underside reacted to the pieces that had fallen into the water, shrivelling and seeming to turn inside out.

Tim looked back at the whitish-yellow crystals and suddenly realised what they were. Rock salt. Just like terrestrial slugs and snails, the Sentinels couldn't stand it. That's why they'd cut the channel around the outcrop. To avoid the stuff entirely!

He stuffed as much as he could into the pockets of his jacket, then made a pouch from the front of his T-shirt and scooped more into that. He hurried back, scattering handfuls ahead of him like a farmer sowing seeds. The Sentinel puckered and edged away, deflecting what it could while shrinking from the tunnel walls and elongating itself to reduce its area of exposure. It started moving backwards, but slowly, and would no doubt recapture lost ground as soon as Tim went back to replenish his supplies. He'd need a mountain of rock salt to make any real progress.

The smaller stuff was running low, so he took out a large lump intending to break to it up. Then he had an idea. Instead of pounding it against the wall, he dropped it into the channel, ground it under his heel and sloshed the water forward with his foot. The reaction was immediate. The creature chittered shrilly and flailed furiously away, leaving long slimy tendrils in the salty water behind it.

Tim pursued it, but the Sentinel was in full retreat and moving fast. He had to run to keep up with it. All pretence at defence had vanished. The antennas disappeared as the creature focused solely on escape. Now and then, at particularly tight curves in the passage, Tim was able to add to its distress by peppering its unprotected rear with handfuls of dust.

They passed the Y-junction, the passage straightened, and suddenly Tim knew where he was. There was alarm and confusion ahead as the second Sentinel fought to overtake the first, and the pair of them struggled to ooze back through the iron bars at the far end. Tim gave them an incentive, dumping the last of his hoard, grinding it up and sloshing it ahead.

Their high-pitched screeches faded as they fled. Silence returned. The agitated water in the bottom of the tunnel stilled and Tim moved on towards the darker section, bracing himself for what he would find there.

36 : Stink

'That's weird. What's that?' Coral pointed to a solidified puddle on the rock floor. The ground around it was grey and rough. This patch looked shiny and new. Norman bent to examine it.

'Looks like volcanic lava. Like it's melted from somewhere.'

He traced a line of dribbles back up the wall. 'It's run down from somewhere. Here!'

He pressed his torch flat against the wall.

'Another opening! See it? But circular this time.'

'Looks like the entrance to another tunnel.' Coral ran a hand over the surface. 'Closed off, like the aperture in a camera lens.'

'It's better disguised than the other one,' Norman said, rapping a knuckle against it. 'But it's still metal.'

'More dishwash?' Ludokrus asked.

* * *

Alkemy was propped in a corner of the trough resting on her elbows, her eyes shut tight, breathing in short gasps. She'd tried to drag herself free of the goo, but that was as far as she'd got. Her lower body was still submerged and Tim could see ripples of activity around her as it bubbled and seethed.

'Alkemy! Alkemy!'

He ran towards her, calling her name. Her eyelids flickered and she whimpered like an injured puppy, then screwed them tight against a stab of pain. Although her arms and face were free of the substance, there were deep black burns where she'd been caught by splashes. He shuddered to think what the rest of her must be like.

He got his hands beneath her shoulders and braced himself. He wasn't weedy, but he was no muscle-man either. He might only get one go at this.

He let his mind dwell on the Sentinels and what they'd done to her, let the rage boil up inside him, then channelled every ounce of it into his arms and legs. He moved smoothly, remembering how the goo seemed to lock hard at sudden shocks, and straightened his legs, drawing her up and out of the pool.

There was a slurping, sucking sound, as if it was unwilling to let her go.

He sat her on the edge, gasping, then he pushed up his sleeve, reached a hand beneath her still submerged legs and lifted them free.

The stinging from the goo began immediately. He half-carried, half-dragged her to the water channel and sat her in it, scooping and sloshing water over her.

She shuddered with relief. He could feel it cooling his

arm too. But it wasn't anywhere near enough.

The goo had leached the colour from her jeans and, though it had eaten through in places, they had at least provided a layer of protection. But in the thinner, worn patches where it had got through, the wounds were awful. Deep blue-black pits fringed with fiery red. If she was conscious at all, Tim thought, she must be in agony.

'I'll get you out of here. I promise,' he said, but as soon as the words were out he realised how powerless he was. He didn't know what to do. His hands were shaking with helplessness and rage. But if water was good, more water must be better.

He couldn't carry her, but he could drag her. He took off his jacket, looped it underneath her arms, and used the sleeves like a tow rope. She groaned as he took the weight, but they were soon moving steadily through the smooth-walled passage. As they went, water banked up behind her hips then flowed down around her sides, flushing over her legs, cleaning out the last vestiges of goo.

He plodded on, moving steadily, checking her from time to time. The water was soothing her wounds, but she looked very pale. Back past the Y-junction, through the cathedral-like cave with its glorious ribbon of light, all the way back to where they'd first entered the maze of pink passages.

In the back of his mind he was hoping the Sentinels had triggered the door release. Perhaps by accident in their desperation to escape the salty water, or perhaps just to get rid of them, but as he rounded the last bend he saw his hopes were dashed. The door was still shut tight.

* * *

'Oh man, what is that stink?' Coral said as the first streaky holes appeared in the circular hatch.

'Not fresh air, that's for sure,' Norman said. 'Which means it's probably not a way out.'

'There you go, being cheerful again.'

The holes grew larger and the drift of nanodust kept Ludokrus busy, scraping it to one side, adding it to a pile where other nanomachines were busy reconstituting the metal.

Norman peeled off one of the strips between the dribbles. 'It doesn't smell that bad. Just rotten meat.'

'At least we won't starve then.'

The last shards came away, still bubbling with nanomachines. They dragged them aside and stood studying the smooth wall of the circular passage.

'How did they cut this?' Norman ran a hand over the surface. 'It's like it's been melted.'

'High-energy laser,' Ludokrus said.

'That's what we need.'

'Yeah, I wish.'

Norman scrambled in.

'Hey, who said you were first?' Coral said.

'I discovered it, didn't I? Anyway, you keep complaining about the smell. If you go first and woof your cookies, we'll have to crawl through it.'

She turned to Ludokrus for support but found him smiling. 'Yeah, is right. You last!' Then his manner became serious. 'But careful, yes? Go slow. One by one.'

Norman disappeared. A minute later his voice came back up the shaft. 'All clear. Another dead-end, but come and look at this.'

Ludokrus made his way up the passage. Coral held her nose and followed.

'Is that one of those killer robots?' Norman said, keeping his distance from the object on the ground. He'd heard about the damage they could do.

'No, the eyes are wrong. Not enough of them.' Ludokrus said. 'The Emissary have eyes all round the head.'

He moved closer. Coral leaned back into the passage they'd just come through and took a gulp of air. The stench in the closed space made her feel sick.

A machine of some sort lay crushed beneath a mountain of rock. It was clearly robotic – the head and shoulder and extended arm showed that – but the revolting part was the lumpy puddle in which it lay, a soup of what looked like half-digested meat.

'Also, looks like it once have skin to cover,' Ludokrus added. 'That is smell. Something make decay.'

Norman edged closer. 'What happened to its head?'

Whatever corrosive fluid had attacked it, it had focused on the head. In other places, shiny metal parts shone through, but the skull was dull and deeply pitted. Norman nudged it with his foot. It had been lying side-on. Now it rolled back and stared straight up at them. Ludokrus gasped and drew away.

'What is it?'

They stared at him. His face was pale in the torchlight.

'Albert,' he said in a choking whisper. 'Is Albert.'

'Are you sure?' Norman got down on his hands and

knees.

Ludokrus shrunk back, slumped against a rock and nodded.

Norman, who hardly knew the syntho, was fascinated. He studied the intricate connections of the metal skeleton, awestruck by the complexity and the finely made parts. He was surprised he could identify many of them. Servos, actuators, hydraulic linkages, dampers ...

Coral moved to comfort Ludokrus, but he seemed more dazed than anything.

'I do not mean for this,' he said. 'He make me mad sometime. Always with the secret. So annoy. But this. This he does not deserve.'

'It's all right, it's not your fault.'

He looked down at the remains. Coral put an arm around him, but he didn't respond. Still in shock, she guessed.

Norman raised a skeletal arm from the meaty soup. Fibres and strands still stuck in places, tearing and dropping off with soft plops.

'Do you have to be so gross?' she said, but he ignored her, lifting the arm higher, excavating some of the loose stones around the shoulder with his free hand and directing his torch into the gap.

'This might sound a bit insensitive, but there's a lot of raw material here, you know.'

'Insensitive? *Insensitive?* Ludokrus has just discovered his guardian's dead and you're already dissecting him!'

Norman ignored her and asked quietly, 'How was he powered?'

Ludokrus blinked and disengaged himself from Coral.

'The biologic part is like us. By eat and drink. But core machine power come from micro-fusion generator.'

'I don't know what that is, but it sounds like it could produce a lot of energy.'

'Of course.'

Norman pointed to the side passage. 'Enough to cut a hole like that?'

37 : Beating Heart

Norman dug away as much of the loose rubble around Albert as he could, but the skeletal frame was still pinned by a boulder the size of a shopping trolley.

'Wouldn't it have been flattened anyway?' Coral's voice was muffled by the handkerchief she was holding over her mouth and nose.

'The frame is strong there. Special, to protect,' Ludokrus said. 'The generator work by nuclear. Dangerous to break.'

Norman stretched full length on the cold stone floor and angled his torch under the boulder. 'I can see it. A bluish-coloured box, right? That boulder's right on top of it. Can you make something to dissolve it?'

'Yeah, but the by-product will be gas.'

'Who'll notice?' Coral said.

'Not smelly. Poison.'

'Oh.'

'What about making a sledgehammer from those raw materials?' Norman said.

Ludokrus looked at the huge boulder and smiled. 'Have

idea for something better.'

He dived down the passage to the main shaft and returned with the lumps of metal from the dissolved doors. He lined the ingots up, end to end, added blobs of nanomachines to each gap and within a minute, the seething machines left behind a long steel pole.

'Remember your uncle say how to move the world?' he said to Coral, slipping one end of it under the boulder and using a smaller rock as a fulcrum. 'Now we try.'

He swung down on the metal bar and was rewarded by a fall of stones from the back of the boulder.

'Wait. Hold it there!' Norman wedged some rocks in the growing gap. Ludokrus released the lever, adjusted the position of the bar, and swung on it again.

The front of the boulder rose higher. More dust and stones fell off the back. Coral abandoned her handkerchief and added her weight to the lever while Norman scrambled for larger and larger rocks to wedge in the growing gap.

'A little more. Keep going. Yes!'

He rammed home the last supporting rock. Ludokrus and Coral released their grip.

'We're set. I can get my whole arm in there now.'

Norman held out a cupped hand. Ludokrus tapped a blob of his dish-washing formula into it, and Norman reached in, positioning it as far down the spine as he could. Then he jammed his torch in behind and switched it on to activate the tiny machines.

A minute later there was a snap and the boulder shifted slightly as Albert's torso separated from his imprisoned legs. Norman withdrew the torch, waited a few seconds to make sure the nanomachines were extinguished by the darkness, then together he and Ludokrus dragged Albert's upper body free.

Coral told herself it was just scrap metal, but she still gasped at the sight of the skeletal frame. One arm was missing, the spine had been dissolved below the ribcage, but there was still something recognisable, almost human, in the form.

The ribs on one side were flattened while on the other total collapse had been prevented by strong bracing around a kidney-shaped blue-metal device that sat a little to the left of where a human heart would be. It was as thick as a dictionary and covered in a tracery of fine, copper-coloured filaments.

'That's it, right?' Norman said.

Ludokrus nodded, crouching over it.

'Is it still working?'

'Feel.'

Norman reached out uncertainly. The metal casing was warm. Then he jerked his hand away in surprise. 'It's beating, like a real heart!'

'Ugh!' Coral said.

'No, is good,' Ludokrus told her. 'Albert would want this. To be still useful.' He looked down at the battered frame. 'And so much use. Many raw material. Optic from the eye to make the laser. Part for circuit. Dielectric for capacitor. And power,' he touched the micro-fusion generator. 'Much, much power.'

* * *

Alkemy was cold. Tim saw her shiver and touched her cheek. No wonder. The water she was sitting in was icy. At least he could do something about that.

He half-lifted, half-dragged her into the fungus chamber. She groaned as one of her damaged ankles clipped a rocky outcrop, and he winced at the sight of her wizened flesh, but once past the entrance, the soft spongy floor made things easier.

He dug up a mat of fungus and swaddled her in it up to her chin. She sighed and smiled and her shivering stopped.

He slumped beside her catching his breath, almost succumbing to the sleep-inducing fumes. Leaning on his injured arm, he noticed how the warmth of the fungus seemed to drain away the pain. It clearly had anaesthetic qualities, which was good news for Alkemy.

He considered their position. He'd driven off the Sentinels – for now – but they'd almost certainly regroup and stage a counter-attack, so he had to move fast. After a quick check that Alkemy was comfortable, he made his way back out.

* * *

They dragged Albert's remains through to the start of the cave-in. Ludokrus set to work with the calculator and the other raw materials while Norman wandered off, playing his torch over the nearby walls.

'Where you go?'

'We've found two hidden doors. There must be at least one more. Where they took Tim and Alkemy.'

'OK, but build first, search later. Yes? The nanomachine need much light.'

Norman returned and added his torch beam to the pool formed by the other two. He watched as three solid struts took shape, anchored to the ground. They formed the legs of a tripod, slowly growing up towards each other before fusing together in the middle. Nearby, a complicated box-like device was forming around the micro-fusion generator. Circuits, optics, electronics. It was fascinating to watch, but Norman grew restless.

'Do you need this?' He picked up an unused part. The upper half of Albert's little finger.

Ludokrus shook his head.

'I'll head back down.'

'What, in the dark?' Coral said.

'I can feel my way along the side.'

'And do what?'

'Keep looking.' He tapped the finger against the rock wall 'The other doors were metal so I should be able to hear the difference.'

They watched as he edged away into darkness. *Tap-tap-tap ... tap-tap-tap ...*

Ludokrus said quietly, 'You do not tell me you have the boyfriend.'

'Had,' Coral said. 'Past tense.'

He looked at her.

'Didn't you hear that bit?'

'I ... go back to work.'

'It seems that my so-called boyfriend took up with my so-called best friend about ten seconds after I left to come down here.'

'I'm sorry. Bad way to find out.'

'Yeah, well at least I know now.'

Tap-tap-tap … tap-tap-tap …

Ludokrus reached out and covered the back of her hand with his. Coral looked at him sadly but didn't draw away.

* * *

'*Oooohh!*'

'*Stop moaning. Let me think.*'

'*Look what that wretched monkey boy has done to me. It will take decades to grow these slime fronds back.*'

'*They needed trimming anyway.*'

'*What do you mean?*'

'*Well, you were always slurping about with your curly frills. Very unsentinel-like.*'

'*I thought you liked the way I could juggle snot with them.*'

'*Yes, yes, very clever. But who do you think you are? You're not a movie slug, you know.*'

'*I might be. One day.*'

'*Might have been, you mean. Not now. Look at those puckered fronds.*'

'*Oooohh!*'

'*Shut up and let me think!*'

'*What is there to think about? The wretched creature escaped the dissolving tank and we can't take live monkeys on our ship.*'

'*It's not due until tomorrow. And they can't go anywhere. There may still be a way to get that syntho's memory module. But first we have to get back to the control room and see what's happening out there.*'

38 : Phmmm

The cooler air outside the fungus room helped clear Tim's head. He knew what he had to do. Set up defensive barriers against the Sentinels. Keep them at bay while he tried to find some way out or summon help.

He moved quickly, heading straight for the outcrop of rock salt. Once there, he made a swag of his jacket, loaded it up and slung it over his shoulder. Then, gathering as much as he could carry in his free arm, he kicked a few of the larger boulders into the channel behind him and headed back.

There were three other passages running off from the junction. All of them barred. He piled pieces of rock salt in front of each, leaving the larger lumps to dissolve slowly while grinding up the smaller ones and sloshing the water through the bars.

He thought about the fungus and how it was a source of food. They hadn't seen any other rooms like it in the Sentinels' lair. What if it was the only one? A good pile of salt around it would keep them away. And hungry. Perhaps he could use it as a bargaining chip: food in exchange for freedom.

He returned for another load and piled the whole of it around the narrow fissure in the wall.

Finally satisfied, he went back to the entrance passage and checked again for buttons or switches or levers that would release the outer door, certain he must have missed something. But once again he found nothing.

* * *

Phmmm.

'It works!'

A circular area of rock a metre in diameter glowed dull red as the laser pulse struck it. Coral and Ludokrus felt a backwash of hot air roll over them.

The cutter made a deep whine that grew steadily until it went beyond the range of normal hearing. Then, for several seconds, the air crackled with static electricity until the charge was suddenly released with a second *phmmm* of sound that accompanied another crimson bolt.

This time, the circular area glowed cherry red and the first few millimetres of rock sagged and melted, dribbling away to congeal around the base of the tripod the laser cutter sat on. The charge built up again, slowly and inexorably. Twenty seconds later – *phmmm* – another layer of rock dribbled away.

The cutter was a boxy, briefcase-sized device with a tapering, conical end. It was aimed upwards at a slight angle so that melted rock ran back and kept the tunnel it was cutting clear.

'How long's it going to take?' Coral shielded her face from the blast of hot air.

'Hard to say. One hour maybe.'

Norman returned, drawn by the sound.

'Find anything?' Coral asked.

He shook his head. 'But all that means is they're not behind a metal door. Which kind of makes sense. That shelf and access tunnel were quick jobs. This one's obviously better disguised.'

'So how do we find it?'

'The way we started searching in the first place. There must be a line or a join or a seam where the two sides fit together.' He took back his torch.

Phmmm.

Another wave of heat washed over them.

'Let's check it out.' Coral fanned her hand. 'Better than slow-roasting here.'

* * *

The sound of a car turning into the reserve drew Alice back from her vantage point overlooking the coastal track. A green station wagon. The TV people. What were they doing back? She didn't want them disturbing the mice.

Eric was looking over the closed-up caravan when she emerged from the bush. Crystal was still in the car.

'Still no sign of the tourists?' he said.

'No.'

'Just thought we'd pop in as we were passing.'

'Are you leaving then?'

'Heading to Fox Glacier. One of the missing men lives there. Those guys that were lost in the bush when the first meteorite came down. We're going to interview him for tonight's bulletin.'

'Does that mean you won't be using me?'

'Not tonight.'

Alice sighed. There was still time to redeem herself.

'Any luck with Glad Smith?'

He shook his head. 'But there is one thing you could do.' He opened the rear door and took a brown leather bag from the seat.

'What's this?'

'Concealed camera. The lens points out here, see? There's full instructions in the side pocket. And here's my card in case you have problems.'

'What do you want me to do with it?'

'Fox Glacier's about two hours drive so we'll stay overnight. Be back sometime tomorrow. In the meantime, if the tourists show up and you manage to get an interview with this Albert character ...' He gave her a knowing wink.

'Yes, all right,' she said and watched them drive away.

* * *

'Ooohh!'

'Oooww!'

'What's happening?'

'The salt contamination's getting worse.'

'That wretched monkey boy! He's trying to kill us. We have to do something or we'll never make it back to the control room.'

'There's only one thing we can do.'
'Do it then. Quickly. It's us or him!'

39 : Awful Secret

Phmmm.

Coral looked back up the shaft as a stream of red-hot lava ran down from the steadily lengthening hole, congealing in waves at the base of the laser cutter. A waft of warm air reached her as the charge built slowly for the next pulse.

At least her clothes had dried out after the downpour, she thought, and she turned back to the wall she was examining.

Phmmm.

* * *

Tim waded back to the entrance of the fungus room. Was it his imagination, or was the water level higher? The flow seemed faster too. He watched it tug at the sides of a small piece of rock salt before carrying it away, tumbling it end over end down the smooth-walled passage. Before, the water had been close to the tops of his shoes. Now it was ankle deep.

He climbed back into the fungus room and checked on Alkemy. She was resting and seemed comfortable enough, but tendrils of fungus had begun attaching themselves to the side of her face. They pulled away easily enough, but he didn't like the way it seemed to be growing on her. When he brushed it from her skin, it left tiny pockmarks.

'Alkemy? Alkemy, can you hear me?'

She stirred and sighed lazily.

'Try and keep this stuff off your face, OK? Just give it a wipe now and then.'

'Mmm,' she said.

He reached down to take off his cold wet shoes and found a young possum staring at him, its large brown eyes dark pools in the torchlight. It was less than a metre away. It blinked back at him and yawned.

'What the heck?'

Possums were wild creatures, but not this one, apparently.

He reached out a hand to it. It sniffed at him cautiously then backed away.

'How did you get in here?'

He moved towards it. It shuffled backwards, not comfortable, but not really taking fright.

A thought struck him: it got in, so there must be another way out. The one place they hadn't explored was the far end of this chamber. He picked up his torch and followed the possum.

The roof at the back tapered sharply to the floor. At first sight it looked like a seamless line of fungus, but as he drew closer Tim saw there was a gap about a hand's-breadth wide between the ceiling and the ground. He could smell something too. Fresh air. There was some sort of opening or vent back there.

The air seemed to revive the possum. It took a long sniff then suddenly seemed to remember it should be scared of humans and scampered away, racing through the gap and disappearing up a small hole in the rocks behind.

Tim reached out and pulled the fungus away from the sides of the opening. It was much too small for him, but the fresh air smelled good and he sat back wondering what was going on.

Something gave way beneath him. A slight shift in the heavy fungus mat. Curious, he started tearing it up.

He dug deeper. The stuff was half a metre thick, but he finally managed to pull out enough to make a decent hole. He found his torch, shone it down, then started back in alarm.

Bones.

Hundreds of them.

Thousands.

The bones of small animals stripped completely bare, the roots of the fungus wrapped round and round them.

He suddenly realised the awful secret of the fungus and rushed back to Alkemy, calling her name, desperately. 'Alkemy, wake up. Wake up, we can't stay here!'

The tendrils had grown back over her face. He swept them aside.

'The fungus, it's carnivorous,' he gasped. 'The smell makes you sleepy. Like an anaesthetic. You fall asleep, then it eats you.'

He could imagine the far end of the opening where the

possum had crawled in. A fissure in a rock face or an opening in a cave somewhere in the bush that surrounded Gizzard Gully. Drawn by the alluring scent of the place, a procession of small animals – rabbits, possums, rats, mice, weasels and stoats – had come down here to rest and fall asleep. And die. Thousands upon thousands of them over the years. And the fungus fed on their remains.

Back at the entrance of the fungus room, water was lapping around the lower rocks. The level was rising steadily. It took him a moment to register what was happening, then he realised his mistake. Filling the passages with salt had been a good defensive move. Too good, because now the Sentinels were trying to flush them clean.

'We really are going to have to move,' he told Alkemy.

Torn scraps of fungus floated in the pooling water. Tim had an idea. He tore off a thicker piece and submerged it. It bobbed to the surface.

'Yes!' he muttered and got busy, tearing off a mat of the stuff then securing it around Alkemy. Hopefully, away from its roots, it would lose its carnivorous tendencies. And if it didn't, well, it probably wouldn't matter now.

By the time he was finished, there was five centimetres of water in the base of the room and Alkemy was already partly floating. He zipped up his jacket, stuffed some more bits of fungus inside to help his own buoyancy, then made for the exit, guiding Alkemy along behind him, her head cradled on a pillow of the stuff.

The passage outside was now one-third full. The current was steady and growing swifter, sweeping back towards the junction and the barred grilles beyond. He didn't want to get caught against them if it got any deeper, so he struggled against the flow and guided Alkemy back to the short passage they'd first entered. The water there was just as deep, but it was a dead-end. That meant there was no current.

Alkemy slept on, floating on her fungus life raft.

The level was up to his waist now and kept rising. Tim shivered and wondered how much deeper it would get.

* * *

'At last, the relief! I can feel it already.'

'Wretched loathsome monkey boy. I'll make him pay for what he's done to me!'

'Oh, he'll pay all right. Doubly so. When his companion dies that memory module will self-destruct, remember?'

'I remember. I just wish I could watch it happen.'

* * *

The torch bobbed about near the top of the tunnel, illuminating the last few centimetres of air. At least the rising water let him check the upper edge of the closed entrance door. Before, it had been an awkward stretch. Now, with his fungus-padded jacket acting like a life preserver, it was easy to make a minute examination of the rock wall.

Not that he expected to find anything. But at least it kept his mind occupied.

And then he saw it: a pinhole on the left-side disguised

by a fold in the surface rock. It was near the roof. A perfect circle of darkness barely about two millimetres wide.

Of course! It all made sense now. He thought of the Sentinel driving him away with finely pointed antenna tips. Such gooey creatures would have trouble with regular buttons or switches, but they could make fine, jabbing needles. He could still feel some of the wounds it had inflicted.

And that was all he needed. A needle. A pin. A paperclip. A piece of wire. He searched his pockets. String, coins, bits of soggy paper, the leftover scanner block already falling to bits from the damp. The stub of a pencil, some forgotten chewing gum – but nothing he could use.

He took another breath. His nose was pressed against the ceiling now. And still the water kept rising. He could feel it lapping around his mouth. One or two deep breaths was all he had left.

He tilted his head, pressed his face to the glassy ceiling, and filled his lungs. The water closed over him, leaving a few tantalising bubbles of air in the roof of the passage, but that was all. When this breath was gone, that would be it. His struggles would be over.

40 : Last Gasp

'That soon cleared up.' Emma Townsend peered from the kitchen window as the last of the dark clouds passed overhead. 'Funny little storm. All over in no time.'

'That'll be the opposite of "mainly",' Frank said. 'The weather bloke said it'll be "mainly fine", so that must be the other bit. And speaking of funny little storms ...'

Alice swung into the drive and pulled up outside. She got out of her car slowly, then gently closed the door, as if there was someone sleeping inside that she didn't want to disturb. As she headed for the house, she held out the key and pressed a button on it. The car gave a chirp and flashed its lights.

'She's locking it,' Em said.

'Smart move. There's some pretty dodgy cows around here.'

'Ssshh!' Em said.

'Hi Em. Hello Frank.'

'You sound like you've had a good day,' Em said.

'Yes, I have rather.'

'Been shopping?' Em nodded out the window. There

was something on the back seat under an old blanket.

'Oh ... just an old birdcage I picked up in town.'

'Birdcage?'

'Mmm. It's a bit tatty at the moment. Needs cleaning up and painting.'

'I didn't think you liked caged birds.'

'No, no you ... put plants and things in them. For interior decoration. They're all the rage right now.'

'Did you speak to that reporter?'

'She's gone away. To Fox Glacier. Might be back tomorrow.'

'Will you talk to her then?'

'I might. I'm ... still thinking about it. Shall I put the kettle on?'

'We've just had a cuppa, but help yourself.' Em glanced out the window and laughed. 'Oh look at Smudge. Straight up on your bonnet. It must be the warmth of the engine.'

Alice let out a squawk, slammed the kettle down and raced out.

'Nooooo! No Smudge. Off. Get off. Go! Scat!'

'What on earth is wrong with her?'

'I gave up asking that question years ago,' Frank said.

* * *

A droplet of water ran down the wall. The movement caught Coral's eye. It was followed by another. She turned to investigate, then Norman's voice said, 'Hey, hear that?'

'What? I don't hear anything.'

'Exactly. The tunneller's stopped. Either it's broken

down or it's broken through.'

They paused and listened. He was right. There was no more steady build-up whine, no static pause, no *phmmm*.

They raced back to check. Ludokrus led the way and let out a whoop of joy. 'Can see the daylight. Look. She is through! Now all we need is time for her to cool.'

'How long?'

Coral and Norman sighted along the sides of the cutter, peering at a small circle of sky and shifting clouds at the far end.

'Rock is still red-hot, but the new air will help. Half-hour, maybe.'

'We'd better get back to finding the others then.'

They headed back down, their steps lighter, their mood brighter, three torch beams playing over the bottom of the mineshaft. They walked side by side, then stopped mid-stride.

'What the heck?' Coral muttered.

* * *

The pink glow continued beneath the surface of the water. At least it wasn't dark, Tim thought. Maybe drowning wouldn't be so bad.

Alkemy's head bumped against him, her hair swirling round him in the half-light. How much did she know of their predicament? How much was she aware of through her pain and the anaesthetic fungus? Not much, he hoped. And soon her suffering would be over.

He felt like crying out at the injustice of it all, like

yelling one last defiant insult at the Sentinels, but fought it back, holding his breath as long as possible.

Alkemy's head bumped him again. He touched her. The skin of her cheek was still warm. He wanted to tell her he was sorry he'd broken his promise, that he hadn't been able to get her out after all.

Silvery strands of hair drifted past his face, clouding the cold clear water.

Her hair.

She didn't wear it loose. She brushed and tied it back, securing the wispy bits at the sides with clips. The recollection of her doing so that morning in the caravan came flooding back to him; Alkemy brushing her hair and pinning it back.

Pinning it back.

With clips.

Hair clips!

He scrambled frantically, tugging at her hair until he found one of them. It was tangled in a swirling knot, took precious seconds to work loose. A doubled-over piece of wire with blobs of resin on each end to blunt the sharp points. He straightened it, bit on one end, and dragged it through his teeth to remove the resin.

It jerked free and he dropped it.

He wasted precious seconds, torn between diving down to try to find it or searching out another one. Forcing himself to ignore his clumsiness, he resumed combing his fingers through her hair.

There! Another one! Careful now ...

He repeated the process as his breath strained to escape, his body wailing that he had to breathe. He held on, focused on his task, straightened and cleaned the wire, then swam back in search of the pinhole.

It was a tight fit, but it was his last chance. He pushed it in. Hard.

A centimetre in, it struck something. Resistance. He pushed harder, jamming the other end into the palm of his hand, breaking the skin. But he didn't feel a thing because the rock wall in front of him slid silently away.

For one absurd moment it seemed like it had been a waste of time. The door vanished, but the force field still held things in place. He remembered pushing through it from the mineshaft. Like battling a strong wind. He could see through it. Could see what looked like the faces of his friends gawping at him. The view a fish must have from inside its bowl.

Then the pressure grew too much, the force field collapsed, and he and Alkemy tumbled out in a cascade of water.

41 : Another Problem

Coral, Ludokrus and Norman leapt back as a wall of water surged towards them, rushing up the floor of the mineshaft like a tidal wave. Their torch beams swung about wildly as they leapt back, but the mineshaft sloped down, angled like a beach, and the wave broke with a rushing sigh that left two lumps of debris in its wake. One was coughing and splashing about in the shallows. The other floated on a raft of green matting and looked like she'd been on a gentle cruise.

'That has to be the most amazing entrance ever,' Norman grinned. 'It looked like you were swimming around like a couple of goldfish, then someone broke the bowl.'

'That's exactly what it felt like,' Tim said, going over what had happened while drying out his sodden clothes by the still-glowing exit passage.

He looked over at Alkemy. She was still unconscious, but her breathing was slow and steady. The fungus anaesthetic had slowed down her whole system, which was probably what had saved her.

He looked at the laser cutter set on a sturdy tripod, the

feet of which were now permanently welded to the floor by streams of cooling lava. Then he squatted to examine the passage it had cut. It was a metre wide and inclined at an angle of ten degrees. At the far end, he made out a patch of late afternoon sky and felt his heart leap at the prospect of the open air and a view of distant hills.

'Careful,' Ludokrus said. 'If machine restart, it mine your head!'

He ducked back as Ludokrus swivelled the tunneller to one side then detached it from the tripod.

'Safe now.'

'The level's still rising,' Coral said, coming past with a saucepan of water and sloshing it up the exit tunnel. A great cloud of steam engulfed her for a moment. 'It makes our job easier though. Not so far to go each time.'

Ludokrus had fashioned a couple of pans from leftover scraps of metal and now he and Coral were using them to cool the glowing rock.

'We've got one more problem,' Norman said, stopping them before they could go back for another load.

'Great, what now?'

'I think we're all agreed this whole thing's been a set-up from the start,' he said. 'The Sentinels caught Albert and used him as bait to get us, right?'

'Right.'

'So how did they know where we were? What we were doing outside there in the gully? How did they know when to start and stop the flashing lights? To set off that landslide? There's only one way they could have known: they've got the gully under surveillance.'

'So?' Coral said. 'Watching doesn't mean they can

actually do anything. We'll give them a wave as we go.'

'You probably won't get a chance. We know they set off explosions above two of the mines already, one to trap Albert, one to trap us. They must have the whole place rigged. They could bring the entire gully down on top of us before we get halfway to the hut.'

'Can't we just wait till it gets dark?'

'They'll have infra-red cameras and image intensifiers too. It was getting dark when they got Albert.'

'So what do we do?'

'Whatever it is,' Tim said, 'we should do it now. While they're still flushing out that salt water.'

'Well?' Coral turned to Norman. 'I hope you've got a plan.'

'As a matter of fact ...' he said.

42 : Odd Man Out

The fungus made great insulating material, Norman thought, leaning on a wad of the stuff, elbows down, kicking with his feet as he pushed his way up the exit passage. The slope was gentle and the surface glassy smooth, but the sides were still hot, especially near the middle where the cooling air and splashed water hadn't yet reached it, so he went as fast as he could. The fungus mat dried quickly, becoming crisp and brittle. It began to smoke. The toes of his runners began to melt too. He could feel the heat in his feet and sensed them sticking to the scorching rock.

He pushed on, harder. He had no choice. He couldn't stop now or he'd be barbecued.

As he neared the exit, the rock began to cool again and fresh air hit him like a cold shower. The late afternoon sunlight was blinding after the gloomy mineshaft and he staggered out shielding his eyes to find himself in a very different place to the one he'd entered a few hours earlier. The plateau where the bikes had been parked, the bikes themselves, and the switchback track to the gully floor were gone, swept away by the explosion and landslide.

'OK, I'm out,' he called back down the shaft. 'Heading off now.'

'Good luck.' Tim's acknowledgement echoed back, accompanied by a waft of steam from another tunnel-cooling splash of water.

The slope was steep, the rocks loose, but there were no mineshafts above him. That meant there were no more hidden explosives above him either – or so he hoped.

The good thing about being the odd man out was that the Sentinels wouldn't pay him much attention. At least that was the theory. Why bring a rockfall down on one hapless human they hadn't seen before when it was Alkemy and Ludokrus they were really after? If they were watching, the Sentinels would be waiting for the others to emerge, keeping one last surprise in store for them.

He paused and caught his breath. There was no point climbing all the way to the ridge at the top. He just needed to stay high enough to skirt the highest mine as he made his way around to the valley entrance.

It took almost half an hour – plenty of time for the tunnel to cool properly – and when he reached the hut he grabbed Ludokrus's bike and hit the starter.

The engine coughed faintly and his heart sank.

Don't tell me it's still water-logged!

Then he remembered the bikes' silent running. He kicked away the stand, let go the handlebars and gave it a shove. It wobbled slightly then bounced upright. It was working!

He wheeled the rickshaw-like trailer out from where Ludokrus had assembled it, attached it to the tow bar and rode away up the zigzag path, leaving the gully behind. The trailer moved smoothly, its wheels were well sprung, and it didn't affect the bike's performance. That was good. No, that was critical.

At the summit, he paused briefly by the warning signs, picked out a route, then headed off, blazing a new trail along the top of the gully's eastern slope. The view was spectacular but the drop down both sides of the sharply pointed peak was alarming. He tried not to think about it and kept his eyes fixed straight ahead, searching out the safest route and anticipating every turn and bump.

Suddenly, behind him, the trailer slipped into a dip and slid sideways off the narrow peak. The back end of the bike was dragged with it. Norman felt it go and battled the temptation to leap off and save himself. Without him, the bike and trailer would go crashing down into the gully below.

Instead, he threw his weight forward, forcing the bike's auto-stabilisers to lean with him, then accelerated hard. The back wheel skidded, gripped, then bit, hauling the trailer back in line so suddenly he was forced to brake to stop from going off the other side.

He paused for a second, caught his breath and wiped his clammy hands on his T-shirt.

That was close, but not far now.

Two hundred metres from the exit hole, he edged off the ridge and angled down towards it, still half-expecting the ground beneath his wheels to erupt at any moment.

Nothing happened. He reached the opening without incident, swung the bike around to face the way he'd come, left the motor running, choked the wheels with stones and called down to the others.

Tim was first to emerge, blinking and squinting, his damp clothes dishevelled. Coral followed, her blonde hair thick with grit, her face streaked with grime. Neither said anything as they breathed in great gulps of fresh air.

Norman pointed out the trail he'd left, and Tim and Coral headed off. Norman waited, watching their progress and relayed the details down to Ludokrus.

'That's it, they're back at the hut now. They've collected the other two bikes and are heading back up.'

'OK. We come now.'

Ludokrus slid Alkemy, still wrapped in fungus, into the exit passage, got behind and pushed for all he was worth. She moved easily enough, but he had to keep going. If he paused, they'd both slide back down the smooth slope.

As they neared the top, Norman reached in and took the strain, helping to slide her out into the open air. Ludokrus scrambled out behind her and stood poised, waiting. This was the moment of truth. If the Sentinels were watching, if they had anything explosives hidden above them, this would be the time to trigger them.

Nothing happened. Norman let out a breath. 'Let's get her in the trailer,' he said, taking one end of the fungus matting.

With Alkemy strapped in and Ludokrus dubbing on the back, Norman eased the bike back up the trail he'd left then followed the ridgeline back to the warning signs at the head of the gully.

Tim was back with the second bike by the time they arrived and he hurried over to check Alkemy. The fresh air and the bouncing traverse had woken her and she blinked wearily at him.

'How do you feel?'

'Numb,' she said. 'But thank you. I remember what you do.'

He smiled in relief and touched her shoulder.

The sun was sinking steadily. Gizzard Gully was calm and still. It looked like nothing had stirred down there for a hundred years or more.

'This is the last I ever want to see of *that* place,' Coral said.

They all heartily agreed, mounted the bikes and headed for home.

3

Rata
Day

43 : Declaration of War

To the people of Wellington, the mirror-windowed office block was just another bland government building amongst dozens of others. Except this one had a number of surveillance cameras concealed in bubble-like blisters on the underside of its broad verandas and exceptionally strong stainless steel bollards around it, spaced along the pavement at regular intervals to prevent people from parking there – or ramming their way in.

On the fifth floor, Director General Johnson Johns turned from his window at the knock on his door and watched a smart young man in a smart new suit enter.

'Morning Darling.'

'Morning sir.'

The young man was carrying a red manilla folder. Johnson Johns hadn't been in the job long, but he'd been there long enough to know that red meant trouble.

'Thought you'd better see this, sir. 'A pri one sit-rep from the Yanks.'

'A priority one situation report from our American cousins, Mr Darling?' The DG couldn't abide service jargon.

'What is it this time? The ambassador caught speeding again? Mrs Ambassador got a parking ticket?' He took the folder and flicked through the closely printed pages.

'Bit more than that, sir.' Darling's eyes were bright with anticipation. 'It seems that one of their comm sat nets ... er ... commercial satellite networks responsible for relaying satellite phone messages went off-line yesterday. Sixteen satellites in total. They swivelled away from Earth, broadcast a sequence of coded signals into deep space, swivelled back, and came back online again.'

'What's that got to do with us?'

'Seems they were hijacked. Someone told them to do it, and the techs have traced the originating call to a handset registered to the Nine News Network.'

Johnson Johns raised an eyebrow as Darling moved to a pair of detailed maps on the wall; the North and South Islands side by side.

'What's more – and our base at Waihopai have confirmed it – the call came from here.' He indicated a remote spot on the West Coast of the South Island.

The Director General got up for a closer look. 'What, in the middle of nowhere?'

'Not quite nowhere, sir. Did you see the TV news last night?'

* * *

'More scrambled eggs anyone?'

'No thanks.'

'No thanks.'

'Yes please, Mrs Townsend!'

'At least someone's got an appetite.' Em glanced at Tim and Coral as she topped up Norman's plate. They looked tired. Yesterday's walk must have worn them out, especially getting caught in that storm. They'd arrived home damp and dirty. 'You really don't have to be up so early, you know. It is a holiday.'

It couldn't have felt *less* like a holiday.

Tim made a shot at a smile. 'Don't want to miss the day,' he said, his voice sounding brighter than he felt.

Coral gave him a look. He knew what she meant. It was the last day. The adventure was over. By late this evening Alkemy and Ludokrus would be heading for home. This time tomorrow, the three of them would be getting ready for school.

'What do you reckon they'll do now?' Norman whispered.

'Who?'

He glanced over his shoulder and checked under the table, looking for the cat. 'The you-know-whats?'

'You mean the Sentinels?' Coral said.

'Yeah.'

'There's not much they can do now. Not stuck in that old mine.'

'Don't underestimate them,' Tim said.

Coral gave a brittle laugh. 'Are you serious? The Eltherian ship will be here in ...' she checked her watch, '... less than twelve hours, and all they've got to use against it is a cat and an ancient school principal. Colour me terrified.'

Norman helped himself to another slice of toast. 'What'll the Sentinels do when they've gone?'

'Pack up and go too, I guess,' Tim said.

'We should go back up there later. In a few weeks' time, I mean. Once everyone's gone. Have a proper look around. We've got a way in now, and who knows what cool stuff they'll leave behind.'

'Have a nice walk,' Coral said dismisively.

Norman glanced at Tim. He hadn't been planning on walking.

'Besides,' she added, 'in a few weeks time it'll be the end of term. We'll be heading back to Auckland.'

Tim made a face.

'At the very least I'd like to see that trough they pushed Alkemy into. You said she seemed to dance on it at first.' Norman piled scrambled egg on the toast and crammed it in his mouth.

'It was weird. It seemed like while she kept moving she was OK, but as soon as she stopped, she sank.'

'Oobleck,' Norman said.

'Don't talk with your mouth full.'

'I'm not!'

'What did you say then?'

'Oobleck. I said it sounds like oobleck.'

'What the hell is—?'

'Oh, it's great fun. Have you never made some?'

Tim shook his head.

Norman scooped up the last of the scrambled egg with a crust. 'You can make it yourself by mixing water and corn starch. I once went through the shop's entire stock and made a whole bath tub full. It was really neat. But Mum wasn't too happy.'

'What's so special about water and corn starch?'

'It makes a liquid that doesn't behave like a proper liquid. They call it a non-Newtonian fluid. You can dip your finger in it if you do it slowly, but if you give it a sharp tap it behaves like a solid.'

Tim thought of Alkemy's odd side to side dance.

'Any sudden shock makes its molecules lock together. Once the shock's been absorbed, it behaves like a liquid again.'

As soon as the Sentinel blocked her and stopped her moving, Alkemy started sinking.

'So if you step in it and try to snatch your foot out ...?'

'It'll lock. Solid. But you'd be able to pull it out if you moved slowly.'

Which was exactly how he'd dragged her out.

'Obviously that Sentinel stuff was a lot nastier than water and corn starch,' Norman continued, 'but the principle's the same.'

'What was that stuff for?' Coral said.

Tim shook his head. He didn't know. But the Sentinels singled her out for it. He remembered the greasy-looking antenna pad that seemed to study his face before pushing him aside.

'Speaking of Alkemy,' Coral picked up her plate. 'We should get these done and see how she's doing. Provided of course that Dustbin here has finished.'

Norman wiped a finger round his plate and licked it. 'All done.'

'I'll get my stuff,' Tim said, once they'd done the dishes.

Smudge lay in wait in the hallway, coiled like a spring. The moment he trotted past, she launched herself at him, sinking her claws and teeth into his jeans-clad leg. Tim leapt back in shock and spun around, but that made Smudge cling tighter and sink her claws in deeper.

'Get her off! Get her off!' he cried, but Coral and Norman stared, stunned and a little frightened by the ferocity of the attack.

Alice appeared. 'Oh! No, no, no puss. No,' she called. 'Bad cat!'

Smudge wasn't listening.

Em rushed in from out the back and helped Tim pry the cat loose. Even then, Smudge continued snarling and lashing at him as she was dragged away.

'I don't understand it,' Em said, dabbing antiseptic on his wounds. He had a few scratches and the dent of teeth marks, but they hadn't broken the skin. His jeans had saved him. 'She's never done anything like that before. You must've startled her.'

'What was that about?' Coral said as they headed for the shortcut to the reserve.

Tim's leg still stung from the disinfectant. 'I reckon it's revenge for what I did to the Sentinels. Especially that one I splashed with salt water.'

'Nah, it's more than that,' Norman said.

'What do you mean?'

'It's more like a declaration of war. They're saying they haven't finished with us yet.'

44 : Special Friend

Alkemy was out of the full-body suit Ludokrus had zipped
her into the night before. They found her reclining on a
lounger in front of the caravan. She wore a broad-brimmed
hat and sunglasses, her legs covered with a brightly
coloured beach towel. Around her lay a litter of cups and
plates, along with several books. She looked up and waved
when she saw them approach, saving a particularly warm
smile for Tim.

'How are you feeling?' he asked.

'Bored but much better, thank you.' She lifted the towel
to reveal the pair of inflated silver boots that encased her
legs from the knees down. The most exposed area. The area
the goo had done the most damage. A small pump nestled
between her ankles, coordinating the activity of the healing
gel.

'Only two more hour to go.'

'Will you be able to walk OK?'

'Muscle will be new and not so strong. I must go
careful.'

'You would not think so careful if you see her eat.'

Ludokrus came out of the caravan carrying a tray laden with fruit, energy bars, nuts, raisins, cheese, chocolate and two slices of cold pizza. He set it on her lap. 'Already she gobble all the cereal, egg and toast we have.'

'I cannot help!' Alkemy said. 'My body need the energy for the remake.'

'Well on that basis,' Coral said, 'Norman must about to clone himself.'

'Hey!'

Ludokrus collected the empty dishes and returned to the caravan. Coral followed him in.

'And how are you?' she asked.

He shrugged. He looked drawn and tired.

'Did you get any sleep?'

He gestured towards his sister. 'Busy night. Checking. Keeping watch.'

'More nightmares, huh?'

He shrugged.

She studied his face. 'It's not your fault, you know.'

'Whole thing is my fault. All the danger is down to me. I nearly kill us all.'

'That's ridiculous.'

'Who else then? Who drive Albert away by saying the rude thing to him? Why else does he go out to place the scanner blocks at night? Excuse. To get away from me.'

'You don't know that.'

'And who should be in charge when he is gone? I let Tim and Alkemy go into mine. Then I take us three there also.'

'But you got us out again. You built the laser cutter.'

Ludokrus bit his lip. 'I was scared.'

'We were all scared, Ludokrus. People handle things in different ways. Everyone does what they can. We're a team. We're a good team.'

Norman stepped into the caravan.

'Now here's nerd boy to say something inappropriate,' Coral said with surprising gentleness.

'I ... just came ... for the ...' He gestured at the receiver lying on the bench, but Coral put an arm around his shoulders.

'I never said thanks for what you did yesterday. It was team work, but I reckon you did the most. If you hadn't found those secret passages, we'd all still be stuck down there. So good work. And thanks.'

'Yes, thank you,' Ludokrus said.

Norman turned a beetroot colour. 'I ... it's ... you're welcome.' He grabbed the receiver and scuttled out.

'But you're still a nerd!' Coral called after him.

* * *

The morning air was warm and still. Gulls soared overhead and the sound of distant surf was soothing. Alkemy leaned back and watched Tim and Norman as they huddled round the receiver, trying to make sense of the streams of information coming in from the activated scanner blocks. The Sentinels were alive and active and didn't care who knew it. They had nothing to hide now.

'I almost forgot,' Coral said. 'Aunt Em invited you all for lunch.'

'Albert also?'

'Of course. It's a thank-you for looking after us yesterday.'

'Will need excuse.'

'I'll think of something.'

Mention of Albert made them go quiet.

Coral dragged a hand over the ground, plucking at tufts of grass. 'Your ship's due about seven o'clock, right? It'll still be light.'

'Should be OK. Is why we chose this place. Remote.'

'Albert said it'll avoid potential witnesses. Does that include us?'

'Friend is OK. I put you in the signal. But if others come, she will go elsewhere.'

'Well Alice is going home this afternoon, and Aunt Em and Uncle Frank always watch the six o'clock news. There's no one else around here.'

'Do you have that memory bulb thing?' Norman asked Alkemy. 'Can we see it?'

Alkemy took it from her pocket and held it out, cupped in the palm of her hand.

Coral said, 'It doesn't look like much.'

'I think it's pretty neat,' Tim said. 'It looks old fashioned and really advanced at the same time. See that? It's like there's a little world in there behind that swirling cloud. You almost catch glimpses of things now and then. How does it work?'

Ludokrus shook his head. 'I never see a thing like that before.'

'What is it exactly?' Coral said. 'I mean, what's in there?'

'Albert,' Alkemy said.

'Albert?'

'From what he tell us, it is a copy of his mind.'

'You mean like a backup?'

She nodded.

'*Of his mind?*'

Ludokrus said carefully, 'Maybe you make mistake from what he say.'

Alkemy shook her head. 'Is new technology. Very secret. Tim hear this also.'

'Actually, he said it was a special storage and recording module,' Tim said.

'He means mind. That is how he talk.'

'But is not possible to copy a whole mind,' Ludokrus said.

'Maybe this is why is secret. New. The normal syntho do not have.'

'But all have memory unit for the math and computation and the storage.'

'Does not look like this.'

Ludokrus conceded the point.

'So what was your silly old syntho doing with secret new technology?' Coral said.

'Albert was not silly.' Alkemy closed her fingers around the bulb and drew it to her chest. 'He was special. He was friend.'

Norman leaned forward and tilted her fist to look at the bottom of the bulb.

'That's interesting. That's where it was plugged in, right?'

She nodded.

'Look at this.'

He picked up the receiver and turned it sideways.

'Remember how Albert rebuilt this thing and added 3D mapping? Well he also added this.' He tapped on a circular socket, an indentation seven millimetres across and five deep. On the bottom of it was an array of fine metal contacts in a distinctive pattern.

'I couldn't figure out what it was. I thought it might be air vent or something. Until now. Look.'

He held it beside the end of the upturned bulb in Alkemy's fist. They saw at once how the patterns matched perfectly.

'I reckon that's designed to plug in there.'

45 : Connections

'Cannot be.' Ludokrus studied the connectors.

'They're the same, look. One's a mirror image of the other.'

Ludokrus looked at his sister. 'You think Albert plan this? Think something may happen? Remake the receiver so this will fit?'

'He make the Temporal Accumulator also,' Alkemy said. 'Why rush? We cannot use. We have no ship. And back then we cannot even call for one.'

'Are you saying what I think you're saying?' Tim said. 'That he built the Temporal Accumulator and modified the receiver, then went off knowing he might not come back?'

Norman said, 'Maybe he guessed where the Sentinels were from Mum's maps. Maybe he went looking for them and left a little insurance behind. He knew we'd go looking for him if he didn't return.'

Alkemy bit her lip and studied the bulb. 'You think I should try to plug it in?'

Ludokrus shook his head, 'Does not make sense. How can he know he does not come back?'

'Not know for certain, but like Norman say; insurance.'

'He mentioned a mission too,' Tim said to Alkemy. 'Remember? He said he'd completed his mission to the best of his abilities.'

'What sort of mission?'

'Didn't say.'

'The old receiver,' Ludokrus said to Norman. 'She have this socket also?'

'Definitely not.'

Ludokrus sighed. 'Albert, always with the secret.'

Alkemy held the bulb out. Norman set the receiver in her lap. 'He say I must keep it close. Will still be close, yes? Can keep my hand on.'

Tim nodded.

Still, she hadn't quite decided, but as she moved it near the socket, the bulb decided for her. It jumped from her fingers like a paperclip brought close to a strong magnet. The two surfaces met, the bulb rotated half a turn, then sank in as it made the connection.

There was a pause. A thin red band lit up around the receiver's edge and a voice said, 'Restricted recollection parameters activated. Five sentient beings present. Please identify yourselves.'

Tim recognised the robotic voice immediately. 'It's the one from the mineshaft. From when we first found Albert. Just say your names.'

They did so.

There was another pause.

'Identities confirmed,' the voice said. 'Access permitted.'

The shallow basin of the receiver filled with grey static

that slowly formed into a recognisable shape.

'It's the gully!' Tim said.

It was early evening. A view from the hut. Dark clouds gathering overhead. The picture panned from one side of the valley to the other. Around the edge of the display were graphs and indicators, all in green.

'This must be from Albert's perspective. We're seeing what he saw.'

'What's that overlay?' Coral asked.

'Threat assessment,' Ludokrus replied.

Albert took his time, checking through three hundred and sixty degrees. The indicators all stayed green.

The image zoomed to a high point on one of the rock walls, then scanned the slope below. Calculations flashed in the bottom corner. Estimates of time and distance. A clock overlay appeared briefly. He started to move.

'Looks like he's going to put a scanner block up there and worked out how long it'll take,' Norman said.

'Don't go. Don't go,' Alkemy muttered.

Albert went. He moved with surprising speed, pausing at the gully floor before starting up the slope. There was a flash of lightning followed by a boom of thunder. The image inclined skyward. A view of boiling clouds.

'It's that storm the other night. He's right underneath it!'

'Just like we were.'

As he continued up the slope, the air filled with pounding rain. His pace quickened.

Another flash of lightning showed the outline of a mineshaft ahead. A slight hesitation, more threat assessments, then he made straight for it. There was a brief blur followed by a view of the valley below, framed by an oval of rock.

'He's taking shelter.'

A hand came into view and set a scanner block outside the entrance.

Lightning crackled close by. More thunder. Albert backed a little deeper into the mineshaft. A single indicator on the lower left turned yellow.

Alkemy closed her eyes and looked away.

Another roar of sound. For a moment it seemed that lightning had struck the cliff above the mine. Rock exploded outwards and the images became a confusion of tunnel walls, boulders, dirt and dust. But the thunderous booming didn't stop. It went on and on, as if a series of charges were being detonated, one after the other.

The receiver went dark then lit up again in ghostly green as Albert switched to low-light mode and sprinted down the shaft, the roof caving in behind him. He was beating it! Then another explosion brought down a section directly ahead. He had no choice. He dived into it like a swimmer plunging into a raging stream. Jumbled images showed him fighting through the falling rock. The chaos cleared for an instant. An open space ahead. Then something enormous caught him in the back and threw him to the ground.

The sound stopped. The picture froze on the open space ahead. A low angle, skewed, tilted to one side. Dust settled as the glowing indicators – now all red – flickered out one by one and lines of static scored the fading image.

There was a long respectful silence. Alkemy stared at the flickering static with tears in her eyes. Finally Ludokrus said, 'OK. But I think we work this out, yes? How they catch him?'

'Wait,' Norman said as Alkemy moved to withdraw the bulb, 'I think there's more.'

46 : Weapon of War

Shapes formed in the static haze. A seething blue-grey mist. There was a rumbling hiss, like the sound of a mistuned radio. It came in surges, like waves crashing against rocks.

'Are you all right?' a voice said.

The focus sharpened and they saw that's exactly what it was; a stormy sea.

'I think so, yes.' Albert's voice, so clear and uncannily close that Alkemy looked around. 'A little light-headed, that's all.'

'Not surprising in the circumstances,' the voice said. 'That's quite an implant you've received.'

The view shifted and centred on a tall, slender man in early middle age. He had a long face, dark eyes and sallow cheeks. Unremarkable except for midnight blue hair that was tied back in a ponytail. He wore a flowing brown robe and had a monitor balanced in his lap that looked remarkably like the receiver.

'Uncle Krilen!' Alkemy said.

Albert looked around. The room behind him might have belonged to a small private hospital. The walls were painted pale green. A mirror on one side showed Albert seated on a reclining chair on the balcony. He wore a wad of bandages around his head.

'Did the procedure go satisfactorily?' he asked.

'Flawlessly.'

The movement of Krilen's mouth didn't match his words. Tim guessed some sort of automatic translation was taking place. It was like watching a foreign movie that had been dubbed into English.

Albert touched a hand to his forehead. 'When can I access the enhancements?'

'They'll come online automatically over the next few weeks as your brain adapts and the lace grows to form new connections, but you should be able to access some of the basic functions now.'

The view shifted back to the sea. The image held for a moment, blurred, then suddenly transformed into numbers. The waves became moving graphs of mass and volume, the rocks a grid of surfaces and angles. An overlay indicated the wave's impact points and calculated the trajectory of every droplet, a prediction that, half a second later, was mapped and matched to reality.

He turned back to Krilen who was studying the projections on his monitor, a puzzled look on his face. 'Sorry, I think I had this on the wrong setting. Can you repeat that please?'

Albert did so for the next wave then turned back.

Krilen frowned, got up and left the room, returning with another man dressed like a technician. A small, cheerful man with a round face, a shaved head and a tatty lab coat, its pockets bulging with tools and gadgets. He carried a clipboard and had a badge pinned to his lapel. The Eltherian script was unreadable till a translation overlay appeared: Andop Scolyfol, Theia University.

The technician checked the dressing on Albert's forehead, fiddled with the monitor, then produced a second one and asked Albert to run through the procedure again.

Scolyfol and Krilen stood to one side, talking in low voices for five full minutes, studying and comparing the readouts. There were glances at Albert and much head shaking.

'Is there a problem?' Albert said.

'Not ... a problem,' Krilen said. 'Just something unexpected. You shouldn't be able to do that, you see. What you did with those waves. The computations involved are staggeringly complex. You might one day reach that level, but not within four hours of the beads being implanted. That's barely any time for a neural lace to begin to form a network. This is quite unheard of.'

The image froze and dimmed. The static returned.

'What were they talking about?' Coral whispered.

'I think they put something in his brain,' Tim replied.

After a brief interlude, the static cleared and a new picture formed.

They were now seated in a clean white room. An office. There were artefacts that might have been tribal artworks hanging on one wall, shelves of equipment, two cupboards, a sofa and armchairs to one side, a large white desk on the other. Behind it was a window and a nighttime view out over a vast city. Krilen was seated behind the desk.

'You're an oddity, Albert. Irrational, unpredictable and given to whims and fancies. Those, you might argue, are the characteristics of many of your class of synthetic, which is true, but only to a degree. *You* are an exception: an oddity amongst oddities. Predictably unpredictable. You're exactly what we want.'

'What do Marileon and Dudilo say?'

'It was the parents' idea. They approached me. The coincidence of the coordinates, I believe. Transpose two groups of numbers and instead of heading for their new archaeological site, you end up at our target.'

He waved a hand. The office lights dimmed and a three-dimensional projection of the Milky Way appeared above the desk in front of him. Using a series of gestures, he zoomed in on a tiny portion near the edge of one spiral arm where two regions were highlighted by red and yellow cubes.

'Maril's always had an interest in Thanatos affairs,' he continued. 'It was her speciality once, and she's kept abreast of what little new information has come down to us over the years. It's the time scales, you see. The Thanatos work on scales almost beyond comprehension. But I suppose when you've been around for ten billion years, what's a few hundred million here or there?

'All we know for certain is that aeons ago they annexed this portion of the galaxy.' He gestured at the red-tinted cube. It was labelled KSX-119. 'We also know they've been conducting experiments there since before we Eltherians were little more than pond slime.'

'Experiments? Doing what?'

'Searching for the essence of the Old Ones. The beings that occupied our galaxy when it was in its infancy, then vanished. Now they appear to have found it. Or at least something that's excited a great deal of interest.'

'Sentient creatures?'

'Obviously. Solar systems coalesce into suns and planets. Planets with liquid water form life, and eventually that life becomes intelligent. It's almost inevitable. But there's something different about this lot. Something special. What do you make of this?'

The projection transformed into a spiky wave.

'A first primitive radio transmission.'

'And this?'

The waveform shrank to one side and a scatter static appeared beside it.

'The signature of a thermonuclear explosion.'

'Precisely. And what space of time would you say separates these two events?'

'In our own case – and we are exceptional – it was half a millennia. Five hundred years.'

'Would you believe that in this case it's less than fifty?'

'What?'

Krilen nodded. 'Perhaps now you see why they've excited the Thanatos's interest – and ours. If they can go from radio to atomic bombs in just fifty years, in a hundred they could have interstellar travel. What then becomes of us?' He waved a hand and the galactic atlas reappeared, focused on the red and yellow cubes.

'From our perspective, this has occurred in the worst possible location. That system is a mere fifty light-years away. What happens if they do develop interstellar travel? What happens if the Thanatos decide to give them more room to play in? More uninterrupted space uncontaminated by outside influences?' He widened two fingers and the red box engulfed the yellow. 'What will become of us?'

'They wouldn't. Surely?'

'Have you heard of the Erynitis artefact?' Albert shook his head. 'No, of course you haven't. It's still highly classified. And the reason it's classified is that if the Thanatos know that we know ... well, it could make things difficult.

'The Erynitis were a thirty million-year-old civilisation. They occupied more than four hundred systems. The Thanatos ... tolerated them. At least until a consul made an inappropriate remark to His Darkness. Then the Thanatos wiped them out. Condemned and methodically exterminated them from every system they occupied. More than seven hundred planets. Half a trillion beings. We wouldn't have known they'd ever existed if it hadn't been for the artefact; a piece of space junk buried in an asteroid that turned out to be an archive and encyclopedia of their species.'

'Wiped them out?' Albert repeated, shocked.

He leaned forward and brushed the image of the galaxy aside, returning to the earlier projection. 'What's happened since this?' He pointed to the nuclear scatter. 'We must have been inundated by signals after that.'

Krilen shook his head. 'That was one of the last things we received. The Thanatos have thrown a Dyson sphere around the entire system. An electromagnetic shield that lets signals in but blocks anything coming out.'

'A shield the diameter of a solar system? Impressive.' Calculations flew across the bottom of the screen as Albert worked out the energy that would require.

'You see what we're up against?' Krilen said. 'At the

moment that sphere only blocks signals. We can still get a ship in and out. But once whatever occupies this system starts shuttling between planets, you can guarantee it'll be upgraded. That's why we must act quickly. We need reliable intelligence. We need to know what's going on in there.'

'I understand that, and I'm happy to take on the job, but how do the children fit in? You say they're to know nothing of the mission?'

'Certainly not. They're your cover, Albert. Innocence is their shield – and yours. We can harden your systems, add probe traps and self-deletion circuits, but wetware brains don't work like that. The Thanatos would discover all they know in a matter of hours, but if all they know is that their eccentric syntho misprogrammed the flight computer ... well ... we'd have more chance of recovering you if anything went wrong. And we *must* recover you. Once you're inside that sphere, all communication with us will be blocked.'

'I understand. And I now understand why you hinted my implant was a failure. Why you asked me to act more and more eccentrically in public.'

'I've kept you a secret because your surgery was remarkably effective,' Krilen said. 'You're our biggest success to date, Albert. Our biggest success by far. In fact, you're the most powerful thinking machine we've ever produced. The depth of your perception and insights have been evident from the outset. And they continue to grow. Do you know what your official classification is? "Weapon of War." Or at least it would be if the Military Council got hold of you. They'd want to dissect you and see exactly what went so right this time. Or plug you into one of their command centres and have you run battle simulations.

'I also kept you secret to see how you develop. Now the possibility of this mission has come up, I think you're the syntho for the job. It could be dangerous, and will almost certainly require a great deal of resourcefulness. Should I risk one of our greatest assets on such a mission?

'In truth, I have little choice. The future of our civilisation may depend on what you find out there.'

47 : Man on a Mission

'Presentation concluded,' the robotic voice said. 'No further access permitted.' The memory bulb popped from the receiver back into Alkemy's hand.

'Presentation?' she said. 'Does that mean Albert make this special for us?'

'Like edited highlights.' Tim said. 'Notice how it was translated too?'

They sat staring at the static till Norman took the receiver back and switched it off.

'It's starting to make sense,' Tim added. 'Like Norman said yesterday, the Sentinels set the whole thing up. They caught Albert, tried to get his memory bulb, and realised there was something special about it. So they used him to lure us there, used Alkemy to get it, then tried to dissolve her around it so the bulb wouldn't self-destruct.'

She said, 'Remember in the fungus room, when we first go in and hide? We go to sleep, but something shake and make us wake.'

Tim recalled the slimy goo on his shoulder and in her hair. 'The Sentinels didn't want to leave us there for the fungus to digest. They *wanted* us to find that trough so they could use it to digest you.'

Coral said, 'So they gave Albert some kind of brain implant. Who was the guy with the blue hair? You called him uncle.'

'Not real uncle. Old family friend. But important man. Head of the Science Council.'

'And the other people he mentioned? Marileon and Dudilo?'

'Our parent.'

'Your *parents*? You mean your parents helped set this whole thing up?'

Ludokrus shrugged. 'To mix the coordinates seems like a good plan.'

'Yeah, when you left. Twenty-five years ago. You've probably got a whole new family now.'

Tim saw the look on Alkemy's face and put in quickly, 'I had no idea Albert was so special.'

'He is always special,' she said.

'Special all right,' Coral said. 'What did that Krilen guy say? The most powerful thinking machine you've ever produced. Wow!'

'So, a secret plan,' Norman said, 'but why reveal it now? You heard blue-hair. If the Thanatos catch you, they'll find out everything in a few hours. We already know the reason you came here: to find out what's going on. Albert told us that himself the other day, before your ship was blown up.'

'I think he was being more subtle than that,' Tim said. 'If they get caught now, the Thanatos won't believe they're just a couple of lost travellers, not after all that's happened with the Sentinels. But by showing them that presentation he's given them a memory of how they were duped. That they're innocent. It really was nothing to do with them. So the Thanatos will be more likely to let them go.'

'What about the memory bulb?'

'Obviously the Eltherians want to get that back. But if the Thanatos catch them before they get home, they can just drop it and it'll self-destruct.'

'He really was a man on a mission, then.'

'More. He *was* the mission,' Ludokrus said. 'Now is our job to complete and take his thought and memory home with us. You all have help. Our peoples and our planet will be much grateful.'

Tim and Norman grinned. Coral bit her lip.

'Coo-ee!' a voice called across the clearing.

'Oh no,' Coral groaned.

'What ...?'

'Alice!'

'Maybe she bring more piglets.'

'*Pikelets*. And it doesn't look like it.'

All she was carrying was a brown leather shoulder bag.

'Is Albert about?' she called, eyeing the Cadillac.

'He ... go for walk.'

'Oh. When will he be back?'

'*Long* walk. Not back for some time.'

'I see.'

She stood, uncertain. Then they heard the sound of a car approaching on Rata Road. They turned and looked. It turned their way. Flashes of yellow paintwork showed through the gaps in the intervening trees.

'I know that car,' Tim said. 'It's Cakeface.'

48 : Straight from the Monkey's Mouth

Millicent Millais stood before them in a tweed suit and extremely sensible shoes. She regarded them with her pursed mouth and powdered face. 'Good morning children.' It was all they could do to stop themselves from leaping to their feet and chanting *Good morning, Mrs Millais* in response.

She took a clipboard from her car and surveyed the reserve, raised one disapproving eyebrow and said, 'I should like to speak with a Mr Albertus Kattflapp, please. Perhaps you can direct me.'

'He's out,' Tim said, repeating Ludokrus's lie.

'Then perhaps Mrs Kattflapp.'

She turned to Alice. Alice backed away.

'There isn't one,' Tim said.

Cakeface regarded him stonily. He felt like a bug under a magnifying glass.

'It is rather important, Timothy.' Then her mood lightened and she added in voice that was somehow both reasonable and threatening at the same time, 'I wouldn't have driven all this way on my jolly holiday if it wasn't, you know.'

'He might not be back for a while,' Coral said. 'Once he gets out in the bush, he loses all track of time.'

Cakeface regarded her with a look that would have wilted flowers. 'Coral Townsend,' she pronounced. 'I believe that *we* are due to have a discussion about your absence from school last Friday afternoon.'

Coral said nothing, but held her gaze.

'But that can wait until tomorrow. *First thing tomorrow. My office.*'

Her mood changed again and she brightened. 'Well, if Mr Kattflapp is out, I shall await his return.'

With that, she took a folding chair from the boot of her car, a book from the back seat, and settled in a patch of shade under a nearby tree.

Coral nudged the others towards the awning, leaving Alkemy stuck on the recliner with her injured legs. 'What the hell's all that about?' she hissed. 'The Sentinels know Albert's dead. *They* killed him. What's she playing at?'

'They've fed her some excuse to get her over here,' Tim said. 'They're up to something.'

'Well we don't want her sitting there all day. What happens when your ship arrives?'

'It will be some hours yet.'

'Look out, she's watching us,' Norman said.

'Like she can hear anything at that distance!' Coral snorted.

'You think they make her wait all day?'

'It's possible. They might even make her follow us

around.'

'Then we have to get rid of her!' Coral said.

'How do we do that?'

'I dunno. But it might help to find out what she wants Albert for in the first place.'

'How do we do that?'

'You're her pal, why don't you go and ask?'

'Since when was I her pal?' Tim said.

'Didn't you have a good old chat with her on Friday about my *absence from school*? If you hadn't, she'd never have known. And I wouldn't have to face her in the morning.'

'Hey, you three had disappeared. I didn't know what was going on. I had to turn to someone.'

'She's a Sentinel agent.'

'I didn't know that then. None of us did.'

It was that interview – with her odd answers and sudden shifts in conversation – that finally convinced Tim she was really under Sentinel control.

Coral crossed her arms and stared at him, unmoved.

He looked around at the others but found no support.

'Oh all right,' he said.

Cakeface looked up from her book as Tim approached.

'I was ... going to put the kettle on. I wondered if you'd like a cup of coffee.'

'That's very thoughtful of you Timothy. But not at the moment, thank you.'

His eyes dropped to the clipboard propped against the chair and he saw it contained a single sheet of paper headed *Rata Area School – Pupil Registration*. The form Coral had filled out for Alkemy and Ludokrus after their first day at school.

'Is there a problem with that?' he said. 'Only, I might be able to help because Mr Kattflapp's English isn't very good.'

That was the lie he'd told her on Friday, a trap to determine whether she really had met Albert. And she'd fallen for it. Perhaps she'd remember.

Millicent Millais considered the offer. 'Perhaps you can, Timothy,' she said slowly. 'You see, Mr Kattflapp took the children out of school, but he never completed the paperwork. Technically, they are still on our roll. It will cause all sorts of confusion with the Education Department.'

So that's how they got you to come over here!

He said aloud, 'I could get him to sign it when he comes back and bring it in tomorrow if you like.'

Cakeface blinked. There was a fractional hesitation before she said, 'I'm afraid it has to be witnessed and countersigned by another adult.'

Tim glanced at the bottom of the form. If it did, there were no boxes for it. But it would be pointless, and possibly dangerous, to challenge her. He recognised the flicker that had passed across her face. He'd seen it before on Friday afternoon when he'd enquired about his sister and his missing friends. It meant the Sentinels were actively tampering with her memories.

'Oh, right,' he said. 'How come he didn't sign it the other day?'

That flicker again. 'I'm afraid he was rather argumentative. It didn't seem an opportune time.'

'What was he upset about, if you don't mind me asking?'

'Family troubles, I believe. He was somewhat

emotional. He is foreign, as you said.'

It was creepy the way the Sentinels filled in gaps and built up whole new recollections, but he should stick to the present, he thought.

'Hey, I've got an idea. My aunt is waiting for Albert too. But she's staying at the farm which is just down the road. Why don't I get her to countersign the form with him when he comes back?'

Cakeface stared at him blankly. A longer hesitation this time. Tim thought he'd overdone it.

* * *

'Stop wittering to that monkey boy and look at this.'

'What is it?'

'I applied magnification, image enhancement and lip-reading analysis to that little group in the awning to find out what they were saying. It seems their ship is due.'

'What?!'

'See for yourself. One says, "What happens when your ship arrives?" The other replies, "It will be some hours yet."'

'I don't believe it!'

'There's your evidence. Straight from the monkey's mouth.'

'But how can they have summoned a ship? What about all that transmitter nonsense?'

'A ruse. An attempt to divert us. These monkeys are smarter than they look.'

'What can we do?'

'We need to act quickly. The first thing to do is to get your little spy out of there. The situation's changed and I have another *job for her ...'*

* * *

Cakeface suddenly smiled. The effect was chilling.

'What a splendid boy you are, Timothy Townsend. The ideal solution! Do you think your aunt would mind?'

'No, not at all.'

Cakeface was already on her feet, folding up her chair.

'Dear boy.' She patted his head and handed him the clipboard. 'You've saved my morning. I have *so* much else to do.'

49 : Telling Stories

'That was easy.'

'Too easy.' Tim watched Cakeface depart. 'The Sentinels are up to something, I'm sure of it.'

'Well I can sign that for Albert.' Coral took the form off him. 'Since I signed for him originally.'

'Get it countersigned while you're at it.' Tim nodded towards Alice. 'It's your turn.'

'Why me?'

'Aren't you and Alice special pals?'

'Just because I was reading one the books she left at the farm.'

'*Old Norse Myths and Legends*,' Tim told the others. 'The special pals had a good old chat about it the other day.'

Coral scowled at him. 'Oh, all right. Since you did your bit.'

'It's hard to tell the two of them apart sometimes,' Norman said as she set off. 'Side by side, they look like twins.'

Coral made a rude gesture behind her back.

'I've been thinking about Albert,' Norman added.

'Everyone wants to see him. Your aunt, Cakeface, Mr and Mrs Townsend for lunch. So how complicated was he really? I mean, apart from his brain and that memory bulb thing?'

'Depend on the level you are talking,' Ludokrus said. 'How complicated are you? Deep down you are just the skelington.'

'Exactly.' Norman looked around the awning. 'You've still got plenty of raw materials here.'

Ludokrus gave a half-laugh. 'You do not mean ...?'

'Why not? Got anything else to do while we wait for your ship?'

Coral returned with the form and said to Tim, 'Alice says she'll sign on one condition. She wants to talk to us first. Both of us.'

'What about?'

'Guess.'

'We can't do that!'

'Why not? We can tell her what she expects to hear. After all, she doesn't know that we know what she *thinks* she knows.'

'Eh?'

'That interview she did with Crystal Starbrite hasn't been broadcast yet. And we know what she said. But she doesn't know that we know.'

'Right, but—'

'C'mon, it'll be a laugh! We can wind her up. Who's going to believer her anyway? It's not like it's being recorded or anything.'

* * *

Alice sat cross-legged on the ground holding the leather bag in her lap. Tim and Coral sat opposite. It was a nice angle with the caravan in the background. Not that she would ever let them use the footage. Not of the children. Not after her promise to Em. But it would add weight to her own story, and maybe give her leverage when she finally talked to Albert.

'I should tell you from the outset that I know *exactly* what's been going on around here. I mean about the spaceship, and the mice, and what you did to them.'

Coral's jaw dropped. Tim watched her with grudging admiration. She was better at this stuff than he was. 'How on earth ...?'

'Never mind that. Let's start at the beginning. Tell me what you know about the mice.'

'Nothing really. Just that they're visitors.'

'You mean from another planet?'

'Yeah. But we don't think they're really mice. They just took on that shape to explore the place.'

'I see.' Alice fought to suppress a delighted smile. She'd been right all along! 'And what happened to them?'

'They escaped. We've been searching for them ever since. That's ... what we were doing yesterday. Albert has this theory they're headed south.'

'And ...?'

'Nothing so far. That's where he's gone today. We were supposed to go too, but we're all pretty tired, and Alkemy's got blisters.'

'Tell me about the meteorite.'

'There was no meteorite. That was an explosion. Their ship blew up.'

Alice turned to Tim, swivelling her whole body his way. The bag too. 'But you said you saw a flash of light in the sky before it hit.'

'I ... um ... made that up.'

'We had to say something,' Coral said.

Alice swivelled back. 'Do you know why it blew up?'

'Albert reckons it was on a timer so that if something happened to its inhabitants it would self-destruct.'

'So by capturing its inhabitants you effectively caused the destruction of their ship.'

'Yeah, well, we know that now.'

'Who is Albert? What's he doing here?'

'Dunno. All we know is he's some sort of government agent. But he really is their uncle.' She gestured at Alkemy. 'He just borrowed them for a few weeks to add to his cover story about being a tourist.'

Alice took a breath and tried to think of the sorts of questions Crystal Starbrite would ask. 'What would you say to the mice now if you could see them again?'

'Sorry, I guess. About their ship and all. We didn't know.'

'But you've left them stranded.'

'Well, maybe ...'

'Only maybe?'

'Albert reckons they'll have a backup somewhere out in space. That when they're safe they'll signal for it to come and pick them up.'

'*Really?*' Alice struggled to contain her excitement. 'So *that's* why he's so keen to find them.'

Coral nodded as Alice looked around the reserve. 'Has he really gone for the day?'

Tim thought about what Ludokrus and Norman were doing. 'Nah, he'll be be back for lunch.'

'Will he now? Well, I shall speak to him them.' Alice got to her feet and hooked the leather bag over her shoulder. 'But a deal's a deal.' She took the form and signed it, and as she handed it back she added, 'There's no need to mention our little chat to Albert, you know.'

'No, of course not,' Coral said, biting back a grin.

* * *

Millicent Millais held the phone away from her ear as tinny music erupted from the earpiece. 'Can you believe it? They've put me on hold, *again*.'

Roderick Millais shook his head and helped himself to another slice of cake. 'You are sure about this, aren't you dear?'

'Of course I am. I know what I saw.'

'I was just thinking that if they're the sort of people you suspect, and they realise it was you who dobbed them in ... well ... they might not look on it very kindly.'

'Roderick! I'm surprised at you! Are you suggesting I should keep quiet out of fear of reprisals?'

'Not in so many words—'

'One should never, *ever* let oneself be intimidated, Roderick. Is that clear?'

'Yes, dear.'

The music stopped and she snapped the phone back to her ear. She covered the mouthpiece, whispered, 'Someone senior at last!' then spoke into the phone.

'Yes, I'm still here … Good morning, Inspector … Well, as I told your sergeant, we are a farming community and weapons are not uncommon here – for pest control and hunting – but it was the quantity that attracted my attention … Oh I'd say fifteen or twenty crates … Yes, crates … Well that was the other thing. I can tell a shotgun from a .22, but the ones in the open crate weren't like anything I'd seen outside of a war film. They had those curving magazines that plug in underneath … Yes, that's what my husband said. He's much more into that sort of thing than I am.'

'Semi-automatic assault rifles?' Roderick whispered.

She nodded.

He looked pleased with himself.

The voice on the other end said something.

'Ah, now I didn't realise the significance of *that* until I returned home,' she continued. 'It was stacked up in cartons beside the guns. One of them had been ripped open and you could see plastic-wrapped packets stacked inside. They were a sort of brickish colour and I assumed it was modelling clay – we use it all the time at school – though I didn't recognise the brand name. That's why I made a particular note of it. I thought it might be cheaper. We're always looking to save a few— Yes, yes, I'm quite certain about the spelling, Inspector: S, E, M, T, E, X.'

Roderick looked at her expectantly.

'That's what my husband said. How foolish of me not to have known.'

'Well?' he whispered.

She cupped a hand over the receiver. 'You were right, Roderick. It's not modelling clay at all. It's high explosive.'

50 : Making Friends

Alkemy eased off the inflated leggings, wiped away the remains of the healing gel with a towel then flexed her toes. Then she set her feet on the ground and, using the back of her chair for support, stood up and took a few careful steps.

'How does it feel?' Tim held his arm out and she took his elbow.

'Strange. Like wearing new shoe. Only there are no shoe.'

She slid on a pair of jandals and they made one shuffling circuit of the caravan, then another – this time without the arm for support. At the start of the third, she'd gained enough confidence to walk without watching where to step. She turned to him and said, 'My memory is in pieces from the time I am in the tank, but I remember you come back for me.' She touched his arm. 'Thank you.'

Tim looked at the ground and shuffled his own feet.

'You save my life. I do not forget.' She put an arm around him and kissed his cheek.

'Hey guys,' Norman called as they passed the awning again. 'Come and look at this.'

Inside, stretched out on the workbench, they found the shiny skeletal framework of a mechanical man.

Norman picked up a thin piece of transparent plastic and slipped it over his left hand. It fitted snugly and was almost invisible against his skin. Then he raised it and waggled his fingers at them. They saw the outline of a number of control surfaces on the palm and fingers. He tapped a couple with his right hand and the figure sat up and turned towards them, its bare metal skull gleaming in the half-light. Alkemy and Tim stepped back in surprise. When it spoke, they almost fled the tent.

'Hello,' it said, 'I'm Artificial Albert.'

Alkemy clutched her chest. 'The voice ...!'

It sounded exactly like him.

Tim looked round and found Coral grinning at them, a tiny microphone in her hand.

'I must say it's rather chilly in here,' the machine said and rubbed its hands together. 'I could do with some flesh on my frame.'

'Yeah, yeah. Coming,' Ludokrus muttered from the corner where he was crouched over an old paddling pool. He reached in and lifted out a long thick piece of dripping plastic, the colour and texture of raw meat.

'Oh no. Too much!' Alkemy cried and hobbled out.

* * *

'What is it now, Darling?' the Director General said as his assistant hurried in brandishing a sheet of paper. 'Another *sit-rep?*'

'A UA from PHQ, sir. A PTA. But it does tie in with that earlier rep.'

Johnson Johns closed his eyes. 'In plain English, please!'

'Police Headquarters, sir. An urgent advisory of potential terrorist activity called in by a GP – a member of the general public. Sighting of weapons and what appears to be a large quantity of explosives.'

'Explosives?'

'Situationally and locationwise, it ties in with that satellite hack.'

Situationally? Locationwise? Johnson Johns wondered if such words actually existed. He studied the document. 'Who reported this ... potential terrorist activity?'

'Local school principal, sir. Head-mistress.'

'What have we got on her?'

'Nothing.'

'Nothing at all? We're the Security Intelligence Service, man. We should have something on everyone.'

'I've asked MinEd – the Ministry of Education – to email her file. My contact there had a quick recce. Seems she's as clean as a whistle.'

'So to all intents and purposes a solid and reliable witness.'

'Yes, sir.'

Johns studied the grid reference, rose and walked over to the wall map where a small yellow pin now protruded from a remote spot on the West Coast of the South Island. 'Do we know any more about that meteorite the other night?' He'd reviewed the news clip his assistant had forwarded. 'Anyone track it? Any other witnesses?'

'No sir. Just that boy they interviewed.'

'What if it wasn't a meteorite, Darling? What if those potential terrorist chaps were trying out their Semtex?'

'Exactly what I thought, sir.'

'Better get the Prime Minister and the Chief of Defence Force on the line. *Now*, please.'

51 : Artificial Albert

'That right arm's still a bit sticky,' Norman said.

'My fault,' Ludokrus replied. 'I should not make him do the cartwheel.'

'It was pretty funny though.'

Artificial Albert turned his head and glared at them. '*I* didn't think so.'

Norman and Ludokrus had a control glove each. Coral had one too, but hers was just for head movements. She also had a whisper-mic – a fine wire strand tucked in her abundant hair. When activated by her glove, Artificial Albert would say whatever she whispered.

'Not very natural, guys,' Tim called.

Albert was striding ahead of them, following the gravel road that led to the farm, but with his head turned completely backwards.

'Oh chill out, Timmo,' Coral said through Albert as Ludokrus made him dance.

Alkemy shook her head. She didn't approve of the undertaking and was unnerved at how life-like the replica had turned out. With flesh on the bare metal skeleton, some of Albert's clothes, and a voice pattern copied from the memory bulb, the likeness was uncanny. At least until he started to break dance in the middle of the road.

The robot actually walked more smoothly than Alkemy, and even though they adjusted their pace to hers Tim could see she was struggling. She insisted she was fine, saying the sooner her new muscles got used to it, the better, but when he offered to find her a stick she accepted gratefully.

Round the back of the farmhouse, in the shade of a rata tree, they found a long trestle table set with plates, cutlery and a selection of side-salads. On one end was a mountainous pavlova topped with fresh strawberries and cream.

'Yum!' Norman said.

Frank had taken charge of a smaller table covered with bottles and glasses.

'There's water, fizz and fruit juice over there. Help yourselves, kids.' He turned to Albert. 'What I reckon you need is a beer.'

'I reckon you're right,' Albert said.

Frank poured him one and raised his glass. 'Cheers.'

'Cheers,' Coral whispered and glanced at Norman.

Norman stroked his glove and Albert raised his glass.

It stopped halfway.

He stroked it again, harder.

Nothing.

And again.

Alice and Em emerged from the house, carrying steaming dishes. Frank turned towards them as Albert's arm suddenly engaged and flung the contents of his glass over his shoulder – most of which hit Coral.

Frank turned back. 'Now that's what I call a thirst! Here, let me top you up.'

'You did that on purpose!' Coral hissed at Norman.

'It's that right arm again.'

'Well use the left! Look at me, I'm soaked. And you can stop laughing.' She slapped Ludokrus, who laughed even harder.

Lunch was serve-yourself, but Coral attended to Albert to avoid further mishaps.

'More lamb, Albert?'

'Yes please.'

'Bean salad?'

'Thanks.'

Tim grinned and nudged Ludokrus. 'Talking to herself again. She's a natural.'

'Stop whispering, you lot,' Albert snapped at them. 'It's not polite. And sit up straight, Ludokrus.'

The three controllers were forced to pick at their food. They couldn't eat much as they had to stay focused on manipulating Albert.

'Don't you want those chicken wings?' Tim said to Norman.

'Yes, I—'

'Here, I'll swap you for some brussels sprouts.'

'No way!'

'More chips, Alkemy? I don't think Norman wants these.'

'I'll get you for this, Townsend!' Norman hissed.

Albert apologised to Em and Frank for their late return the day before.

'I have to admit we were getting a bit worried,' Em

said, 'but you did the right thing in waiting out that storm.'

Albert smiled and shoved a forkful of lamb into his chin.

Norman snorted, then pretended to choke on his food, which distracted everyone long enough for Ludokrus to correct the mistake.

'Still got a spot of gravy there,' Tim said out the corner of his mouth.

Norman made a wiping gesture on his glove, but nothing happened.

'Use his left—'

But Norman forgot and tried again and Albert suddenly slapped himself in the face.

Everyone stared.

'Sandfly,' he muttered.

The meal continued.

Alice, seated diagonally across from Albert, gave him a curious glance. Tim noticed and had a look himself. It took a moment to realise what was wrong.

'He's not chewing,' he whispered to Coral.

'Oh give me a break. I'm trying to hold a conversation here.'

'Yeah, well, someone's noticed.'

Coral corrected the problem. Then, when only Alice was looking, she made Albert swallow a boiled potato – whole. It travelled down his throat in a lump, looking like he'd swallowed a tennis ball.

Alice stared in horror. Albert grinned at her. She looked away.

'Where's he putting it all?' Tim said to Norman.

'You're asking *him?*' Coral said. 'Old Dustbin?'

'Hey!' Norman said.

'You want to know?' Ludokrus said quietly. 'Listen.'

They heard a faint sloshing sound.

'What's that?'

'Look under table.'

'Not all at once!'

They took turns, sitting back in their chairs, glancing under the tablecloth. One of Albert's legs was raised and he shook it vigorously.

'Is the beer. Reservoir is in the foot,' Ludokrus said.

'Not the first glass. Coral's still wearing that.'

'Very funny. He's got hollow legs. Just like Norman.'

'Hey!'

'Actually,' Coral added, 'you probably don't want to do that too much.'

'Why not?'

'Because it's beer. It fizzes.'

As she spoke, a froth of foam burst out from Albert's nostrils. Norman tried to steer his hand to cover it, but the arm jammed halfway. The only thing Coral could do was stick out Albert's tongue to catch it.

'Oh, gross!'

Em and Frank looked up the table. Coral turned Albert's head away just in time, but not before Alice caught a glimpse. A look of mute horror crossed her face.

They were laughing so hard that no one knew what to do. Fortunately, Albert's head was turned towards them, the same way as the other adults. Unfortunately, foaming bubbles were still streaming from his nose. The sight of it made them laugh even harder.

'What on earth's got into them?' Em said.

Tim nudged his sister. 'Open his mouth.'

'God no, he'll puke it out!'

'He won't, trust me. It's a pressure thing.'

'I'll point him at you if he does.'

Coral stroked her palm and Albert's mouth opened. There was a faint hiss, like a sigh, and the nose foam stopped bubbling. Norman worked his left hand, bringing it up with a serviette, and Coral managed to make him shake his head in a disapproving, adult fashion.

'I reckon they've been at my beer,' Frank said.

'Not us,' Tim said, and the others laughed even harder.

* * *

'I wonder if I could have a word,' Alice said to Albert when they'd finished dessert. 'In private.' She moved to the seat directly opposite him.

'We'll do these.' Em took an armful of dishes from Tim and handed them to Frank. She nodded at Albert and Alice, then said in a lower tone, 'You lot make yourselves scarce.'

Em still had hopes for her sister. A few days earlier – before all this talk of spaceships – Alice had seemed rather keen on Albert. So much so that she'd made him a plate of her special wholemeal pikelets. He was a sensible chap. Perhaps he could talk her round. Perhaps he could help her shake off some of the silly ideas she had.

'Can't go far,' Ludokrus said. 'The gloves have not much range.'

'My bedroom,' Coral said. 'It's nearest.'

Out of range of the transmitters, Albert slumped a little

as they went inside. Alice didn't notice. She was fiddling with something in her bag as she set it on the table.

Albert straightened again as they reached Coral's room and he came back in range of the control gloves. Through the open window, they could hear what was going on.

'Well,' Alice said.

'Well, well, well,' Albert replied. 'Three holes in the ground.'

Coral sniggered.

Tim elbowed her.

'Ow!' Albert said.

'What?'

'Nothing. You wanted to talk to me, Alice?'

'Yes. I want to know who you are for a start. And what you're doing at the reserve.'

'I want a cup of tea,' Albert said. 'And some ice cream. And a bowl of cherries. And to look into your lovely bloodshot eyes.'

'What?'

'Nothing.' He gave her a silly grin.

'You can't distract me, you know. I won't let you. I know what you've been up to. I know everything. I know all about the spaceship,' she leaned forward significantly, '*and* the mice.'

'Pipi and Paua?'

'Pardon?'

'The mice. They're called Pipi and Paua.'

'Oh ... are they?'

'You didn't know that.'

Alice checked herself. He'd distracted her again.

'Look,' she said, 'I want to know who you're working

for.'

'The government.'

'Which department?'

'Pest control.'

'I don't believe you.'

Coral whispered to Ludokrus and Norman, 'Lean him forward.'

Albert leaned forward and said quietly, 'Well, I suppose I could tell you ...'

'Yes?' Alice leaned closer.

'... but then I'd have to kill you. *Bwa-ha-ha-ha-hah!*'

Alice lurched backwards, startled, and fell off her seat.

* * *

Coral was still laughing when they reached the shortcut. Ludokrus and Norman were making Albert walk like a zombie: stiff-legged, arms outstretched, his head lolling to one side.

'That was *so* funny!'

'You shouldn't have said that,' Tim said. 'You know what she's like.'

'Oh relax. Who's she going to tell? No one will believe her anyway.'

52 : Psst!

Crystal Starbrite woke in the passenger seat of the green station wagon, blinked and looked around. 'Where are we? Why are we stopping?'

'Approaching the turn-off to Rata,' Eric said. 'Looks like there's some sort hold-up.'

Three cars were stopped in front of them. The lead car did a u-turn and headed back past them. The next car paused then carried on south, re-joining State Highway 6, while the third also u-turned and headed back towards Haast.

Eric stopped in front of a police car parked sideways across the road, its red and blue lights flashing.

'Sorry sir, road's closed,' a fresh-faced constable told them.

'Accident?'

'Army exercise.'

'How long for?'

'At this stage, till first light tomorrow.'

There was thunderous roar as a heavy-lift helicopter came in, hovering over a field to the south, a Unimog truck swinging from a cradle beneath it. Four figures raced out the moment the truck touched down, released the cradle, and the helicopter soared away.

Crystal leaned across to the driver's window. 'You can't close a public road for an army exercise.' She flicked her hair in case he didn't recognise her. He clearly did.

'You can if it comes from high enough up, ma'am.'

'What does that mean?'

'This lot are just backup.' He gestured to the truck and troops behind him. 'I heard the SAS went in half an hour ago.'

'The SAS?'

A ute pulled into a marked-off bay on the other side of the police car, evidently coming from Rata. An army unit sprang into action. The driver was directed out of the cab, taken to one side, searched and interviewed, while another team inspected his vehicle, inside and out. They even had mirrors on sticks, checking underneath it. Four soldiers conducted the inspection. Four more stood back, automatic rifles at the ready.

Finally, after a radio consultation, the driver was cleared. He returned to his cab and was waved through a grassy chicane. A second policeman withdrew a set of portable road-spikes and directed the ute away from the roadblock.

'Park up,' Crystal told Eric. 'Let's find out what's happening.'

'I'm sorry, I can't let you stop here,' the policeman said. 'I've been ordered to move everyone on.'

'We're not everyone. We're the press.'

'*Especially* the press.'

Crystal smiled, ignored him, and undid her seatbelt. The words were like music to her ears. They invariably signified a big story.

As she opened her door, a loud voice barked, 'Stay in your vehicle.'

She paused, half in, half out, and saw it came from an army sergeant who'd emerged from a field on their left. He was walking smartly towards them, flanked by a corporal and a squad of four armed soldiers.

'Good afternoon … Sergeant.' She checked the man's stripes and gave him a winning smile.

'Staff Sergeant,' he replied, completely unwon. 'Now, get back in your vehicle and leave, please. This is a restricted area.'

'Since when?'

'Since now.'

'I'm sorry? Do you know who I am?'

'Do you know who *I* am, madam? Round here, I'm god almighty, and you will do exactly as I tell you.'

'On whose authority?'

'On this authority.' He gestured to four soldiers. They circled the car.

Crystal looked from one to the other. At the stern faces and the rifles held at the ready.

'You can't—'

'I bloody well can.'

They glared at each other. Seconds passed. Neither of them blinked. Then the Staff Sergeant stretched out an arm, checked his watch and said to the man at his side, 'Corporal, if this vehicle's still here in thirty seconds, have the men shoot out its tyres and detain its occupants under the

Terrorism Suppression Act, 2002.'

'Yes sir,' the corporal snapped.

'What?' Crystal said. 'The Terrorism Suppression Act? What the hell is—?'

Eric leaned across the passenger seat. 'Get in the car, Crystal.'

'Twenty seconds.'

'You can't treat members of the press like—'

'Shut up and get in the car,' Eric told her.

There was the sound of another helicopter approaching.

'Ten seconds.'

Still Crystal didn't move.

The corporal snapped, 'Shoulder weapons!'

She looked round and saw four armed men aiming at the tyres of their car.

She shut up and got back in.

* * *

Alkemy looked around the caravan that had been their home and sighed. 'Nothing to pack. Really, we need only one thing.'

Ludokrus nodded and opened a cupboard from which he took a small cardboard box. Coral gave him a quizzical look.

'I forget, we do not show you yet,' he said. 'Albert build her before he go missing. The reason we are come here in the first place.' He opened the lid, removed a fold of bubble-wrap, took out a spun glass orb the size of a grapefruit and handed it to Coral.

'This is it? The Temporal Accumulator?' He nodded. 'It's beautiful.'

She held it close and saw that inside the orb were other orbs, each slightly smaller than the last. Trapped between the surfaces were moving sparks, like tiny fireflies that came into existence for a few seconds then flickered and died. Staring into its depths was like staring into a tiny swirling galaxy.

She became lost for a moment, thinking of the larger galaxy and wondering how she was going to manage once they'd gone. Once *he'd* gone.

'How does it work?' Norman said to Ludokrus.

'Why do you always have to know how stuff works?' Coral said. 'Why can't it just *be*? Look at it, it's lovely.'

'Are those sparks some sort of quantum thing?'

She sighed and handed it back. 'I'm going for a walk,' she said.

Ludokrus watched her go, wondering if he should follow, but Norman was asking him about the caravan and the Cadillac and what would happen to them when they left.

'I make these.'

He took out a collection of self-adhesive discs, explaining that everything constructed by nanomachines had a telltale molecular signature. Originally designed as a safety measure in case they ever ran amok, the signature also allowed rapid identification and recycling of unwanted items.

'Easy to use. Just stick and press in centre,' he said, handing some to Norman and some to Tim. 'Car, caravan, Artificial Albert. The bikes also. Remember, we leave them up behind the resource pit.'

'Oh right. Mustn't forget the bikes. Eh, Tim?' Norman gave his friend a significant look.

Coral's walk took her round the rim of the crater and out to a patch of rocky foreshore where the sea surged listlessly. The tide was in and she sat and watched it for a while, lost in thought, feeling the way she often felt at the end of a long holiday. But this time even more so. In a few hours Alkemy and Ludokrus would be gone. A few hours after that and they'd be back to the old school routine, as if the last few days had never happened. And in a few weeks' time they'd return to Auckland. The time they'd spent here, the adventures they'd had, would become memories that grew fainter day by day.

Already it was hard to believe half the things that had happened to them.

Fifty light-years, she thought. Four hundred and seventy trillion kilometres. An impossible distance. Three weeks travel to those on board, but here on Earth she'd be an old woman by the time they got home. And if they returned? A hundred years would have gone by here.

But there was one consolation. Batty old Albert – who hadn't been so batty after all – had rebuilt the Temporal Accumulator before the Sentinels got him ...

'Psst.'

... and Ludokrus said he'd added in whatever was needed to test his theory about countering the effects of time and light-speed travel. If he had, and if it worked ...

'Psst.'

... maybe she would see them again one day.

'Psst.'

It wasn't much. But it was something to hold on to.

'Psst!'

Coral turned, annoyed, surveying the toitoi, flax and kanuka immediately behind her.

Nothing.

'*Psst!*'

That came from a different direction. Either whoever it was had moved without making a sound, or there were two of them. She got to her feet.

'*Psst!*'

Or three.

'Who is that?' she said, advancing a few steps into the waist-high undergrowth. 'If that's you guys horsing around ...'

There was a sudden rustling up ahead.

'Yeah, yeah, big joke.' She advanced further. 'Like I'm really fright—'

A figure rose from the undergrowth behind her. A gloved hand shot out and clamped her mouth. Other hands appeared and dragged her swiftly out of sight.

53 : Evacs

'Jeez Crystal,' Eric said, 'learn to pick your battles! Men with guns trump reporters with cameras every time.'

'They can't treat *me* like that.'

'They can under the Terrorism Suppression Act. They can throw you in jail for up to thirty days and not even give you a reason. You won't get much reporting done from there.'

Crystal pouted, still smarting at the sergeant's treatment. She was a star. *Nobody* treated a star like that.

'So what's going on back there?'

'I wish I knew. But it seems like a hell of a coincidence after everything else that's happened.'

Her satellite phone rang. She didn't recognise the incoming number.

'What?' she snapped, then, 'Oh, hello.'

'It's Alice Jones,' she whispered to Eric, covering the mouthpiece.

'No, he can't talk now, he's driving,' she said into the phone. 'But I can relay a message.'

She listened intently for a full minute, not saying

anything. Then she said, 'All right. Look, we'll meet you at the Old Oak Café in Haast. We're heading there ourselves. But you should know the army have closed the road. They're not they're letting anyone in, but they are letting people out, so you should be OK.'

'Well?' Eric said.

Crystal clicked the phone off. 'She's heading out, heading for home. She's got some footage for us to backup her story. And apparently she's had a death threat.'

* * *

'Where have you been?'

The others were lounging in the sun when Coral returned. Tim sensed there was something wrong immediately. Her face was blank, like a mask, and she walked at a measured pace, like a robot. He thought she might be trying to imitate Artificial Albert, but there was no joking, no light of fun in her eyes.

She stopped, rested her hands on the back of a folding chair, leaned forward confidentially and said, 'Don't look now, but we're surrounded by a bunch of soldiers.'

'What?' Norman turned.

'I said don't look, idiot. Just get your things and pretend we're going for a walk.'

'Are you serious?'

Coral's expression didn't waiver. 'Just make sure you've got everything you need. I mean *everything*.'

Alkemy reached for her pink backpack, the outline of the Temporal Accumulator box visible inside.

'What about Alb—?'

'They said to stay away from the caravan. They've got all sorts of stuff trained on us.'

'Really?'

'Really.'

They got up, exchanging glances, gathered their things and headed for the entrance of the reserve, moving as instructed – casually but carefully. Tim glanced at his sister, still half-expecting a hoot of laughter and a cry that they'd all been sucked in, but her face remained grave.

'Are you sure about this? I never heard anything.'

'It's the SAS, Timmo. I think that's how they operate.'

Nothing seemed out of place, even when they reached the road, but the moment they stepped into the shadow of a stand of trees, six figures emerged from the undergrowth. It was an odd sensation. A moment before, a casual glance showed nothing but stripy shade, then suddenly it was full of bulky figures in heavy camouflage carrying guns.

'Nice one girlie.' A hand patted Coral's shoulder. It too was camouflaged. 'Anyone else back there?'

Coral glanced helplessly at the others before answering. 'No.'

'Perimeter Patrol,' a low voice said. 'Five, repeat five evacs coming your way. All minors. Over.' There was a crackle of static and an acknowledgement.

The first soldier nodded to another who jerked his head and gestured they should follow him. He moved briskly, leading them up the road towards the farm. After a hundred metres, they met with a regular unit coming the other way. Tim saw the soldiers stiffen at the sight of their camouflaged companion. He clearly commanded respect.

'Can I get a couple of you guys to escort this lot back to the farm for me?' he said.

'Certainly, sir!' one of their number snapped.

'Take care, kids.' He turned and slipped away, half vanishing against the background, even in the light of day.

Aunt Em was pacing the veranda when they came into view, her expression a mixture of relief and *What-have-you-been-up-to-now?* A large khaki tent had been erected in front of the milking shed and the drive was littered with vehicles and people moving to and fro.

'Army *and* police,' Norman said. 'Awesome!'

Their escort fell back and they walked up to the house, amazed at the transformation from farm into a bustling headquarters.

'I take it this is them?' a police sergeant said to Em.

She nodded.

'Never a dull moment with you lot around,' Frank said.

'Is everyone OK?' the sergeant said. 'It's all right, you're safe now.'

'Safe from what?' Coral asked.

He ignored the question. 'We'll want to talk to you all later, but just take it easy for now. OK?'

'Where's Albert?' Em asked. 'Is he not with you?'

'He's ... gone for a walk,' Tim said.

Norman nudged him.

There was a crackle of radio traffic from the tent. They could hear it from the veranda. 'Repeat,' a voice said, 'perimeter secure. No sign of weapons or explosives. But we've found a body.'

'Description?'

'Male. Caucasian. Late forties or early fifties. Medic

says he's cold. Might have been here a while.'

Norman nudged him again.

'Injuries?'

'Nothing obvious. Just checking for ... What the hell?'

'Repeat, Tiger One-Nine.'

'Tiger One-Nine. Looks like we might have a situation here after all.'

At the third nudge, Tim whirled round and hissed, *'What?'*

Norman didn't say a word, just rolled eyes towards the western horizon where a faint, pencil-thin vapour trail was visible, heading their way.

Tim looked at his friend in alarm. Norman mouthed, 'The ship.'

54 : House Arrest

Alice approached the roadblock, her heart pounding so loudly she thought the soldiers would hear it through the open window of her car.

'What's the problem?' she asked as casually as she could, keeping both hands on the steering wheel to steady them.

'Just a routine exercise, ma'am,' one of them said, leaning in the window. 'Would you mind stepping out of the vehicle please?'

Alice did so.

'May I see some identification?'

She took her license from her handbag as a squad of soldiers examined her car, popping the boot and bonnet, checking the underside with mirrors. They opened all four doors and checked the inside too.

'What's this?' one of them snapped, pointing at the blanket-draped cage on the back seat that had been secured with a seat belt.

'Parakeet,' Alice said quickly. 'He's dozing. Please don't disturb him. He can be very noisy in a small car.'

The soldier used the barrel of his gun to lift a corner of the blanket, enough to confirm it really was a birdcage.

Alice held her breath. The mice stayed hidden.

The first soldier returned from radioing in her details. 'Where are you heading, Ms Jones?'

'Home. To Greymouth. I've been visiting my sister.'

'Right you are,' he said and handed back her license. 'Thank you, Ms Jones. Carry on.'

* * *

'Brilliant! Your stupid robot got us arrested!' Coral hissed as a stern looking policewoman closed the lounge door on them.

'You didn't think it was so stupid when you used him to threaten Alice,' Tim said, checking the doors that led to the veranda and finding them locked. 'Anyway, we haven't been arrested. We're "wanted for questioning" once that army guy gets back.'

'And what are we going to tell him? "Oh, we just built an advanced robot for fun."'

'Hey, you're the one who said don't go near the caravan. We could've brought him with us. Or at the very least I could have stuck a disassembly disc on him.'

'And got yourself shot in the process.'

'I didn't know you cared.'

'Yeah, well, blood splatters and I like this T-shirt.'

She sighed and slumped into one of the armchairs. 'Look, I saw some of the gear those guys had pointed at us: audio, video, infra-red, telescopic lenses and god knows

324

what else. I don't know what they thought we were up to, but if they'd spotted us slipping on control gloves and tapping out commands they'd have been on to us straight away. And then they'd want to interview Albert. On his own. The way they're carrying on, they must think he's some sort of terrorist. You heard that radio broadcast. They're looking for guns and explosives.'

Tim went to the window and looked out at the activity outside. 'I know who's behind all this: Cakeface. We should never have let her leave the reserve.'

'OK, so the Sentinels meddled with her memories. To what end? They don't know about the ... ' Coral checked herself and looked around in case Smudge was nearby, '... about the you-know-what. Or even Artificial Albert. So why call the in the Feds?'

'I think it's like that Smudge attack. They can't really do anything. They're just harassing us.'

'Speaking of the you-know-what.' Ludokrus said, studying the calculator. 'You are sure of what you see? I get no signal.'

Tim and Norman exchanged a look; nodded.

Ludokrus frowned. 'Maybe she is still too far.'

There was a knock at the door and Aunt Em entered with a pitcher of raspberry cordial and a plate of biscuits. She was escorted by the policewoman who cautioned her against saying anything. But she didn't need to speak. Her expression said it all.

As she left, they heard a key turn in the lock.

'What are they doing that for? It's not as if we're going anywhere.'

The sound made the lounge feel like a prison cell. A

comfortable cell – there was TV, a sofa, armchairs and plenty of books and magazines – but the prospect of being interviewed by the major in charge of the operation hung over them like a cloud. What could they say? How could they possibly explain Artificial Albert?

Ludokrus scowled at the calculator. 'Also, the you-know-what is early. Should not be here for one more hour at least. But this show me nothing. No arrive time, no where she is heading.'

'What sort of range does it have?' Norman said. 'I was thinking that if the you-know-what avoids the reserve and heads, say, to the other side of town, would the calculator still pick it up?'

'Twenty kilometre? No, too far. Would need a good aerial.'

'We would never find her in time anyway,' Alkemy said. 'Albert say she will not wait.'

'What about using the scanner blocks? They're designed to pick up signals and they are scattered all over the place. Could we reprogram them remotely and use them as receivers for the calculator?' He drew the receiver from his backpack.

'Signal type from spacecraft is much different, but maybe,' Ludokrus said.

They hunched over the receiver, trying different combinations.

'And *we* should get our stories straight,' Tim said to Coral. 'For when that guy gets back from the reserve.'

Coral shook her head. 'No, we shouldn't, because we shouldn't *be* here when he gets back from the reserve. These guys have a you-know-what to catch.'

'How do we get away without the army and police coming after us?' He gestured at the locked door. 'And how do we get out of here for a start?'

'Ssshh. Let me think.'

Coral paced the room while Norman and Ludokrus worked on the receiver. 'No, no, try ... How about ...? Maybe if we ... Yeah ... Yeah, that's it!'

'It work?' Alkemy asked anxiously.

Ludokrus, still hunched over the screen, nodded. 'But this cannot be right. You check please.' He handed it to Norman.

'What's not right?' Tim said.

Norman studied the display, made some adjustments, then shook his head. 'No, that's what I get too. No doubt about it. And I suppose it is out of the way.'

'What? What?' Tim demanded.

'The ship is headed straight for Gizzard Gully.'

55 : Need to Know

'Cannot be.' Alkemy exclaimed. 'How can our ship go there? That place is full of Sentinel!'

'It's not the ship's fault,' Norman said. 'Albert the super-brain didn't spot them either.'

'And it's probably the nearest unpopulated open space round here right now,' Tim added, thinking of the area around the hut.

'We must warn her. Say to go elsewhere.'

'How? You have a satphone, or maybe a transmitter?'

Alkemy sighed and stared at the locked door. 'Does not matter now anyway. We cannot reach.'

'Actually, I think we can.' Coral said, snatching up a sheepskin rug from in front of the fireplace and throwing it to her. 'Here. Raw materials. You're going to need the calculator. Meanwhile, you guys come and help me with the sofa. I want it directly in front of the TV with its back to the door.'

'What do I make with this?' Alkemy asked, holding up the rug.

'Wigs,' Coral said. 'One for each of you. Exactly the

same colours as your current hair.'

* * *

Coral studied the carpet. 'About there, I think,' she said to herself, then dropped the cordial jug. It landed with a thud, throwing a crimson pool over the beige carpet. In a much louder voice she yelled 'Oh you idiot!' then raced for the door and rattled the handle.

The policewoman was quick, but Coral was quicker. 'Spilt the drink,' she snapped. 'That stuff stains!' and pushed her way past, making for the kitchen.

The policewoman looked at the line of guilty faces turned towards her from the sofa. They turned back and slouched down so that only the tops of their heads were visible. Tim turned up the volume on the TV.

Coral returned with a mop, sponge and bucket, and began working on the carpet.

'Can you get me a refill please?' She held out the bucket and continued working on the stain. 'Warm water'll be fine.'

The policewoman hesitated, glanced back at the sofa, then went across the hall to the bathroom. As she emptied the bucket into the bath, Alkemy and Ludokrus followed her out, walking on tiptoe before darting up to Tim's room.

The policewoman glanced back and started refilling the bucket.

Tim and Norman adjusted the wigs, balancing them on cushions and the upturned legs of an occasional table. Coral checked their positioning and gave them a thumbs-up. They readied themselves behind the door.

'And some towels as well please,' Coral called. 'In the cupboard on your left.' The figure across the hall turned. Coral waved Tim and Norman out, then dipped her fingers in the pitcher and splashed some of the remaining cordial on herself.

The policewoman returned and stood in the doorway, watching Coral finish up. When she was done, she handed her the bucket and mop, then looked down at her T-shirt. 'Oh great! I'm going to have to put this in to soak. Can I change into something else?'

The policewoman nodded, checked the back of heads arranged along the sofa, then escorted her out.

'I'm all sticky too. I need a shower.'

'Don't be long,' the policewoman said, relocking the lounge door.

* * *

Coral turned on the shower then left the bathroom – via the window. Ludokrus helped her out and she dropped into the garden beside the others. 'I reckon we've got about ten minutes. Have you guys got our next move figured out?'

'Yes.'

'No.'

Tim and Norman spoke together.

'Oh c'mon, I've done my bit!'

'I say we go over the garden fence then straight across the fields,' Tim said. 'It's the quickest way.'

'Too exposed,' Norman said. 'They'll see us from miles away.'

'It'll be all right once we get to the road. There's plenty of vegetation along the far side. And a ditch.'

'But we actually have to get there without being seen. The safest way is up the drive. We'll be under cover all the way.'

'Yeah, and the guys on the gate are just going to let us march straight through.'

'Look, it's the army. People only get told what they need to know. The guys on the gate won't have a clue about Albert, or us being held for questioning.'

'I can't believe they'll let us walk straight out.'

'Why not? Just act normal. Be casual about it. Like you really don't expect to be stopped.'

'You're mad!'

'Let's try it. You and I. If we get caught ... well, it doesn't matter. We haven't got a ship to catch. And if they do pick us up, we can make a fuss and create a diversion so the others can get away across the fields.'

Tim frowned. It wasn't much of a plan, but he couldn't think of a better one.

A minute later, the pair of them pushed through a stand of flax partway down the drive and walked casually towards the gate. Two soldiers wearing disruptive pattern camouflage uniforms stood at ease on the far side of it. They stiffened and turned when they heard footsteps behind them.

'It'll be late,' Norman said to Tim. 'It always is.' He called to the soldiers, 'Has the bus been past yet?'

They exchanged a glance and shook their heads.

'Told you,' he said to Tim.

'Should you kids be—?' the one on the right began.

'I've got to make sure this lot catches the Haast bus,' Norman continued. 'Don't want them missing school tomorrow, right?' He gave Tim a playful punch.

Tim scowled. The guard on the right grinned and unlatched the gate.

'C'mon you guys, get a move on,' Norman called over his shoulder.

The others emerged, wary at first, only relaxing when they saw the soldier holding the gate for them.

'The bus stop's about fifty metres further down, just around that bend.' Norman pointed left, the opposite direction to the reserve.

The others moved on. Norman lingered, nodding at the gate guards' guns. 'Are they Steyrs?'

They nodded.

'You should join the SAS. They get M4 carbines. They look much cooler!'

Tim elbowed him. 'Come on Norman, don't want to miss that bus.' When they were up the road and out of earshot he hissed, 'You can overdo that *being casual* bit, you know!'

56 : Vapour Trails

Crystal Starbrite sipped her coffee, flicked her hair and drummed her fingers on the tabletop, willing her satellite phone to ring. Seconds later it complied.

Eric looked up from the newspaper he was reading.

She checked the caller ID. 'It's the office.'

'Aren't you going to answer it?'

'Let it ring for a bit. I don't want them to think we're just swanning around waiting for them to call us back.'

'But we are just swanning around waiting for them to call us back.'

Crystal let it ring twice more before answering.

'Crystal! Love it! Awesome stuff!' She held the phone away from her ear. The voice was loud enough for Eric to hear. 'Barry and the team have reviewed what you've got so far and given you the green light. We'll do a live cross on the news, so get yourselves set up somewhere interesting, and the In Depth team want a half-hour special on what's going on down there. Play up the aliens and the mystery angle. You know the score.'

'Budget?'

'Whatever it takes.'

Crystal smiled. 'So Barry liked my pitch?'

'Don't get too cocky. The army and police that really swung it for you.'

'What d'you mean?'

'All this "training exercise" nonsense. Normally their PR people are over us like a rash with something like that, but all we can get this time is "No comment" and referrals to the Chief of Defence Force. And his people have stopped taking calls. There's talk of terrorist plots, the Prime Minister's called an emergency Cabinet meeting, and on top of all that we've had several reports of vapour trails in your area.'

'Vapour trails?'

'Yeah, but get this: according to Civil Aviation, there are no scheduled aircraft movements anywhere nearby. None. Zero. Zip'

'You said "trails". Does that mean there's more than one?'

'One coming in from the south, one from the west. Both heading your way.'

'Heading where, exactly?'

'If they keep on the way they're going and you join the dots on a map, they'll meet near the coast about twenty K from that town you've been staying in.'

'You mean Rata?'

'That's the spot. So drag your bums out of the jacuzzi and get out there and get me that story!'

The phone clicked off. Crystal stared at it. 'But we're not *in* Rata,' she told it. 'We can't get back there.'

Eric put down his newspaper. 'Maybe we can.'

* * *

Tim had never paid much attention to the land opposite the farm before. It was part of the same conservation estate that protected the reserve and was consequently overgrown and wild. Its roadside border was an unbroken line of toitoi, which made for perfect cover once they forced their way through it and doubled-back, and there was even a track of sorts along the far side.

Opposite the farm entrance, Norman burrowed back into the foliage, returning to report no change in the gate guards' attitude. Their deception hadn't been spotted yet.

They proceeded at a steady jog, pausing now and then so that Alkemy could catch up. Several times Tim saw Ludokrus glance anxiously at his watch.

'I hope the bikes are OK,' Coral said. 'How far out would the army cordon go?'

'Probably to the edge of the reserve,' Norman said. 'If it goes out any further, we're stuffed.'

The toitoi had been cut back around the Rata Road intersection so they were forced to climb up through some low scrub, but it did give them a clear view of the reserve. A ring of troops surrounded the campground, vehicles were parked haphazardly on the verge nearby, and the caravan was illuminated by bright lights inside and out as forensic teams examined every surface.

'So much for leaving only footprints,' Tim muttered.

'What will you tell them when we are gone?' Alkemy asked.

'Doesn't really matter then, does it? We just need to get

close enough to stick a few disassembly discs on things.'

They followed the scrub down to a bubbling stream then scrambled along its bank until they reached a culvert running under Rata Road. 'Through here,' Norman said, leading them into the low concrete tunnel. 'We can cross the road without being seen.'

The stream skirted the back of the resource pit. They found the bikes where they'd left them, past the pyramid of appliances, hidden in some waist-high ferns. As they eased them out, the sound of raised voices and barked orders reached them from the reserve. A vehicle took off with a furious skid. They froze, fearing they'd triggered an unseen alarm. It raced directly towards them, then, at the intersection, it swung hard left and headed for the farm.

'Must discover we are gone,' Ludokrus said, helping his sister on to the back of his bike. 'Good idea to make them think we go the other way.'

They started the bikes and proceeded cautiously, edging along the grass verge at the side of Rata Road, moving one at a time, keeping close to the fence line and the shelter of the overhanging trees. But once they reached the first bend, they accelerated hard.

Norman crouched over the handlebars like a speedway rider, forcing Tim – riding pillion – to do likewise, but they were now so familiar with the bikes that when they reached the turn-off to the old mining track none of them even bothered slowing down. Three bikes and five riders crashed through the undergrowth, shot up the side of the low hill that hid the start of the track, soared through the air in graceful, exhilarating arcs, and landed smoothly on the other side.

Tim found himself agreeing with his friend. They really should try to keep these things!

A shadow passed over them as they navigated the long incline that led to the entrance to the gully. They looked up and saw the smooth underside of the Eltherian ship. It was travelling at little more than treetop height, silent except for a low hum and a rustle of air, and as it reached the brow of the hill ahead it dropped out of sight.

Ludokrus checked his watch. 'Where has she been? According to the receiver, she already land more than one half-hour.'

Norman checked the receiver attached to the cradle on his handlebars. 'Dunno,' he called. 'Looks like this thing's playing up. I'm getting a double reading. Maybe our programming's mucked something up.'

'Watch the track!' Tim yelled as they bounced into a deep rut and headed for the cliff edge.

Norman swung the bike back in a long low skid.

They reached the warning signs at the top of the gully in time to see the ship settle in the open space opposite the hut below. It hovered briefly as four support struts extended from its smooth hull, then settled lightly, balanced and level on the uneven ground.

It was the same basic design as the one they'd seen in the forest – like two silvery saucers, one upside down and placed on top the other – but this ship was larger.

'It's a lot bigger,' Tim said.

'Last was just escape pod. This is proper evac ship. Take more peoples.'

Flaps appeared in the ship's upper surface and a loud whooshing sound began. It was now making more noise than when it was in flight.

'What's it doing?'

'Thermo-dump. She has shield. See how she does not get all burn from coming through your atmosphere? She store the heat from entry, but now must be expel. Will take some minutes.'

Tim recalled the blackened underside of their former craft. This ship was unmarked.

'Are you sure it's safe to go down there?' Coral said.

'Ship would not land if it was not. She make a survey first. Besides, look.'

He pointed. Beyond the *Hope* and *Sanity* signs, a huge slip blocked the far end of the gully. A wall of boulders had come crashing down from both sides. It looked recent. Dust still hung in the air.

'What happened there?'

Ludokrus shook his head. 'Does not look good for the Sentinel. But our ship is here now, and we have time to make a proper goodbye.'

'Great,' Coral said quietly.

They headed down the track, still cautious, alert to any change in their surroundings. Tim even kept one eye on the weather, but the gully was as lifeless as it had ever been.

The ship's exhaust volume dropped an octave as they neared the hut and an opening appeared on its underside. A metal ramp slid out and settled on the dusty ground.

Norman set his bike on its stand and unclipped the receiver. 'Can we take a look inside?'

'Sure.'

As they made their way towards the ship, a rumble sounded further up the valley. Something stirred. They looked to see rocks falling from the slip that blocked the far end.

'That's weird.'

Suddenly, a second ship rose from its hiding place, streaming dust and debris, shaking off its camouflage. Its design was vastly different from the other craft. A slope-fronted box studded with a dense mass of complex fittings that crackled with static electricity as it swung towards them.

They stared in awe.

'The vapour trail we saw,' Tim said. 'That wasn't *your* ship.'

The words were barely out of his mouth when it opened fire; a staccato blast of laser light aimed squarely at the other ship.

'Take cover!' Ludokrus yelled as the ground around them erupted in white-hot jets.

57 : Deflection Profile

Alice parked across the road from the Old Oak Café and told the apparently empty car that she wouldn't be long. She locked up carefully and crossed the street.

As soon as she entered, Alice could that Eric and Crystal weren't there yet. Only three tables were occupied. An elderly couple, a family group, and a man on his own. She checked her watch, took a table from which she could keep her eye on her car, and ordered herbal tea.

It was delivered by a chatty waitress. 'You just missed all the excitement. We had a TV star in here. That one from the news. The one that's in all the magazines.'

'Crystal Starbrite?'

'Did you see her?'

'I'm supposed to be meeting her here.'

'Really?' The waitress looked sceptical.

'How long ago did they leave?'

The girl glanced at the wall clock. 'Fifteen minutes, maybe. Looked like they were in a hurry.'

Alice took out her cellphone and switched it on. Now she'd returned to civilisation it was working again. It beeped immediately. A missed call. She listened to the voice message.

'Hi Alice. Eric here from Nine News. Guess you're still on the road and have your phone off. Look, we have to dash out for a bit, but we're staying in town tonight. We're at Archer's Hotel on the main road. Grab yourself something to eat and drink – say it's on the Nine News account – and we'll see you in an hour or so. Something big's going on down here, and you might be our star witness.'

Alice replayed the message then looked up at a flutter of noise outside. She was just in time to see a helicopter rise from a field behind the town and head south.

* * *

The last view Tim had of the Eltherian ship was of the ramp withdrawing and the hatch slamming shut. A second later, still stunned by the ferocity of the attack, he was racing away with the others.

At first, they headed for the hut, but when a white-hot fragment the size of a fist punched right through both sides leaving nothing but two smoking holes, they changed their minds. Norman, in the lead, dived into the low trench formed by the dry stream bed. The others followed. It was, at best, a marginal shelter, but at least they were out of the direct line of flying fragments.

'Everyone OK?' Ludokrus gasped.

Tim, who'd been trailing them, found the others staring at him in horror.

'What?' he said, then looked down at his jacket. There

were two blackened holes in it; one front, one back, just below his left armpit. 'Whoa!' he said, raising his arm to prove – partly to himself – that the fragment had passed straight through the fabric. 'I never even felt that.'

Another burst of fire. Another wave of searing fragments whistled overhead. They crouched lower.

There was a brief lull. Up the valley, the Sentinel ship rose higher, seeking a more commanding position, then the firing recommenced. Five fiery fingers jetted out in parallel from the five barrels of the centrally mounted gun, all focused on a single spot.

Tim risked a peek and was surprised to find the Eltherian craft was still there.

'Why doesn't it *do* something?'

'She is lifeboat. No attack. Only shield.'

As the next wave came in he saw the shield's deflection profile a metre proud of the ship's surface, a shape that matched its smooth contours.

'Why not fly off then? At least get out of the firing line.'

'Lifeboat mission is to rescue. If danger, other ships should defend. But those we do not have.'

During the next lull, Tim checked again. The shield's outline was now partially visible, illuminated by five glowing dots that matched the five parallel lines of fire.

'How long can it hold out?' he asked.

'Not long,' Ludokrus said.

Another barrage started, targeted squarely at the five weakened points in the shield. They began glowing amber.

Fragments of energy shrapnel whizzed overhead, sizzling as they struck the ground, each one another knick in the rapidly depleting shield. All they could do was cower in the ditch and await the ship's imminent destruction. Then what? Tim thought. Then where would the Sentinels direct their fire?

58 : No Time for Goodbyes

'They're incredibly accurate.' Norman studied the Sentinel ship as it hovered on thrusters, bobbing slightly in the breeze that moved across the rim of the gully. 'They're hitting the exact same spot every time. Like they're triangulating somehow.'

The five glowing dots expanded as more and more energy was sapped from the Eltherian ship's shield. The centres now glowed dull red. As they watched, another barrage came in, striking them again with pinpoint accuracy. The dull red colour turned a fiery orange.

Typical Norman, Tim thought, admiring their attacker's technical skills when they all knew what was coming next. He fingered the hole in his jacket. Maybe it would be like that. Maybe it would be so quick he wouldn't even notice.

He looked around desperately, but there was nowhere else to run. Apart from the creek bed and the mineshafts, there was no cover at all. The Sentinel ship's elevated position meant it commanded the gully from end to end.

Norman settled the receiver on the ground in front of

him and fiddled with the controls. Tim was surprised he was still carrying it. Another barrage came in. They all ducked except Norman.

'You know I said yesterday I reckoned they had the whole gully under surveillance? Well according to this there's a camera array on the hut.'

'How do you know that, and who cares anyway?' Tim yelled back as dust and whizzing fragments fell like rain.

'It's transmitting, and this is a receiver. We reprogrammed it to pick up everything,' Norman said. 'There's another one on that signpost up the gully. They're using them to triangulate their fire. We have to do something.'

'Yeah, like what?'

But Norman was already on his feet, taking advantage of a lull in firing to scramble up the bank.

'No, wait!' Tim yelled.

Norman ignored him and sprinted across the open ground. The Sentinel ship swung in his direction and five shots sliced up the earth a metre from his pounding feet.

* * *

'Quickly, quickly, shootee monkey!'

'Stop, you idiot! Focus on the ship. We'll deal with them later.'

'But I like to make them run.'

'We'll make them run all right. And jump. And dance. But after we've finished off that ship.'

* * *

Norman threw himself into a low roll as the five shots hit the ground behind him. The impact actually helped his momentum and he came to rest flat against the side of the hut. If he was right about the camera, he should be safe here. They wouldn't deliberately shoot out their own targeting device. But if he was wrong, they'd blast the hut – and him – to pieces.

He gritted his teeth, held his breath and glanced up at the wall above him. It was peppered with holes, some of them still smoking. It would come in the next barrage. They were spaced at five-second intervals, maybe to recharge the gun. He counted down. Four ... three ... two ...

The gunfire resumed, but the focus returned to the ship. He let out his breath.

'What the hell is he doing?' Coral said.

Tim pointed to a blinking dot on the discarded receiver. At this range it showed the precise location of the camera: on the highest point of the roof at the back of the hut. 'I think he's going to try to take it out.'

They watched Norman clamber onto one of the fuel drums. The camera was on the roof directly above him, half a metre from the end of his outstretched arms. He jumped and hooked his hands over the bargeboard it was fixed to. His arms flexed as he tried to raise himself up. One foot shot out, scrambling for purchase against the side of the hut. It didn't find anything to lock against and he dropped back.

'Go on, you can do it!' Tim muttered.

Norman tried again. He swung his whole body this time, almost hooked a foot over the edge of the roof, but it slipped off and he dropped back once more.

The jolt loosened the board. He was still hanging on and felt it give a little, so this time, instead of climbing or swinging, he just held on and bounced up and down, tugging with all his weight.

The top of the board tilted as one rotten corner pulled through the nails that secured it. He felt it give. Bounced harder. Then suddenly the whole thing came away, catching him off balance. He staggered off the edge of the fuel drum, still hanging on to the board. Gravity did the rest.

He fell backwards, taking the board with him and loosening others it was attached to before landing flat on his back. Winded, he sat up just as the falling timber caught up with him. A long, solid piece cracked against his skull and he slumped back down again, unconscious.

* * *

'We've lost the targeting lock.'

'Must be the shrapnel. Never mind, we're almost through the shield.'

* * *

Ludokrus saw the next barrage strike an undamaged portion of the ship's shield. Norman had been right. He'd bought the ship a couple of minutes at least. Now it was his turn to buy them a little more.

'You still have the memory bulb?' he called to Alkemy.

'Of course.'

'Look after it,' he said, giving her arm a quick squeeze

as he sprang to his feet and started running.

* * *

'*Look, another monkey!*'
　　'*Focus. Focus.*'

* * *

'Ludokrus!' Coral screamed. 'Where are you going?'

He ignored her. There was no time for goodbyes. He followed the line of the creek bed as it wound deep into the gully and raced towards the Sentinel ship.

59 : Suicide Mission

'Norman!' Tim yelled.

No response. Not even when a shower of fizzing shrapnel scored the ground all around him. He'd been right about the camera. Though the incoming fire was still well aimed, it no longer had the pinpoint accuracy of before. Already, the five weakened impact points had lost their angry red appearance, dropping back to a deeper glow as the shield regenerated. But the withering attack continued. He might have stopped them working at the weakened points, but the shield as a whole was still taking a tremendous pounding.

'Norman!'

Tim looked round for support, but the others were focused on Ludokrus sprinting up the gully. He must have heard what Norman said about the signpost because he lashed out with a foot as he passed by, shearing the partly rotted timber off at the base. It fell to the ground. The Hope board flew into the air while Sanity was driven into the earth by the weight of the falling post. Ludokrus ran on.

Directly below the exit passage, Ludokrus took cover

behind some boulders and studied the rock face above. The way up was rough, steep and stony. And very exposed. It was close to the attacking ship too. He could hear the whine of its thrusters and stabilisers, a constant roar beneath the intermittent sound of its guns. It would only take a single shot to finish him. Even if they missed, even if they just dislodged some of the loose rock above, he'd be done for. Still, it always had been a suicide mission. And it really was their only hope. He took a breath and continued.

'Oh my god, what's he doing?' Coral pressed her hands to her face.

Tim watched too, his fallen friend forgotten for a moment as Ludokrus sprang from cover, tripped and stumbled on a piece of the shattered signpost, then pounded up the scree almost directly beneath the Sentinels' ship. It seemed impossible. There was no way he'd make it even halfway without being noticed.

A distraction, Tim thought. He needs a distraction.

With that, he leapt from the ditch and sprinted for the hut.

'Tim!'

* * *

'Another one. Oh please!'
    'Concentrate. Work first, play later. Finish off the ship.'

* * *

Miraculously, incomprehensibly, the shot he'd been

expecting never came, but Ludokrus didn't pause to wonder at his luck and dived straight into the gloomy, glass-smooth exit passage. His momentum and the gentle incline carried him to the end where he was stopped abruptly by the mining laser's tripod, now a permanent fixture welded to the floor with lava.

His outstretched hand took most of the impact, but he still managed to crack his head on one of the legs. He got to his feet. A trickle of blood ran down his face. He brushed it aside and felt about in the dark. The laser cutter lay where he'd left it, propped on some stones. He grabbed it and hauled it to the exit, straining at the weight. Then he got a shoulder behind it and pushed for all he was worth.

* * *

Tim reached Norman's sprawled form and threw himself flat as another barrage struck the Eltherian ship. A fragment of shrapnel fizzed through the air above him, practically parting his hair.

'Oi!' He shook Norman's shoulder.

Norman groaned.

'You're alive then,' Tim muttered, grabbing his ankles and dragging him back into the comparative shelter of what was left of the hut.

* * *

Ludokrus felt around the laser's chassis and flicked on the power switch, knowing it would take twenty seconds to build the necessary charge. The steady whine began at once, rising slowly, and he counted off the seconds as he pushed towards the exit.

There was no time for proper positioning. He'd reached fifteen already by the time he got there, but the Sentinel ship was in sight, its squat shape hovering almost directly overhead. He paused, aiming the heavy instrument as best he could.

Sixteen ... seventeen ...

The charging whine, shrill now, faded. He aimed and zoomed the beam.

Eighteen ... nineteen ... twenty ...

Nothing. He thought he'd bumped the *Off* switch or damaged something in his haste to push it up the shaft.

... twenty-one ... twenty-two ...

Still nothing. A wave of despair ran through him. No! It couldn't be ... Then he realised that in his excitement he'd been counting too quickly.

Phmmm.

The glassy walls flickered crimson. He snatched his fingers from the cooling fins and saw a faint red flash strike one corner of the Sentinel ship, making it shudder and dip as if caught by an unexpected gust of wind.

'Ha!' he muttered.

As he hoped, they hadn't bothered with their own shields. Why would they, attacking a defenceless lifeboat? He imagined them scrambling with their controls, trying to work out what had happened. With a bit of luck, he might get in one more shot before they spotted him.

* * *

'Ooo, fireworks!' Norman sat up dreamily as another volley struck the Eltherian ship, scattering sparking fragments like a geyser.

'Get down, you idiot,' Tim yelled. 'You're concussed.'

'I can what?'

'You've had a whack on the head. We've got to get out of here. Can you stand? Can you run?'

'Where to?'

'Over there. The ditch.'

Norman staggered to his feet, saw Alkemy's anxious face peering at them and waved. 'Hey, Althingy!'

A white-hot fragment whizzed between them.

'Norman, concentrate!'

'Why?'

'Because they're shooting at us!'

'Not doing a very good job. Look. Ha, ha, missed again.'

Tim felt like slapping him which, since he was already concussed, really wouldn't help.

* * *

The guns started up again. Further down the valley, Ludokrus saw the deflection splashes from his ship's shields. Its whole outline was now visible, glowing an ominous orange. It wouldn't hold out much longer. Another minute, tops. He *had* to get this right.

Basic starship layout always followed certain principles, it didn't matter who the builders were. Component placement was governed by physics and efficiency – at least in primitive craft like the one in front of him – but he couldn't remember whether the stabiliser was the domed unit on the side or that boxy thing near the back.

'Come on,' he told himself, 'you know this. You build many model when you are young.'

The mining laser was too heavy to hold so he balled up his jacket as a support and set it in the mouth of the tunnel. Then he stretched out behind it, studying the target.

The domed unit. It was bigger and an easier shot.

Another portion of his brain counted the seconds between recharging. Slower this time.

Fifteen ... sixteen ...

He aligned the cross hairs and hit the *Lock* button. Checked again, made sure his hands were clear of the cooling fins, reached nineteen, then heard the model-builder part of his brain shout, 'No, it's the boxy thing!'

He jammed the laser hard left, sighted down its side and released the lock button a fraction of a second before he felt the *phmmm*.

A puff of blue smoke was the only visible damage on the underside of the Sentinel ship.

Did he get it wrong after all?

Then the boxy unit started glowing as if lit from inside. Oily black smoke vented from the hole.

The Sentinel ship shuddered and swayed, rocking like a boat in a storm. A moment later it swivelled in his direction. They'd evidently been scanning for the source of the incoming fire.

Ludokrus didn't hesitate. He locked the cutter's targeting computer once more, vaulted over it, and sprinted down the scree, running diagonally, hoping to draw fire away from the tunnel. With a bit of luck, the laser cutter would get in one more shot.

The slope was steep. He stumbled, slipped, regained his footing and sprinted on as a barrage of shots vaporised the sheer face above, bringing down a thunderous avalanche of rock that roared towards him.

60 : Tremors

Crystal Starbrite watched the narrow strip of coastal land fall away as the helicopter sped south. Below, she could see the Rata turn-off, the police car and the collection of army vehicles. She thought she could even see the stroppy sergeant. She'd have waved if she was sure he could see her.

The pilot suddenly checked the machine's speed. They stopped moving forward and settled in a hover three hundred metres up.

'Sorry,' he tapped the comms switch and his voice sounded in her headphones. 'Just had a message to say that we're approaching restricted airspace. This is a far as we can go.'

'Have you acknowledged it?' Crystal said.

'Not yet.'

'Well, you wouldn't, would you? Not if you'd never heard it.' She reached over and snapped off the radio.

The pilot stared at her, shocked.

'We'll double your fee,' she said.

He hesitated.

'Triple it.'

He half grinned, suspecting a joke, then saw she was deadly serious.

'I mean it.'

He nodded, eased the control stick forward and the helicopter moved on.

'Jeez Crystal!' Eric called from the back seat where he'd been readying his camera.

'What?' She glared at him.

'Don't ... don't do that, eh?'

'Do what?'

'Go turning things off at random. The ground's a long way down, you know.'

'I didn't turn things off at random.'

'Oh yes you did. *That's* the radio over there!'

* * *

Time slowed. Ludokrus swam against it. For long moments it seemed he was in a race with a mass of tumbling rocks and boulders, sprinting ahead as they came up behind him with the sound of a thousand pounding feet. He even seemed to be winning. Then small stones skittered past on either side and he felt the brush of something huge directly behind. He couldn't, daren't, change direction now. The slightest hesitation would see him squashed like a bug under a boot. He ran and ran for all he was worth.

'*Go!*' Coral screamed, leaping from cover as she watched a tidal wave of debris sweep towards him. He almost reached the valley floor before a rolling cloud of dust obscured her view. From deep in its midst she saw a single stab of red light followed by an answering explosion near the back of the hovering spaceship. She paid it no attention. She was on her feet, racing towards the spot she'd last seen him. But as she drew closer and the dust began to clear, it became obvious that Ludokrus was gone.

* * *

'*Steady! Hold her steady!*'

   '*I can't. The stabiliser's gone.*'

   '*Wretched monkey people!*'

   '*You should have let me shoot them.*'

   '*Forget shooting. Cease fire and trigger the gully destructors.*'

* * *

'Ooo, pretty!' Norman said, pointing back towards the gully.

Tim turned to see a line of blue explosive flashes light up along each side, each one corresponding to the mouth of a mineshaft.

'What the hell ...?'

But something else was happening too. Something more profound. It started as a rumble deep within the earth and he felt it first as a jangling in his bones. A disconcerting shudder. Then the shock wave reached the surface. A tremor that went on and on, rolling across the ground, shaking the earth as if it was a tray of loose sand. Tim could see the surface ripple and dance. Small stones sunk into the loosened earth. His own feet did likewise. It suddenly felt like he was wading through deep mud.

'Keep moving!' he yelled at Norman. The pair of them staggered like drunks.

Beside them, some of the concrete piles the hut sat on sank below the surface. The sudden shift tore the rest of it apart as if it had been made of matchsticks. The whole structure collapsed on top of the bikes parked around the side.

'Oh no!' Norman cried. The sight of the bikes seemed to shake him from his daze. He turned and started back towards them. Tim reached out to try to stop him, but it was all he could do to keep his feet as another shockwave hit.

61 : Bizarre Behaviour

When the edge of the massive boulder grazed the small of his back, Ludokrus did the only thing he could think of. He jumped, leaping high into the air, hoping that instead of grinding him beneath it, it might instead help shove him to one side.

The idea almost worked.

For half a second he found himself balanced on the boulder's edge, like a circus performer atop a giant ball. Then it stopped, obstructed by smaller stones, its momentum spent. He pitched forward, landing in its lee as a cascade of other debris surged over and around the pair of them.

He fought a wave of panic. Now, instead of being flattened, he was overcome and buried in a deluge of loose rubble.

The boulder acted like a dam, leaving him a little air space as the roaring rock slide continued past, but the sheer volume of it swamped him, going on and on before stopping with frightful suddenness. In one instant, it flowed around him like water. In the next, it set like concrete. Before it did, he clamped his right arm to his left shoulder, creating a breathing space, but he could already feel the tremendous weight on his back and shoulders.

The sound and movement ceased and he felt the air space in front of his face grow humid with his breathing.

Coral ran and pointed. She knew the drill from boats. If you saw someone go overboard, you kept your eyes on them at all times, pointing to them or the spot you'd last seen them until the boat could put about and throw a lifeline. It was easy to lose sight of a bobbing head in the immensity of the ocean. But when the dust began to clear, she found herself in a barren wasteland, pointing to a spot as anonymous and featureless as the surface of the moon. The upper edge of what must have been a massive boulder was the only thing to distinguish it from the surrounding ground.

She stopped, her arm still outstretched, only now taking in the full horror of what had happened. Ludokrus had been buried alive.

* * *

Alkemy scrambled from the creek bed as the sides that had once sheltered them began caving in. There was nowhere they could take cover now. The world, once solid, became a shaking, moving mass. Further up the gully, she saw boulders the size of houses bouncing like ping pong balls across the valley floor. A huge portion of one side wall slumped, bursting like water surging from a broken dam.

At least the Sentinels have stopped firing, she thought.

The Eltherian ship was recovering already. The outline of its shield was now barely visible, and as she watched it began lowering its boarding ramp again.

She caught sight of Norman rummaging through the debris of the fallen hut. He was hauling on roof timbers and sheets of corrugated iron. Bizarre behaviour in the middle of an earthquake. Tim apparently thought so too. He appeared to be trying to reason with him, but Norman was acting like a man possessed.

Alkemy raced towards them, shouting, trying to catch their attention, making her way across in a series of short, lurching runs, pointing to the ship as she did so. Tim spotted the direction of her outstretched arm, saw the ramp coming down and grabbed Norman's ankle. He was about to crawl into the space beside the oil drums where the handlebars of one of the bikes was visible.

'The ramp's down on the ship,' he shouted. 'Let's go and take a look.'

Norman paused. If one thing interested him more than the bikes, it was the spaceship.

Then the Sentinels opened fire again.

It was wild, erratic fire. Poorly targeted. Shots went every which way as the Sentinels fought to hold their ship steady. Two glanced off the Eltherian ship's shield. Three others ploughed craters in the ground nearby.

'Hurry!' Tim yelled, pushing Norman ahead of him.

Norman got to his feet and, guided by Alkemy's outstretched hand, started an unsteady jog towards the ship.

Another jolt brought Tim to his knees. He struggled to his feet and was about to race after them when a stray shot struck one of the abandoned fuel drums a metre behind him. It exploded in a ball of flames, engulfing him completely.

62 : War Games

Frank and Emma Townsend studied the line of wigs propped up on the sofa. The policewoman picked one up. 'Where did they get these?'

'I have no idea,' Em said. 'I've never seen any of them before.'

'So they just magicked them out of thin air, did they?'

Em shrugged helplessly. Frank shook his head.

'You brought drinks in to them,' the policewoman said to Em.

'You watched me do it. And saw me out again. Did you see any wigs?'

Frank said, 'The fact is, a bunch of kids have outwitted you lot *and* the army. They've left you all looking like a bunch of charlies.'

A man in military uniform entered the room behind them and cleared his throat. 'Mr and Mrs Townsend. I'm Major Upshott. I'm in charge of this operation.'

'Your first name's not Charlie by any chance?' Frank said.

Em elbowed her husband.

'This is a serious matter, Mr Townsend.'

'Is it? Well your handling of it has been a joke. Why did you lock them up in the first place?'

'There are ... circumstances they may be able to help us with.'

'What sort of circumstances?'

'I'm not at liberty to say.'

'Well the kids are at liberty now. I hear they waltzed past your gate guards. What did you put out there? A couple of garden gnomes?'

Upshott ignored him and turned his gaze to Em. 'Do you have any idea where they might be heading, Mrs Townsend?'

'You say they went left? There's the Robinson's place about two kilometres up the road, but apart from that I can't think of anywhere else.'

'They were talking about a bus.'

'Not today. It's a holiday.'

An army truck came barrelling down the drive.

'Ah!' Upshott turned and went out to meet it. Em and Frank followed, despite the policewoman's objections.

Two men got out from the front, along with a squad from the back. But no children.

'We checked the neighbouring farm, sir,' the driver reported. 'And every outbuilding visible from the road for five kilometres from here. No sign of them.'

Upshott glared at Frank and Em, but Frank looked past him, staring into the distance.

'Are your boys playing war games up there?' He pointed towards what looked like a firework display in the distant hills. Stabs of light flashed through the evening sky, then a

365

brighter flash was followed seconds later by a muffled crack.

Upshott said nothing, turned away and hurried to the tent.

'Can we go back inside please?' the policewoman said. 'I have some more questions.'

Em took one last look at the distant firework display and said, 'Well at least the kids went the other way.'

'Staying out of trouble for once,' Frank said. 'That's a first.'

* * *

Coral cast about the wasteland, her outstretched arm only now falling to her side as she took in the extent of the avalanche. It was twenty metres wide and two metres deep. A broad scar smeared across the valley floor with no sign of Ludokrus anywhere.

A series of blue flashes on the cliffs above distracted her. Something had triggered explosions in the mouths of every mine in the gully. Small explosions, just enough to bring down a few metres of roof, but she was still forced to cower behind the upright edge of the half-buried boulder as a shower of stones and gravel plummeted from the sky.

Then the tremors began. They started slowly but went on and on, as if the whole gully was being shaken by a gigantic hand. She stared at the ground. Several of the larger stones that had fallen around her disappeared and she realised what was happening. The steady oscillations were sifting the loose ground, causing heavy stuff to sink and lighter to stuff rise.

Cracks appeared, earth settled, dust rose into the air. Somewhere further up the valley a tremendous crash announced the collapse of a rock face, but she paid it no attention, entranced by the sight of what the steady shaking was revealing.

The outline of a shoe. Half a metre away, just below the surface. She could see it clearly. She reached for it, muttering his name.

It twitched.

The next half-minute was spent in a frantic scramble of digging, both aided and hindered by the ongoing tremors. The loosened earth was easy to dig with bare hands, but every time she made a decent hole it shook down the sides and half-filled it again.

At first, she dug where she guessed his head must be, but found nothing. For one horrid moment she had a vision of him sliced in two. Then she realised he was bent double in the lee of the boulder and dug there instead, tearing her nails and bloodying her fingers.

An elbow emerged, then an arm sheltering his face and head, protecting a pocket of air. He reacted to her touch, struggling to help, but his eyes were clenched shut and full of grit and his breathing was laboured.

She realised the problem at once and tore at the earth imprisoning his chest. He took a rasping gasp, let out a painful groan and coughed.

His top half free, he sat up, trying to clear the grit from his eyes.

'Don't worry about that. Get your legs out. We've got to get out of here!' she yelled, as further up the gully more rock faces collapsed in crashing tumults.

She grabbed him under the arms and dragged him free. He could barely walk. His left leg had been badly twisted in the fall, perhaps even broken, and he leaned on her heavily as she half-carried, half-dragged him down the slope. Yet suddenly her world seemed brighter. He was free! He was alive!

The tremors began to fade. Dust settled. Silence returned to the gully.

'This way. Quick as you can.'

'The ship ...?' he croaked.

She could see it in the distance. And the others.

'It's OK. The ramp's down. Let's get you aboard. Oh no!'

Behind them, the Sentinel ship started firing again. Wild, erratic fire, but fire that filled the air with sizzling bolts and gouts of vaporising rock.

'Hurry!' she cried.

Then up ahead the world exploded as a stray shot hit one of the fuel drums. It went off like a bomb.

The fireball lasted several seconds. Blackened tendrils drifted skyward. Below it, the burning continued, and to her horror she saw a figure staggering around in flames.

* * *

Tim's world turned white for a moment. The air around him roared. A sudden rush of wind slammed into him and made him stagger, but somehow he kept his feet. Then the orange glow began. Shimmering like a heat haze. There was a smell too. A chemical stink. The air began to boil.

Yellow. Orange. Red. It took him long seconds to

realise it was flames. Then the pain began. Searing. White-hot. He tried to cry out but breathed in fire. He *was* fire. He was ablaze from head to foot.

63 : Battlefield

'My god, it looks like a battlefield down there,' Crystal peered ahead through the helicopter's Plexiglas front.

'I've just picked up a transmission,' the pilot said. He hadn't responded to the earlier warning, but he hadn't shut the radio off either. 'The army are scrambling a helicopter to intercept us.'

'Better make this quick then. Is that link up?' she called over her shoulder.

Eric, who was practically hanging out the door with his camera, gave her a thumbs-up.

She picked up a microphone, checked it was live, took a breath and began.

A dozen kilometres away, Em and Frank Townsend stood in the lounge giving descriptions of each of the children to the policewoman. The TV was still on, the volume low, but they heard the announcement. 'We interrupt this programme to bring you a live report from the South Island.'

Banners at the bottom of the screen read *Live!* and *Exclusive!* and *Breaking News!* The picture showed an aerial view of what looked like a war-torn battlefield with figures running about on it. There were explosions and incoming fire and a shiny circular object that seemed to be the focus of all the attention.

The voice-over was shouted above the thrum of a helicopter. 'This is Crystal Starbrite reporting live, approximately twenty kilometres from the town of Rata in Southland ...'

Frank Townsend snorted as he turned up the volume. 'We're West Coast, you chump!'

* * *

'Backup stabilisers coming on line.'
'Finally! Resume the attack.'

* * *

Alkemy didn't stop to think. She abandoned Norman and raced back as a volley of shots struck the ship. From the corner of her eye, she saw its shields flicker yellow.

Tim was staggering and flailing, a flaming mass from head to foot. She headed straight towards him, ignoring the heat and the smell of burning flesh, and cannoned into him, hard, shoulder to shoulder, knocking him to ground. He fell, face forward, the flames on his front immediately smothered as she dived in beside him, rolling him quickly to smother the ones still crackling on his back.

Coral arrived seconds later with Ludokrus in tow, still blinking blearily through gritty eyes. Both gasped in shock at what they saw.

Coral clamped a hand to her mouth. The blackened shape looked barely human.

'Who ... was it?'

Alkemy felt for a pulse. More shots landed nearby. Red-hot rocky shrapnel whizzed past them.

'Is,' she snapped. 'Is Tim.' She looked up. Judged the distance to the ship. 'Must move him there. Quick.'

Coral turned to Ludokrus. 'Can you manage on your own?' He nodded and hobbled off.

Coral was briefly arrested by the sight of Norman Smith sitting on the ship's extended ramp. It clearly wanted to withdraw it and kept making attempts to do so. More shots were coming in and striking its shields, but his presence was preventing it from closing up again and he rode the ramp like it was a bucking bronco.

'Stay right there, Norman!' she yelled. 'Hold on!'

Guided by Alkemy, Coral slipped her hands beneath Tim's armpits, trying to avoid the sight of his awful burns. She hesitated, fearing that lifting him might make his injuries worse, but when a small explosion nearby pelted them with scorching rubble it helped make up her mind.

With Alkemy clutching his ankles, they half-carried, half-dragged Tim to the ship.

'This thing's trying to get rid of me,' Norman said, grimly clinging to the ramp as it gave another lurch.

'Smart ship,' Coral snapped as three shots ploughed the ground nearby. 'Now get out of the way!'

He scuttled ahead and they followed, dragging Tim up the smooth surface.

Inside, it was almost peaceful. Except for a warning

chime and a featureless voice that intoned, 'Non-Eltherian presences detected. Please expel.'

The ramp, which had started retracting, extended again.

'They are friend,' Alkemy yelled, but the ship repeated its message. As far as it was concerned, it was under attack by an unknown craft. Now, unknown creatures were swarming aboard it.

Outside, the maelstrom continued.

They carried Tim to one of the dozen gel beds arranged end to end around the perimeter of the craft and lowered him into the semi-liquid goo. As it closed around him, Alkemy pressed a walrus-like mask to his face.

Coral remembered the gel beds from the old escape pod. The way they enclosed and protected the occupant while at the same time giving their mind access to the outside world. But mostly she remembered how they'd helped Glad Smith recover from a nasty bullet wound. Was there time to do the same for Tim?

'Is OK to let go,' Alkemy said gently. Coral realised she'd been holding onto his hand as if holding onto life itself.

Alkemy closed the lid.

Coral looked around and found herself in a circular space with a domed ceiling and a dished floor, all bathed in cool blue light. Inside the circle of beds was a circular seating area, itself arranged around a low but complicated-looking console where Ludokrus sat, his eyes still streaming, working the controls.

'Non-Eltherian presences detected. Please expel,' the ship repeated.

'Cannot override,' he said. 'She will not go with you on

board.'

There was a scraping sound from somewhere overhead and a red light started flashing.

'Shield integrity twelve percent and falling,' the ship said. 'Evacuation recommended.'

Ludokrus banged a fist on the console. 'Will not even go to protect herself!'

More shots came in. Rasping screeches now. The blue lights flickered. The flashing red intensified. A second alarm started. An insistent klaxon.

'Told you,' Norman said. 'It really hates me.'

There was a shudder. The ship tilted. 'Shield failure. Destruction imminent,' the voice said calmly. 'All personnel are advised to evacuate.'

Every shot now felt like a physical blow striking the unprotected hull.

'What can we do?' Coral cried. 'We can go, but we can't take Tim.'

Ludokrus looked at her helplessly through red-rimmed eyes.

'Shields gone. Hull integrity twenty-two percent and falling.'

'Ha! Look at that.' Norman pointed at the console. 'There's another one.'

'Another what?' Coral glared at him. He was unsteady on his feet and his words were slurred. Still concussed from the falling timbers, she guessed. What could he possibly mean?

She looked in spite of herself.

'It's another socket,' she yelled. 'Like on the receiver!'

Ludokrus squinted, still trying to focus, but Alkemy

had already launched herself towards it, one hand reaching into her shirt pocket.

'Hull temperature at critical failure point. Evacuation imperative.'

She jammed the memory bulb into the socket. For an instant, nothing happened. Then it was drawn from her fingers and vanished beneath a small sliding hatch in the top of the console. She staggered back, horrified, staring at her empty hand as the attack on the ship continued.

'Albert! Albert!' she wailed. 'What have I done?'

More shots struck the hull. There was a shuddering creak from somewhere overhead, then a speaker crackled and a familiar voice said, 'You called?'

64 : Collateral Damage

'Hull failure imminent,' the robotic voice intoned as another impact shook the ship, this time overlaid by the screech of tearing metal.

'Oh do shut up,' Albert said.

The lights went out.

For a second there was daylight from the open hatch. Then the ramp slammed shut and snuffed it out.

'Diverting all available power to the shields,' Albert said. 'To the gel beds, people. Prepare for emergency take-off.'

'We can't even *see* them!' Coral yelled back.

Four feeble lights flickered on deep inside four of the beds. They all knew what to do.

'Counting down. Three ... two ...'

Like a team of synchronised swimmers, they dived towards the beds, each snatching a walrus mask as they went.

'One ...'

But before they landed, the four curved couches leapt out to meet them. Four coffin-like lids slammed shut and the ship gave a tremendous, jolting, sideways lurch, followed by a vast explosive flash.

And somewhere in amongst it all someone yelled 'Woo-hoo!'

* * *

'Whoa!'

The helicopter bucked in the jet-stream like a startled horse as the pilot fought for control. It was touch and go for a moment, but neither of his passengers noticed, so intent were they on the scene outside.

It was pretty fantastic, he had to admit.

The second craft turned his way now, more lumbering, less agile than the first, but still capable of a remarkable turn of speed. It shot off in pursuit.

A second jet-stream slammed into the helicopter, but he was prepared for it this time and rode it deftly.

Crystal muted her microphone and glared at him. 'Can't you keep this damn thing steady?'

* * *

'Is that it?' Tim's voice sounded in the darkness. 'Am I dead?'

There was a long silence. All he could hear was a ringing in his ears. He remembered the explosion right behind him, then the awful burning. But he couldn't feel it now. Couldn't feel a thing.

Someone groaned.

'Hello? Anybody there?'

'Tim?' A groggy voice. 'Is that you?'

'Coral?'

'Yeah. Are you all right?'

'Not if I'm dead.'

'Well you're not.' She hesitated. 'Or maybe we're all are.'

A deeper groan came from the darkness. 'Can't be dead. Still hurt.'

'Ludokrus!'

'Ship lift off before the couch is proper close. Ow!'

'My neck hurt.' Alkemy's voice.

'Oh man, I've got a killer headache,' a fourth said.

'Norman?'

'My apologies,' Albert's voice cut in. 'Diagnostics indicate you've sustained a number of moderate injuries from the sudden take-off, but I'm afraid I had no choice. I also note one of you has sustained more severe injuries. I'll have the ship draw up a treatment plan.'

The ship's voice said, 'Diagnostics indicate crew members have sustained a number of moderate injuries from—'

'Oh do be quiet,' Albert said. 'I just told them that. You look after the passengers while I pilot this thing.'

'Relinquishing piloting controls to entity—'

'Shut up, ship!'

'Albert?' Tim murmured. 'I thought he was ... And who's he talking to?'

Ludokrus laughed. 'No need to whisper. All can hear. Alkemy plug the memory bulb into the ship and he take over. Other is the ship personality. Just dumb machine, but it will look after us.'

'Did someone shout "Woo-hoo"?' Tim said.

'What?'

'When we took off. I could have sworn I heard someone yell "Woo-hoo".'

There was a brief silence. The ship said, 'Checking recordings ...' Then added, 'The message came from the synthesised voice of—'

'Oh shut up, ship,' Albert said. 'I was merely expressing my pleasure at finally escaping that wretched planet.'

It took a moment for his words to register.

'What?' Tim said.

'But ... you forget we have the passenger,' Alkemy said.

'I forget nothing, Alkemy. My priority is to protect you and your brother. The collateral damage was unavoidable.'

'Collateral damage?' Coral said. 'We are not collateral, we're human beings. Or at least a couple of us are.'

'Hey!' Norman said.

'The choice was simple,' Albert continued. 'Stick around to evict the humans and lose the ship, or launch.'

'What about leaving only footprints?' Alkemy said.

'This ship was under sustained attack from a Sentinel craft witnessed directly or indirectly by an unknown number of humans,' Albert replied. 'There has been explosive deconstruction of the Sentinel base, and sensors indicate that our departure was recorded by the occupants of a nearby helicopter. I'm afraid things are a little beyond the "leave only footprints" stage.'

'Confirming sensor indications of the presence of—'

'Oh shut up, ship!' five voices chimed.

'Besides, there are Tim's injuries to consider. They are severe and will require considerable tissue regeneration. Should I have abandoned him?'

No one said a word to that, although the ship did manage a quick, 'Preparing treatment plan for burn victim.'

'Does that mean we're in space?' Tim said.

'Yes. And in approximately ten hours we will rendezvous with our mothership. Would you like visuals?'

'Yes, please.'

The blackness faded to a gentler sort of blackness, a blackness flecked with points of light. By turning his head – or perhaps just thinking about turning his head – Tim found he could survey the sky in all directions. It had never looked so rich, so clear, so densely packed with stars.

He heard Norman gasp.

Then he caught it himself; a movement behind them; the edge of a blue disc, instantly familiar. He turned until it filled his vision, picking out the long spine of the Southern Alps illuminated by the setting sun.

The image receded steadily, giving way to a vast expanse of ocean streaked with cloud. Tasmania and the southern coast of Australia came into view, drifting north as they soared south towards Antarctica. There, over the ice continent, a palpable shift took place as the acceleration increased dramatically. Though he couldn't feel it cocooned inside the gel bed, he could see the effect and watched in silence as his home planet shrunk until it was little more than a bright speck in an endless sea of stars.

No one spoke for several minutes, then Norman said, 'But we've got school tomorrow.'

If you enjoyed this book …

…I would really, really appreciate it if you would help others to enjoy it, too. Reviews are like gold dust and they help persuade other readers to give my stories a shot. More readers means more incentive for me write and that means there will be more stories, more quickly.

Thank you!

Also by Geoff Palmer

In the Forty Million Minutes series:

Too Many Zeros

Things get seriously weird when Tim Townsend meets a pair of super-intelligent mice with an extraordinary calculator. Suddenly he and his sister Coral are plunged into an adventure full of strange new technology, killer robots, mind parasites, aliens and galactic intrigue.

Lair of the Sentinels

Things get weirder – and even more perilous – for Tim, Coral and their friends from outer space. The slimy, slug-like, mind-reading Sentinels have formulated a fiendish plan to exterminate them one by one ...

The Man with the Missing Jaw

Fleeing Earth with the Sentinels in hot pursuit, Tim Townsend, his sister Coral and their friends face more perils and fiendish plots when they travel to Eltheria. What should be a triumphant homecoming turns into a cat-and-mouse battle with new, sinister forces ranged against them. Meanwhile, an older, darker, more powerful enemy begins to stir ...

In the Bluebelle Investigations series:

Private Viewing

When Jane Child falls under the spell of her new boss, the wealthy but mysterious Damien Trotter, she finds herself trapped in a web of intrigue, vile secrets and murder, where even her most intimate moments are no longer her own. Now she must confront the shadows in her past and the deeper, darker shadows in her present. Shadows that may cost her the man she loves, her happiness ... and her life.

Private Lives

Jane Child's first case: a missing cat. How did she get the boring one? Partner Matt Healy's is far more interesting: someone's counterfeiting top-notch coffee. But sometimes less can be more. More complex, more frightening and much, much more dangerous.

Standalone novels:

Telling Stories

Steven Spalding is a mild, unexceptional civil-servant, overweight and solitary. But he has a secret. An alter ego in the form of wise-cracking, anarchic and exceptionally rude Eric Dombey. As Eric, Steven can become the self he sometimes wishes to be, but as events in his life slip out of control, the boundaries between real and unreal blur – all is not as it seems.

(Winner of the Reed Fiction Award)

Payback

Solikha Duong lives the carefree life of a village girl in northern Cambodia until her world is torn apart by "truck men" from the south. But Solikha is tough, resourceful, and won't give up without a fight.

Alice Kwann is on vacation when she's attacked by thugs at a stopover in northern Nevada. But Alice too is tough, resourceful, and won't give up without a fight.
What binds these women is a shocking secret and a desire for revenge.

Because sometimes your past won't let you go.

Non-fiction:

Reasons for NOT Writing & How to Overcome Them

A complete guide to writing your first book. And your next one.

Of all the creative arts, writing a book is both deceptively easy and surprisingly difficult. There are plenty of How To guides about creative writing, but precious few deal with the actual day to day process of becoming and being a writer. This practical, self-help guide is an exception that will unlock your potential, your creativity and genius.

About the Author

Geoff Palmer is an award-winning novelist and technical writer based in Wellington, New Zealand. You'll find him ...

Online:
www.geoffpalmer.co.nz

On email:
geoff@geoffpalmer.co.nz

On Facebook:
facebook.com/geoffpalmerNZ

On Twitter:
twitter.com/geoffpalmer